Praise for Courtney Kae's novels

"Like the most delicious cinnamon roll, Courtney Kae's *In the Case of Heartbreak* is warm and gooey and the ultimate comfort treat. I wanted to give Ben the biggest hug, and was rooting for him and Adam to get to their happily ever after. I devoured this book!" —**Alicia Thompson, bestselling author of *Love in the Time of Serial Killers***

"*In the Case of Heartbreak* by Courtney Kae is the scrumptiously sweet, beachy romance of my dreams! Brimming with pure joy and sunshine, this is sure to put a smile on your face." —**Amy Lea, international bestselling author of *Exes and O's***

"Charming, sexy, and full of Big Feels, Courtney Kae bakes a subtly intense cake with Ben and Adam's love story that's equal parts sweet and savory. The care taken in the discussion of mental health is exquisite, delicately folded into Ben and Adam's characters in a way that will stick with me for a long time. *In the Case of Heartbreak* is the swoony queer romance of my dreams, where courtship and consent has never been sexier." —**Steven Salvatore, critically acclaimed author of *And They Lived . . .*, and the forthcoming *The Boyfriend Subscription***

"If you're looking for a beachy escape chock full of emotional roller coasters and a quirky cast of characters, *In the Case of Heartbreak* has you covered. Ben and Adam are just the type of fluffy, gooey cinnamon rolls the world needs, and their tender love story will satisfy your sweet tooth. A wonderful indulgence!" —**TJ Alexander, author of *Chef's Kiss* and *Chef's Choice***

"*In the Case of Heartbreak* made me believe in the power of love, despite all odds. I swooned, I cried, I cheered, I swooned some more. Readers will fall in love with Ben, Adam, and Kae's delightful cast of small-town characters with massively big hearts. Courtney Kae's writing sparkles so much on the page that readers will be left with stars in their eyes." —**Kate Spencer, author of *In a New York Minute***

"Forced proximity? Check. Cinnamon rolls? Check. Adorable queer love? Check. This book has all the makings of the perfect summer romance movie!" —**Amanda Lovelace, author of** ***You Are Your Own Fairy Tale***

"*In the Case of Heartbreak* is an absolutely captivating romance that is sure to leave readers swooning and inspired. I teared up multiple times while reading, as I was so touched by Adam and Ben's devotion to each other. I never wanted to leave the world of the book. Courtney Kae creates settings as dazzling as a fairy tale; her writing is simply irresistible." —**Taleen Voskuni, author of** *Sorry, Bro*

"*In The Case of Heartbreak* is a story that unfolds in depth and flavor much like Ben's signature pastry, the cinnamon roll. Kae's novel is soft and warm, and with its alternating passion and tenderness is a perfect combination of sweet and spicy. . . . You'll root for Ben from page one, but you'll fall in love with his entire hilarious family and once again with Fern Falls by the novel's end." —**Nikki Payne, author of** *Pride and Protest*

"Equal parts sexy, sunny, and sweet, Courtney Kae serves up the perfect friends-to-lovers romance. But her secret ingredient is the tenderness she shows for her characters, as they navigate how to best love each other and themselves. This book reads like a happy sigh." —**Brian D. Kennedy, author of** *A Little Bit Country*

"Courtney Kae has done it again. *In the Case of Heartbreak* takes the classic Hallmark movie formula, pours it into a queer stand mixer, and serves up the sweetest, gayest, sweetest confection of a romance. You'll come for Ben and Adam's emotional love story and stay for the delightfully hilarious side characters that surround and lift them up. Kae bakes a delectable, sexy romance that will have you licking your lips with satisfaction." —**M. A. Wardell, author of** *Teacher of the Year*

"A sweet, swoony cinnamon roll of a romance! *In the Case of Heartbreak* is full of romantic yearning, quirky characters, fabulous parties, and, most importantly, healing through self-love."
—**Susie Dumond, author of *Queerly Beloved***

"A loving and tender romance that feels like the best sort of hug, *In the Case of Heartbreak* is everything I look for in a love story. This will be a story I come back to when I need a dose of comfort."
—**B. K. Borison, author of the Lovelight series**

"Much like Kae's stunning debut, *In the Case of Heartbreak* shines in its range—the warmth, peace, and coziness of its charming beachside town setting and the sweetness and sizzle from its dynamic romance between Ben and Adam. The lovable, meddlesome baker boy of *In the Event of Love* is going to be your next favorite romance lead."
—**Carlyn Greenwald, author of *Sizzle Reel***

"Courtney Kae has given us the literal cinnamon roll hero of our dreams! *In the Case of Heartbreak* is filled with beautifully honest vulnerability and an oh-so-delicious romance that will leave readers everywhere drooling. It serves as a tender reminder that life's sweetest moments are best shared with those we love most." —**Chip Pons, author of *You & I, Rewritten***

"Full of swoony steam, heartfelt charm, and laugh-out-loud moments, *In the Event of Love* is exactly the slow-burn, second-chance, friends-to-lovers romance I was craving. Treat yourself to the beautiful magic of Courtney Kae's writing!" —**Ali Hazelwood, *New York Times* bestselling author of *The Love Hypothesis***

"Kae's delightful debut elevates the popular Christmastime trope of someone from the big city saving a small town from a heartless developer in a feel-good queer second-chance romance. . . . Kae leans heavily into holiday magic without letting things get saccharine, balancing the sweetness of reconnection with steamy eroticism grounded in the feeling of coming home at last. The secondary characters also sparkle, providing cozy feelings of community and support. Readers of all orientations will devour this rainbow-tinted confection." —*Publishers Weekly*, **STARRED REVIEW**

"This debut [will] be living rent-free in your brain all through the snow, especially as you pray for it to get picked up as a Hallmark movie." —*BuzzFeed*

"With its charming small town, snowy mountaintop kisses, and dreamy lumberjane, *In the Event of Love* is perfect for the holidays!" —**Helen Hoang**, *New York Times* **bestselling author of** *The Kiss Quotient*

"Courtney Kae's *In the Event of Love* is the small-town winter romance of my dreams; sparkling, pine-scented, and as beautifully atmospheric as the season itself. The sapphic slow-burn love story is both gorgeously soft and steamy, the feelings will wreck you, and the laugh-out-loud moments will make you want to text entire paragraphs to your best friend. A completely charming read for any time of year." —**Lana Harper**, *New York Times* **bestselling author of** *Payback's a Witch*

"With a slow burn that builds into a roaring fire, *In the Event of Love* is the coziest romance I've ever read. It's the perfect read for anyone who can't get enough Christmas." —**Meryl Wilsner**, **author of** *Something to Talk About* **and** *Mistakes Were Made*

"Wintry perfection, a cozy flannel blanket of a book that wraps its reader in the warmest hug, full of wish-they-were-real characters and off-the-charts sexual tension. [*In the Event of Love*] made me laugh, weep, and believe in the fairy-lit magic of second chances." —**Rachel Lynn Solomon**, **bestselling author of** *The Ex Talk*

"Positively brimming with festive small-town heart, *In the Event of Love* is the perfect funny, sexy, holiday rom-com. Move over, Santa—'tis the season for sexy Sapphic lumberjanes!" **—Dahlia Adler, author of *Cool for the Summer***

"*In the Event of Love* is ultracozy, heart-meltingly sweet, and full of warm wit. Courtney Kae shines with a fresh, bright voice and supremely relatable characters including a dreamy lumberjane who instantly stole my heart!" **—Rosie Danan, author of *The Roommate***

"Courtney Kae's debut is filled with charm and the kind of irresistible voice that gripped me from the first page. *In the Event of Love* strikes the perfect balance between the festive sweetness of a Hallmark Christmas movie and the tension and heat I love in romance novels. I couldn't stop smiling." **—Ruby Barrett, author of *Hot Copy***

"Sparkling with both humor and heat, *In the Event of Love* is a cozy, steamy, bighearted romance that will have its readers reaching for a cup of cocoa while infusing them with the hope of true love and second chances." **—Ashley Herring Blake, author of *Delilah Green Doesn't Care***

"*In the Event of Love* is the perfect holiday romance! It has small-town charm, second chances, a sexy lumber-lass, and the perfect mix of sweet and sexy. Reading it is like frolicking in the snow, only you don't have to get out from under your flannel blanket or put on boots. Move over, Stars Hollow. I'm moving to Fern Falls!" **—Lacie Waldon, author of *The Layover***

"Fresh, witty, and hilarious debut author Courtney Kae should be on your reading radar!" **—Marina Adair, *New York Times* bestselling author**

"Courtney Kae's debut sparkles with humor and charm. A tender second chance at first love that will have you believing in the magic of the holiday season."
—**Sonia Hartl, author of** *Heartbreak for Hire*

"Beautifully romantic and as cozy as a homemade quilt, *In the Event of Love* will make your heart soar. A sexy, sparkling debut from Courtney Kae."
—**Annette Christie, author of** *The Rehearsals*

"With the delicious small-town reunion tension of *Sweet Home Alabama* and the deeply romantic childhood friends-to-lovers arc of *Love & Other Words*, *In the Event of Love* is about finding your way home in every sense of the word. This is a joyful, cathartic story to savor . . . if, unlike me, you can keep yourself from devouring it in one go." —**Ashley Winstead, author of** *Fool Me Once* **and** *In My Dreams I Hold a Knife*

"*In the Event of Love* is a holly jolly delight! Courtney Kae's debut is a cinematic second chance romance that sparkles like a Christmas tree [. . .] you'll fall in love with the small town of Fern Falls just as much as you fall in love with Morgan and Rachel." —**Timothy Janovsky, author of** *Never Been Kissed*

"*In the Event of Love* reads like a Hallmark Christmas movie and goes down like a mug of peppermint hot chocolate. Cozy, comforting, and surprisingly steamy—this is the queer Christmas story we deserve!"
—**Alison Cochrun, author of** *The Charm Offensive*

"The heartwarming romance we've been waiting for that delivers on our favorite holiday tropes. Courtney Kae is my new autobuy!" —**Saranna DeWylde, author of the Fairy Godmothers Inc. series**

"Sweet as a cup of hot cocoa (with some spice mixed in), *In the Event of Love* is the feel-good, queer, second-chance holiday romance we've all been waiting for. With a charming, layered cast of characters, it will have you wanting to escape to quaint-yet-progressive Fern Falls alongside Morgan, Rachel, and the rest of the gang for a stroll through the trees and a treat from Peak Perk Café." —**Anita Kelly, author of *Love & Other Disasters***

"*In the Event of Love* is the holiday romance of my dreams [. . .] the sweetness of a Hallmark holiday movie, set in a town that rivals Schitt's Creek, with plenty of steamy scenes to heat things up! This is a delightful debut and I cannot wait to see what Kae does next!" —**Falon Ballard, author of *Lease on Love***

"I was totally swept away by Courtney Kae's *In the Event of Love*. This tender, poignant, heartfelt debut is overflowing with warmth and atmosphere, with a cast of characters you can't help but fall in love with, and a steamy second-chance romance to swoon over." —**Ava Wilder, author of *How to Fake It in Hollywood***

"Courtney Kae's second-chance romance is cozy as cocoa and twice as charming. Even on the chilliest night, the banter, belonging, and belated homecoming in the Hallmark-perfect town of Fern Falls will wrap you up in a warm flannel hug. No matter how far you go, love will bring you home." —**Lillie Vale, author of *The Shaadi Set-Up***

In The
Case of
Heartbreak

Also by Courtney Kae

In the Event of Love

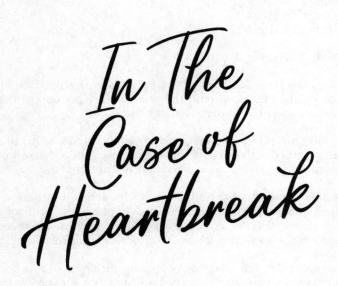

In The Case of Heartbreak

COURTNEY KAE

KENSINGTON
PUBLISHING CORP.

www.kensingtonbooks.com

KENSINGTON BOOKS are published by
Kensington Publishing Corp.
119 West 40th Street
New York, NY 10018

Special book excerpts or customized printings can also be created to fit specific needs. For details, write or phone the office of the Kensington Sales Manager: Kensington Publishing Corp., 119 West 40th Street, New York, NY 10018. Attn. Sales Department. Phone: 1-800-221-2647.

The K with book logo Reg US Pat. & TM Off.

ISBN: 978-1-4967-3898-1 (ebook)

ISBN: 978-1-4967-3897-4

First Kensington Trade Paperback Printing: August 2023

10 9 8 7 6 5 4 3 2 1

Printed in the United States of America

For Norma Lee (G-ma) & Eleanor Adina (Nanny),
Donna Kay & Carol Ann,
Michael & Aisley,
Claire Friedman & Elizabeth Trout.
For you.
For me.

Author's Note

In all my novels, I love to imagine a world that is kinder to queer people, unquestioning, unchallenging. A place where we don't need to explain, defend, or prove ourselves. You'll find that here in Maywell Bay, like you found it in Fern Falls.

Alongside the aesthetic, humor, and quirkiness, I love to create escapes where we're safe to examine the messy, painful, hard things—and learn to believe how very worthy of love we are.

Adam, as a love interest, offers a healing kind of care that we can find in so many places, especially within ourselves.

In writing Ben's story, I went much deeper into trauma than I'd anticipated, and the community in my acknowledgments held my hand while I dove in, whether they knew it or not. Once I stopped wrestling with Ben's arc, he led me to where we both needed to go. Each draft hit a new layer of depth, and step-by-step, we got there. While I did my very best to handle these heavy issues with care, please prioritize and protect your own well-being and mental health with the following content warnings: The main character faces resurfaced childhood trauma from neglect, and mental and emotional abuse from a narcissistic parental figure, as well as depression, and anxiety. The love interest deals with an alcoholic father and an absent mother. Both deal with parental divorce.

Writing Ben's story was raw and painful and healing. This was a process I won't soon forget—one of the most difficult and rewarding things I've ever done. *In the Case of Heartbreak* helped me face down demons, embrace my sensitivity, acknowledge my strengths, relax into the spectrum and fluidity of identity and gender, and lean on and celebrate community.

Like me, Ben has come a long way in his healing journey with the help of family, friends, medication, and professionals. If you need support, the National Suicide Prevention Lifeline can be reached at 1-800-273-TALK (8255) or by dialing 988.

You are brave. You belong. It always gets better.

You deserve every good and wonderful thing.

Love,
Courtney Kae

In The Case of Heartbreak

FILMING NOTICE

Friday, June 30

Delish Dollars Studios hereby announces that it is filming *Take the Cake National* on the premises of Peak Perk Café in Fern Falls, CA.

Being onsite means you release and hold harmless Delish Dollars Studios from any claims or actions that arise as a result of this production. No harassment of any kind will be tolerated.

Chapter 1

You can't be mad at a guy carrying cinnamon rolls, unless that guy dumps those cinnamon rolls on your head. With the way I'm shaking, that's exactly what's going to happen to a poor unfortunate customer if I don't get myself together.

I focus on my reflection in the espresso machine, the only barrier between me and my stuffed-to-the-white-pine-walls café. All of Fern Falls must be here, dressed in their flannel best for the "Hollywood crew" they've hyped since word got out that the bakery is being filmed on live TV.

I can't even make out my glasses in the panel of stainless steel, but I'm gonna act like it's a thrice-cleaned mirror, because looking anywhere else will make me freeze before the million cameras staged around Peak Perk Café.

Okay, there is one camera and one large boom mic, both of which are handheld by women who remain faceless (due to the equipment covering most of their appearance). Dylan, who introduced themself as the show producer (then promptly folded into a downward dog yoga pose, muscles stiff from the five-hour drive from LA), gives me a thumbs-up in my peripheral. They wear a yellow T-shirt that pops against their light brown skin and says Foodies Do It Better in a bold white typeface.

That's been the whole experience of this TV thing. People are supportive and/or placating while I panic.

A couple months ago, I received an email from a scout at Delish Dollars Studios announcing Peak Perk Café was chosen as one of two finalists in the baking competition show *Take the Cake National*. The network-run show selects up-and-coming bakeries with a locally loved product to build into a brand.

Despite my resistance to being filmed, photographed, and perceived in general, I caved when Grandma said, "Ben Parrish, if you don't take this once-in-a-lifetime offer, I'll cancel my birthday reunion, I swear upon my fast-approaching grave."

G-ma (which she then informed me is her preferred title for her ninth decade) does not mess around when it comes to the grandma guilt. Plus, I owe her—not that she would ever want me to feel this way. Five years ago, when Mary Sue, the original owner of this café, put it up for sale, I was eager to take over because I was sure I couldn't fail. I baked with my mom my whole life and had a cookbook full of her recipes. How hard could opening my own bakery be?

Really hard, apparently.

Especially hard in a small town where the tourism season is short, but customers' memories are long, and Mary Sue had a loyal base that was hard to win over. Mom saved me with her menu improvements, and Grandma swooped in with her financial backing, with "To my wonderful grandson" on the more-than-generous check. She still won't let me pay her back, and I can't disappoint her by refusing *Take the Cake National*, especially after she just recovered from a stroke that happened last year.

Talking Mom into letting me participate in the show was another matter.

She finally conceded during our FaceTime call, the conversation going something like: "Ben. I don't want this to open old wounds for you. The media can be nasty and one-sided and I don't want you to suffer again."

"Mom," I said. "This is not the same as when Dad left. I'm grown now. I can handle this."

Was I talking out of my ass? Absolutely. Even imagining my face on TV or news outlets had me back in weekly therapy appointments.

Mom chewed the inside of her cheek. "Grandma's birthday celebration is that weekend. I'll be busy with preparations, so I won't be able to drive up. Are you sure you'll be okay?"

I gripped my phone. "I'll see you the day after filming. I'll be all right. Promise."

She said she would do a tarot spread, but ultimately, the decision was between me and the universe.

So, I signed the contract with Delish Dollars Studios and agreed to take the Parrish Family Cinnamon Rolls to *Take the Cake National.*

Confronting my fear of the media will be a growth opportunity for me. A chance to finally face down my demons. And I'll be doing it with my therapist on speed dial.

Mom sent a "good luck is in the stars" text this morning and said she can't wait to celebrate with me when I arrive at Grandma's beach house tomorrow for the birthday reunion.

Now, here I am, the consequence of my decision before me, wielding cameras.

I'm not sure I can go through with this.

I grip the edge of the counter as images flash in my mind: my eight-year-old school photo plastered on MISSING flyers around town days after I was found in the forest behind my home. That same messy-haired, pale-skinned, lopsided glasses me circulated on news stations as CHILD MISSING IN THE WOODS, then FERN FALLS SEARCH AND RESCUE RECOVERS LOST EIGHT-YEAR-OLD. Finally, a week later: DCFS INVESTIGATES MUSIC INDUSTRY FATHER JAKE GIBBONS AFTER SON IS FOUND IN THE FOREST.

It's great how your body can age to twenty-six, but trauma still hits the nervous system like you're eight years old.

Breathe, Ben. Breathe.

Cinnamon, brown sugar, vanilla. Good.

Producer Dylan and the film crew duo fidget beyond the pastry case, ready to record my hometown montage. Thankfully, since all voting for the show was done online, it's the only episode I'll need to film besides the finale. Both episodes are recorded live. So, there's no messing up here. No making mistakes.

One day. I can make it through one day.

Then, I'll have at least a month to recover before San Francisco, where I'll make my apparently famous cinnamon rolls on live TV so America can vote between me and Sandra Rose from Ohio, who bakes cupcakes in waffle cones. One of our handmade artisan products will then be mass-produced, packaged, and flung onto Walmart shelves. But Walmart once carried Grey Poupon ice cream, a fact that I will mollify myself with in the event that I don't win. But winning isn't the whole point. The point is to take this opportunity, to try something new, to succeed on my own for once. I want to make G-ma proud and show Mom I'm healing, and that she can, too. We can do hard things (thank you, Glennon Doyle and Abby Wambach).

"You can't keep your adoring fans waiting forever," comes a punchy feminine voice.

I find Whitney placing used mugs into the sink along the back wall. Her blue-tipped blond hair is pulled back in a short braid, and her summertime-bronzed skin is flushed from running around filling orders all morning.

"Thank you so much for helping me, Whit."

She winks. "Like I'd pass up free lattes while you're gone? Please."

I chuckle. There aren't many people I'd entrust my bakery to, so when Whitney said her other jobs were slower during the summer (a cozy fairy-themed teahouse and the local tree farm), I asked her to cover for me while I'm away for Grandma's two-week marathon birthday and family reunion. I also needed extra help today.

She reaches into the pastry case and piles a tray with chocolate croissants and lemon bars, then pats my back as she passes by. "You're going to do great, Ben." She throws another wink my way as she rounds the counter and approaches the cameras, handing Dylan a lemon bar, which they readily accept.

I fill my lungs with brown sugar–scented air and whisper my therapist's words from last week's session, something she's repeated to me for years. "Show up. Be myself. I don't need to perform." I sound like one of the many meditation apps on my phone. The words make sense though, and give me a fraction of comfort. This isn't about me, it's about the product, and people already love the Parrish Family Cinnamon Rolls. They've become a viral sensation since the R&R Resort and Events Center opened on the mountain this past spring. Suddenly, my morning deliveries for the continental breakfast popped up on high-profile Instagram accounts of guests who enjoyed the pastries during their stay.

Then came the flood of comments, DMs, calls, and emails asking about national shipping that prompted me to revamp the café's website, which led to being contacted by Hollywood.

Now, Dylan the Producer is thumbs-upping me, ready to document my fascinating small mountain town life in Fern Falls, and the cinnamon rolls that "took social media by storm."

If I keep crouching behind the pastel pink dresser I repurposed as a counter, this will never end, so, another deep breath. I can survive this. I run a hand over my blond hair, smooth my blue dress shirt, and grab the tray of cinnamon rolls tightly enough to combat my nerves—and prevent me from dropping them on anyone's head. No vanilla-glazed hairdos on my watch.

"Hot buns comin' through!" I holler, voice cracking as I

round the counter, swiveling my hips to barely avoid hitting the back of a green metal chair and the elderly person who occupies it.

I catch my choice of words as soon as they exit my mouth and wince, bracing for the butt-related comments.

Someone shouts, "Woo! They look damn good too, Ben!"

"You offer those to go?" comes a clapback from across the room.

The whole café erupts into laughter, and I can't help but reluctantly join in since Dylan smiles like this is the best TV they've ever made.

My cheeks flame—my face. Not the other cheeks in question. "Oh hey, look at that!" I say. "Prices just increased by twenty percent!" Everyone fake-groans and keeps laughing. Small towns and their jokes. Great, really.

My quip earns another grin from Dylan, so I guess morbid embarrassment is good for something. This is not about my personal life, just a little lighthearted joking being filmed. I'll be okay.

The noise dies down a bit, and the camera and mic with bodies move in as I make my way past mint- and butter-yellow–painted tabletops, littered with mismatched plates showcasing all varieties of baked goods. Flea market–found mugs and mason jars hold the wide spectrum of drinks on our menu.

I worked hard to find and create pieces that reflect the charm of this community. Fern Falls may be a small mountain town, but like the cayenne in our egg souffles, it packs quite a punch. We're rustic with flair.

In the years since Mom and Grandma helped me save Peak Perk, it hasn't changed much—save for the decor. I can't mess anything up with a vase, can't ruin our business with a picture frame.

I reach the table where my found family sits, and joy floods my chest. I always feel safe with them.

Before the tray even hits pastel-painted wood, Morgan lunges for a pastry. "You know how much I love your buns," she chides with a wink. Her blond hair falls over her sheer lilac sleeve as she leans forward, blue eyes twinkling like the mischievous person she's been since we were in elementary school.

"Babe, I'm sitting right here. Stop flirting with the baker." Morgan's wife, Rachel, peers at her with a teasing glint in her dark eyes. She wears a backwards gray baseball cap, brown hair falling past her suntanned shoulders, bared in a white tank top. Her trademark flannel is tied around the waist of her jean shorts, like her lumberjane heart refuses to admit it's summer.

"Listen," Morgan says with a smirk, pink rising high on her pale white cheeks, "I may be married—" She bites into a cinnamon roll and moans, licking glaze off her berry-pink lips as she swallows. "But Ben, *icing* your praises."

I snort and roll my eyes. "You did not just make the worst pun I've ever heard."

Rachel throws her head back and laughs, lighting up the whole space. She does that a lot now that she and Morgan are married, and well before their wedding. When Morgan returned home from Los Angeles and literally crashed into Rachel's tree farm, the two became inseparable. Because they were always meant to be.

I grab a roll and tear at it, set it down on the plate before me. Push away the ache that crowds my chest when I'm around other couples, and Rachel, who has the same dimple as her brother Adam. The same crooked smile, full lashes, fuller laugh. I'm happy for Rachel and Morgan, really, but Rachel's brother Adam, who happens to be the person I've loved since I was old enough to realize what a crush was, will never acknowledge me as more than a friend. Which is fair, since I've never actually told him how I feel. Confessing that would mean risking rejection, then having to face it over and over again each time I see him in this mountaintop bubble.

At least when my dad left, I didn't have to be reminded of his rejection face-to-face, day after day. The sad looks from neighbors were bad enough.

When it comes to Adam, I'll take suffering in silence for one, please. It's fine. It's best that way. A pain I can control. Silence is predictable. Safe, secure.

I shake my head, the thoughts along with it. "You're terrible, Morgan."

"Excuse me. I am not the one with a Sir Mix-a-Lot lyric mashup on my building." She jabs an elbow at my ribs.

"Touché," I say, picturing the TikTok videos people have taken out back with the pastel-pink lyrics painted on the window: THIS BAKERY DOOR DON'T WANT NONE UNLESS YOU'VE GOT BUNS, HON. There's a BestBunsBakery hashtag and an accompanying dance. I couldn't pull off the moves if I tried, but patrons seem to like the quirky charm of it along with the cinnamon rolls that lured them here from the resort. And now, I'm on TV.

Dylan the Producer clears their throat.

Right. I need to make conversation. For the camera. That is filming me. "Mrs. Reed, what is it that you like about the cinnamon rolls from Peak Perk Café?"

Morgan opens her mouth to speak, then pauses, glancing behind me.

My face heats. Did I say something wrong?

Dylan's voice is at my shoulder. "Hey, buddy. How 'bout we loosen up a bit?" they whisper. "Have this sound more natural? It's not a business interview, okay? You're among your closest friends."

Yeah, with my dearest friends, being filmed and watched and judged. I nod, tugging at my collar as Dylan retreats. My throat is too tight.

Morgan puts her half-eaten cinnamon roll on her plate. "Something Rach and I really love, Ben, is how your café, and cinnamon rolls in particular, bring people together." She gives me an encouraging nod.

I love my best friend so much.

Rachel leans forward. "That's right. Not only do they draw a massive line at the resort's continental breakfast each morning, but your pastries have become a Fern Falls staple. People don't want to leave town without a pink box filled to the brim with Peak Perk goodies."

They're not wrong. Busy has become the norm in Fern Falls since Morgan, top-notch event planner, ran a fundraiser at Rachel's tree farm last year. When they took over the inn above the farm to combine the land into a resort, they saved the whole town from being flattened by a big corporation. Ever since, R&R Resort and Events Center has drawn tourists up the mountain from Los Angeles and beyond, helping this small town get back on its feet and then some.

I squirm in my seat as I realize it's been too long since I last spoke. Dylan's tapping shoe confirms it. Rachel bites a cinnamon roll. Morgan holds my gaze, silently urging me to say something. Anything.

I pull at my collar.

"Ben." Dylan says my name like I'm an uncooperative second grader. "We know you started Peak Perk Café as a family business. What do you see for the future of the bakery, and for your famous cinnamon rolls?"

It's a simple question. I should have a quick answer. Instead, my lungs deflate like the wind was knocked out of me.

After Dad left, Mom used recipes to create new things for our just-the-two-of-us life.

Dad used to enjoy the cinnamon rolls, so it was the first recipe she changed. She added heavy cream to the rising buns, and they became more fluffy, full, and rich in flavor. She also doctored up the cream cheese frosting until it was so thick it formed upright peaks in the mixing bowl, then, once spread on the baked rolls, melted down into each gooey crevice.

Every time I make them, I remember we survived. Mom made something good.

I'm still looking for my something good, something to create on my own—not that I haven't tried. There were musicals in high school. I wanted to try out, but each time I stood in front of Mrs. Schubert, the drama teacher, I froze on stage. I knew I'd mess up. Be laughed at. Thought of as that kid who got lost in the woods he's lived near his whole life—what kind of idiot gets lost in his own backyard? Messes up so badly his dad left weeks later, when he should have been happy to have me back home? Then, of course, I couldn't even open this bakery on my own. If it weren't for Mom and Grandma, this café wouldn't exist.

Peak Perk has become my whole identity. It's what I do, where I spend all my time. It's who I am. What do I want for my future? What is my something good?

All my neighbors surround me, fill the café.

Whitney brings two mugs to a table by the front window where Ms. Montoya, my former kindergarten teacher, sits with my old high school principal, Ms. Parra.

They recently started dating, and look at each other so lovingly.

Then, I take in my table. Morgan reaches over to swipe icing off Rachel's chin.

I want what these couples have.

I want to be in love and happy. Safe. Secure.

Most of all, I don't want to be afraid anymore.

But those are not things I can say aloud, much less on live national television.

I take a deep breath. "Well, I . . ."

The café door bursts open as a tall, muscular man in a white T-shirt rushes in, his forever-tousled blond hair looking extra-mussed.

I've never been more grateful to see Fern Falls' favorite manic pixie dream himbo.

"Tanner?" I say, getting to my feet. "How may I help you?"

Tanner flashes a wide smile, freckles spreading across his summer-goldened face. "We need you at The Stacks." He juts a thumb over his shoulder toward the bar he owns a few doors down. "For a, um, well, there's a thing."

Whitney crosses her arms and glares at him. "Way to be smooth about the surprise," she whisper-yells.

"It was a surprise until you said that," he replies through clenched teeth.

Oh god. What do they have planned?

"Let's go!" Morgan announces, standing up too quickly to be casual, Rachel following suit.

I eye Dylan. They shrug and usher me forward.

Whatever this surprise is, it has to be better than my blank stares and awkward mumbling.

I turn to Whitney. "Are you okay with—"

She waves her hand toward the door. "I've got the café covered."

I smile my thanks then follow Tanner and the others out the door, camera, mic, and producer trailing us like we're the leads in a reality show. Oh gosh, I guess we are? Outside the bakery, the heat in my face is raised by the temperature of the air as my oxfords hit cobblestones.

I usually love this walk while on a break from the café or delivering baked goods to my neighboring businesses. We pass tourists pulling up to the Fern Falls General Store, boats and trailers in tow. Kids savor ice cream cones at a picnic table out front of the market, most of which drips down their little arms. I dodge a petite person wielding a fishing pole twice the length of their body. There's a locally harvested honey stand outside of Tea and Tarot, the newer naturals shop that took off after my mom closed hers down when she moved in with Grandma a year ago. Normally, I'd stop and sample a taste, pick up a jar for the café, and say hello to my mom's best friends who run the witchy little place, but not today. Not when I'm entourage-ing down Main Street like a Real Housewife of Fern Falls.

"Do you know what this is about?" I ask Morgan.

She motions a zip of her lips. "Don't worry. It's nothing bad."

I swallow hard. Bad could be subjective. She doesn't even like raisins in her oatmeal cookies.

Music keys up as we near The Stacks, a bright guitar strumming I'd recognize anywhere.

My limbs transform like they always do when I hear Adam Reed play: no more solid than raw batter. In high school, he played the electric guitar at assemblies and football games in the small school band. He'd rehearse on the weekends in the barn at his family's tree farm. I'd watch while I pretended to be interested in the crafts Morgan and Rachel enjoyed, the fairy gardens they loved to build, then the Taylor Swift albums they liked to play in the hayloft. The whole time, I'd watch Adam from over the banister. He swayed and kept time with the drummer, Ronnie Elways from science class. I wished I had a teaspoon of rhythm so I could play in the band. I would have even rocked the triangle if I had the courage to approach Adam about it.

Yep, this is bad. I'm about to swoon on live television.

We arrive at The Stacks, but instead of walking through the hunter-green doors that lead to Tanner's gorgeous bar, walls lined with shelves of gem-toned books, we're greeted with a revamped patio, decked out in Fern Falls' finest.

Café lights that will shine even brighter once the sun sets form a high perimeter between the pine trees that stand tall at each corner of the polished deck. Long wooden tables and benches are filled with happy patrons. At the front of it all is a stage, and above it hangs a banner emblazoned with HOME-TOWN PRIDE FOR PEAK PERK CAFÉ!

My chest swells with emotion as Tanner beams. "This is all for you, bud," he says. Then he pats me on the back and goes to check in with his customers.

Morgan puts her arm around my shoulders. "We're so proud of you." Then she goes and takes a seat.

"And so is he," Rachel adds, pointing to her brother, who is positioned center stage beneath the banner, before she joins Morgan at the table.

Adam Reed strums his guitar, smiling like he does every time he plays. There's a certain rhythm his original songs have, a pleasant lilting that mesmerizes me.

I try not to let Rachel's words go to my heart. He may be proud of me as a friend, but that doesn't mean he's interested in being more than that. Especially not when he's always into his ever-changing bandmates. He buys them drinks after shows and they leave together from the bar. I wish I didn't keep track of how many he's had. Fifteen.

A swath of thick brown hair falls across his forehead as he plays, arms flexing in his black T-shirt. His jeans fit more than well and I try very hard not to stare at the perfect lines of his thighs as he balances a foot on the rung of his stool. His black boot bounces in time with the song.

He's so at peace when he plays, a settling of his brows that isn't there when he rushes through the café every morning on his way to his auto shop. He orders black coffee and two cinnamon rolls, says he saves the second for an afternoon pick-me-up. He's always in navy-blue coveralls, the unofficial uniform of Adam's Auto, where he fixes anything that revs with such expertise he's been voted best mechanic in the mountain communities since he opened a few years back, around the time I opened the bakery.

Even though he's exceptionally talented at his day job, he never looks happier than when he's playing guitar; like he's in complete control while blissfully lost in his own universe.

How I'd love to be in that intimate space with him, where he feels vulnerable enough to open up to me for more than brief morning greetings and coffee orders. I miss how he used to talk with me when we were young, before the stresses of life filled in the widening gap between us.

"It's great to see all the support from your hometown," says Dylan.

I startle. Other people are here. I'm being filmed.

Again, this is bad. Unease gnaws at my core. Please don't let this end in viral humiliation. "They're the best," I reply, voice cracking.

As I finish speaking, a blond white woman steps onto the stage and approaches Adam. He smiles and hands her his guitar, then she sits down and strums.

I gulp. Hello to Bandmate Number Sixteen.

But this is different from his Friday night shows at The Stacks. Usually, his bandmate will sing and ogle him while he plays. But today, he doesn't pay attention to her. He steps off the stage and walks . . . toward me.

His teeth flash a brilliant white as he smiles, and his ruddy, perpetually suntanned cheeks glow in a stray beam of sunlight that filters down through the trees.

He only stops when he reaches me, and my heart might, too.

Then, he pulls me into a hug like he hasn't in months.

My forehead reaches his brow, and as he brings me close, my nose skates across his earlobe, sending shivers of pleasure down my neck.

His arms tighten around my back, and each of my cells grows finely attuned to the press of his fingertips, each guitar string–calloused one.

Adam smells like pine and musky motor oil, and Bath and Body Works should get on this.

I could breathe him in forever.

"We're so proud of you," he says, pulling back, his hands braced on my arms.

"Thank you," I manage, untethered by his rare show of emotion.

It's not that Adam is cold toward me, but displays of affection like this are often reserved for monumental occasions.

Maybe this is a big moment. There's a camera crew here, after all.

Adam seems to grow aware of their presence at the same time I do because he backs away from me. The warm air between us chills in his absence.

Dylan steps forward, breaking the awkward pause. "What's your name? Can you tell us about yourself?" they ask.

Adam's cheeks turn even more red. "Adam Reed. I own the auto shop in town, and play guitar here at The Stacks on the weekends and some evenings, for fun, and on special occasions."

"A special occasion it is, indeed," Dylan exclaims, then gestures toward me. "Tell us, Adam, how do you feel about your boyfriend here being chosen for the most popular baking competition show in the nation?"

Adam's eyes fling wide as my heart shoots into my throat.

Time halts. I want to crawl inside of it and reemerge in 1761, or any year that is not right here, right now, when Adam stares at me like being mistaken for my boyfriend is the most horrific thing in the world.

I hold my body still, breaths too, like freezing might make this end faster. From the corner of my eye, my friends angle my way.

My face must be a neon panic alarm.

Keep calm. This is not the same as the media events of your past. You are older now. You can make it through this.

"Oh, shoot," Dylan says, after a lifetime of silence. "Did I misread the heat in the kitchen?"

"I, um . . ." No other words will pass from my brain to my tongue to the godforsaken space between us.

But what if I told him how I feel, right here, right now? I could. The words are on the tip of my tongue. I like you. I always have. "I—"

Adam shakes his head.

My heart plummets.

"Ben and I," he starts, clears his throat, "are good friends, nothing more. We'll always be good friends."

His words are a punch to the gut. A confirmation of what I always suspected, but on live TV. In front of all my friends who've known about my feelings for him for years. It takes everything in me to not double over. God, I'm pathetic. I will not puke on camera. I. Will. Not.

"Okay . . ." Dylan says, shoving their hands into their jean pockets.

Adam parts his lips like he might say something else, then shakes his head and turns, pivoting through the crowd until he disappears through the doors of The Stacks.

His bandmate stops playing, puts down the guitar, and follows him inside—to comfort him, probably. I'm sure he'll love that.

This is why silence was better.

No matter how scared I was of rejection, there was always this hope that I'd find the right way, the right moment, get the right chance to tell Adam how I feel.

I could have, each morning when he came into the café, greeted me with a smile.

That joy was my something good. That's never been more clear now that it's been taken. My chest burns like something vital has been ripped out.

Chapter 2

How stupid was I to hold on to the hope that Adam could return my feelings, just to have years of pining crushed in two seconds flat by Dylan the Producer?

Dylan glances at the film crew then back at me. "Ben—"

I raise my hand. "I need a minute."

I don't wait for them to reply. I don't care that this is live television. If I stay here, I'm gonna sob on camera, and that's not good for anyone.

The mic person turns to follow me, but I lift my hand. "Please. I need a break."

So this is why actors need trailers. But I do have a bakery, and I can make it there before I can't hold back my tears. Hopefully.

I push through the people gathered behind me.

"Ben!" Morgan's voice cuts through the noise.

I squeeze past a backpack and screaming toddler and emerge to find my best friend before me, concern twisting her features. "Are you okay?"

I shake my head, vision already blurring at the edges, emotion clogging my throat. Not this. Not everyone seeing me as pitiful on TV. Again. Will this be in the news tomorrow? All over the internet? Mom was right. I shouldn't have put myself out there, shouldn't have tried.

Morgan squeezes my arm. "I'll take care of them, okay?" She nods toward the film crew. "Go take care of yourself." She gives me a quick hug and heads toward Dylan.

Once I clear the crowd, I cut through a space between two shops and run past the trees to the back door of the café.

If I can just make it there, I'll be okay. I'll lock myself in my little office, eat a five-foot-high stack of day-old sugar cookies, and sleep it off on the old couch beside my desk.

I'll be alone, and I'll be okay.

My gut churns as I crunch through dried pine needles. Dust coats my wingtips by the time I reach my back door.

Everyone must be at The Stacks, because thankfully, no one is taking selfies with the window sign. The front counter is stocked, so Whitney shouldn't need to enter the back kitchen.

I unlock the door, checking over my shoulder to see if Gus the black bear is waiting by the trees. He would be a welcome surprise after this afternoon. Maybe today I would have broken the Fern Falls rule and fed him. I shake my head. I need a dog, cat, succulent, something to hug. Maybe not the succulent.

Sighing, I open the door and my shoulders sag with the slightest bit of relief at the empty space. Sugar cookies, here I come.

I walk through the sea of stainless steel that is my bakery kitchen. It's clean and simple and I love it here. So many memories of community cookie parties during the holidays, baking with Morgan when she first came back last year. The ghosts of those moments would normally give nothing but comfort. Instead, the image of Adam using an unholy amount of sprinkles on a batch of iced cupcakes makes the gaping wound in my chest burn worse. I yank a pink box full of sugar cookies off the counter and head through the door on the far wall that leads to my office.

It's nothing much, and that's everything. This office in the bakery has always felt like my own. At least for a moment, I can leave the outside world where it belongs.

With my home still filled with remnants of Mom's naturals shop, Mountaintop Mystic, there are crystals, herb bundles, and apothecary bottles stacked on walls of shelves in the front half of our home that she converted into a retail space. The rest of our house is small; no more than a kitchen and a living room, two bedrooms, two baths.

It was perfect growing up, but now that she's gone at Grandma's house, it feels like a relic to all Mom did to climb out of divorce and take care of me as a kid.

At twenty-six, I should be rejoicing to have my own space. I would have loved it five years ago, but once we opened the bakery, I pushed off moving out. Life was too busy. And with Mom managing her naturals shop and me running the bakery, we were two ships passing between our businesses.

I close the door and approach the vintage mint-green sofa along the side wall. Sometimes, if I'm catching up on accounting, emails, or orders, I'll crash here for the night. On the light yellow wall above it is a gallery of old kitchen utensils and tools I've picked up at garage sales and flea markets, or antiquing with my grandma, which I haven't done in way too long.

I polished the metals of the whisks and hand mixers, then painted the handles in coordinating shades of pastel pinks, purples, and blues. Taking old things and making them new stitches something back together in me.

The afternoon may have been a disaster, but in this space, everything makes sense.

I'm safe.

I set the box of cookies on my desk, then sit on the couch before the neatly stacked cookbooks, files, and notebooks on the old teal trunk that serves as a coffee table. I pick up yesterday's mail. Anything to take my mind off Adam Reed.

There's a flyer for a discount sale at the sporting goods store in Snow Hill (our neighboring mountain town), an electric bill. And a handwritten envelope from Jake Gibbons Music Management, Studio City, CA.

My stomach flips. This is from my father's company. Mom dropped the Gibbons hyphen from her last name and mine when the divorce became final. I haven't received mail from him in years. Concern bolts through me. Is he okay? Did something bad happen?

I set the envelope down on the table and press my fingers to my lips.

My last and final attempt to see Dad crashed and burned. That was ten years ago.

Things were so fraught between Mom and him, and with the distance of a twelve-hour round trip between us, it was easy to let time pass and stop trying to schedule visits as I grew busy with school, then the bakery—especially when the effort wasn't reciprocated.

I lean forward, bracing my elbows on my knees.

Could this be his way of reconnecting? Hope warms me. Maybe he finally wants to reach out beyond Instagram. I bet he heard about the show from the bakery's profile. Music and Hollywood are similar industries. He might want to congratulate me or meet for lunch.

Gingerly, I lift the envelope by the edges like it might crumble beneath my touch, hold my breath as I pull out the paper, unfold it.

My fingers freeze. This doesn't make sense.

I read it again. Another time.

Phrases pop out, disconnected, scrambling in my brain.

Notice to Peak Perk Café—

Cease and Desist—

Parrish Family Cinnamon Roll Recipe.

My lungs are too tight.

I reread the top lines and my hands shake. A cease and desist letter—from my dad.

From Jake Gibbons Music Management. It explains that Mr. Gibbons recently became aware of our online success and claims the Parrish Family Cinnamon Roll Recipe is his creation, making him the legal owner.

"That's not true," I yell at my empty office.

The letter says that this is a legal serving and must be adhered to until formal proceedings are arranged, or the cease and desist is revoked.

No. He can't take this, too. This show was my chance to finally do something on my own and break free of my past. Now my past is pulling me down by twelve-point Times New Roman typeface on company letterhead.

I stare at the paper and try to keep from crumpling it into a ball.

After all the letters I sent him about high school and life in Fern Falls and nothing at all, he only ever replied with postcards. This is the letter I finally receive.

My famous recipe isn't even my own anymore, and now I can't compete in the Bake-Off without things getting terribly messy. Without having to see my dad for the first time in years. Without letting Grandma down and confirming Mom's biggest fear: The media has made my father resurface in our lives.

I broke my promise to her. I lost the show and Adam in one afternoon. I am definitely not all right.

Chapter 3

The detached garage in my backyard has nothing but miles of forest behind it, which is good news for the nighttime serenity of the neighborhood. My phone has been blowing up since my dramatic exit this afternoon, and Delish Dollars Studios has called no less than ten times. I sent them to voicemail and now, Metallica blares from a scratched-up red boom box on my tool bench, and I've run my palm sander nonstop while the overhead fluorescent lights replace the sunset. Coping mechanism Drown Everything Out activated. I take a deep breath, and a neighbor must have lit a fire pit because a fresh woodsy smoke tinges the air.

There's hardly any blue paint left on this old nightstand, but the sander is loud, so I keep going.

"Enter Sandman" plays its final note, signaling a water break. Gotta hydrate during an existential crisis. I turn off my tool, set it on the sawdust-covered concrete, and take a deep pull from my steel bottle. There should be something stronger in here to match the fuckery of the day, but I'd rather channel my rage through power tools, and those must not be mixed with alcohol.

Too many big feelings fill my body. I can't deal with them at once, so best to numb the sting until I can gather my thoughts, and meet with my therapist.

Adam. My dad. Two different kinds of losses. One brings grief, the other rage. For now, the anger over my father stifles the pain of losing my romantic chance with Adam.

I slam my drink down and water sloshes onto the wooden top of the tool bench. I lean back against the garage cabinets, crossing my arms tightly, muscles aching with tension. My white undershirt will need to be washed as soon as I come to my senses, and it'll require two showers to remove the grit from my skin, but for now, it feels good. Feels right. Nothing in my entire life is put-together, so I might as well match the mess.

Never have I completely ditched a workday before. Then again, never have I had my lifelong crush reject me on live TV, and that's not even the worst of my problems.

Mom has called no less than twenty times, but I can't bring myself to talk to her yet, not when I can hardly form words about this afternoon. Thankfully, Morgan texted me that she and Rachel occupied the film crew with a tour of Fern Falls, and took them to get settled in at the resort for the night. She asked if I was okay, and I said yes. She knew I was lying, so I promised to talk more as soon as I return from my grandma's. Then, Whitney called to say that she would cover the bakery, close up for me, and swing by afterwards for any last-minute instructions before I leave.

Ugh, the bakery. It used to be my escape from memories of my asshole dad. Now, he's tainted that, too.

There are already too many reminders of my father in Fern Falls. Beyond the open garage door, stars shine bright like they always do up here in the Sierra Nevada . . . like they did in the slivers of sky that peeked through the tree branches that night all those years ago when I was eight years old and lost in the woods. I crouched against the trunk of a giant pine and hugged my knees to my chest. If I could survive the night, I'd find the path back out in the morning. I should have brought a flashlight. I vowed to never leave home without one again. Hell, I'd never leave home again. Of course, Dad had the opposite feeling about our home, which he made clear shortly after that night.

I lift my head and take in the ripped and faded rock band posters nailed haphazardly around the garage. The old boom box. These tools he never used.

For so long after he left, I'd sit in here, stare at his stuff, and wonder if he kept it all behind because he was planning to come back. Wonder why the hell he was gone, already knowing the answer.

It was my fault.

I was the one who walked off and got lost that night.

The MISSING flyer with my face on it was pinned to the general store's bulletin board for days after I was found. Mom ripped it down herself.

Then, there were the newspapers, news stations, and news reporters calling my house, waiting outside.

The one time my mother allowed me to speak to a reporter, I told them I'd followed a deer into the forest. A beautiful, gentle doe that let me walk beside her, and brought me to meet her fawn. I don't know if the reporter told anyone because Mom whisked me inside when they tried to ask more questions.

Next was the social worker. I didn't know that's what she was back then. She had red hair and gave me green apple Jolly Ranchers. She asked a lot of questions about the deer, like when I saw it and why I followed it. I thought she was there to help the deer. Which, now that I'm older, I know that's what social workers do, they help.

The visit was short and nothing else came of it, but after the headline of DCFS INVESTIGATES MUSIC INDUSTRY FATHER

Jake Gibbons after Son Is Found in the Forest, there was my parents' fight. The big one. The last one. The one reruns of *Kim Possible* couldn't drown out even at top volume.

The morning after that fight, Dad drove away.

A few weeks later, he sent a postcard from Los Angeles, where he finally had the space, time, and resources to focus on his music management career. He called on holidays, birthdays, sometimes on Sundays. He sent photos of the bands he worked and toured with. He went to Greece, Rome, London. He didn't visit Fern Falls, and he didn't ask me to visit LA. Eventually, the calls thinned out until they stopped all together.

I haven't thought of this shit in years.

I crank the volume on "Nothing Else Matters" then push off the cabinet, reaching for my sander. If I can make everything loud enough, the screaming in my brain might dull.

Along with weekly therapy sessions, this is what helped back then, knowing I could grab tools and tighten the hinges on the kitchen cabinets. Make a frame for a photo of Mom and me. Fix things. Over the years, I continued fixing. Lost things, vintage things. Loved things, discarded things. Most of my completed projects are featured at the bakery, like the antique dresser I painted pink and repurposed as the front counter, the clock and frames, tables and chairs. Here, unfinished projects crowd the perimeter of the garage: chandeliers to refurbish, all kinds of furniture, wine barrels, tin signs, old barnwood and milk cans, bins of beads, fixtures, doorknobs, and other items overflowing from boxes.

I'll get to those more focused projects one day. For now, I need noise.

I put on my prescription safety glasses and re-tackle the nightstand. Vibrations run up my arm, numbing my muscles.

Numb is good.

A cease and desist. From my own father. Didn't have that on my Adulting Sucks bingo card.

Chipped robin's-egg-blue paint disappears in a cloud of dust. This nightstand may become a glossy new piece, or I might plant succulents in the drawers. For now, it's my comfort DIY.

I drive the sander down hard against the wood, grinding my teeth, relishing the volume, friction, physical release of a fraction of rage.

After I opened Dad's envelope, it was easy to google that anyone can send a C&D letter. It's different from an order, and most recipes cannot be copyrighted because they state facts. So, it's not that I'm particularly worried about the legalities so much that I'm pissed off. So pissed off that I called Jake Gibbons Music Management and left a voicemail that this C&D will never hold up in court. I didn't say everything I wanted to, like how dare this be the first letter you reply with after all these years.

Then, I yelled into a throw pillow and ate a cookie or ten.

What did he think this would accomplish? Is it his messed up way of checking in after months of nothing but likes and emoji comments on Instagram? Is this some sort of revenge plot against my mom?

There's now an indent in the wood beneath my sander, so I grind the tool over to a new spot.

The latter is the more likely scenario.

Mom cried for weeks after Dad left. Months. She tried to hide it. I think she thought I couldn't hear her sobs from beyond the bathroom door when she ran the shower.

But for all the tears, there was no more yelling. I felt so guilty even noticing that, being grateful for the ceasefire, for reading romance books again instead of watching shrill TV sitcoms and cartoons at full volume.

As much as I missed Dad, it wasn't a new feeling. I think I was born missing my father. I missed him at my birthday parties when he had last-minute meetings with clients. Missed him at ceremonies at school when I received citizenship awards, when he was absent from the dinner table in favor of his home office. Missed him that night in the woods.

After he left, the added distance to missing him was almost a relief. A permanent marker that spelled out LET HIM GO LIKE HE LET YOU GO across my mind whenever the missing got too loud.

There was no shared custody. He didn't even try for that. There were only intermittent postcards and rushed phone calls and child support checks. At least he sent those. Then, the sparse interactions from @JakeGibbonsMusicManagement on the bakery's Instagram account once I set it up a couple years back.

I freeze, sander blowing dust. My face goes cold. There was the article.

I found it in my mom's room one day when I was a teen scoping out Christmas presents beneath her bed.

It was published a few months after he left. It wasn't even in a recognizable newspaper, something small and probably out of business by the time I found the piece.

The headline flashes across my memory: JAKE GIBBONS DEFENDS CAREER AMIDST DCFS SCANDAL.

They called it a scandal. In the article, he called the social worker's visit a defamation of character. Blamed my mother for being out of town when he had business to attend to, so of course he hadn't seen me wander off; he was trying to provide for his family.

He even threatened to sue the DCFS and media for the damage to his career.

I threw the paper back beneath the bed and swiped at angry tears. Not once did he discuss the harm done to his family, the loss of his wife, his son.

Now there's the C&D.

I push the sander down hard as my vision blurs.

Jesus. Fuck.

The music cuts out and my palm sander swerves.

I turn the tool off as a punchy voice replaces the chaos: "Where is your pressed linen dress shirt?"

I straighten to find Whitney standing beside the stereo, arms crossed.

Heat creeps into my cheeks. I set the sander atop the nightstand and remove my goggles, swipe at my eyes.

She steps closer. "I didn't know that you own work boots? Or jeans?"

I run a hand through my dusty hair. "Thank you so much for closing the shop, covering for me this afternoon."

"Of course," she says, voice softening. Then, she eyes the mutilated piece of furniture.

I rub the back of my neck. "Please don't ask."

"Wasn't gonna."

I sigh.

She fiddles with a belt loop on her jean shorts. "Adam came to the café looking for you."

My stomach dissolves through the concrete. "What did he say?"

"Not much. Just asked if you were okay and when you'd be back."

With the roller coaster my heart has been on today, this is an upswing. I can't help it, can't shoot it down. "What did you tell him?"

"I said you were leaving for your grandmother's tomorrow, and to give you a call, but then his bandmate came in, said they had rehearsal, so he had to go."

And there's the swift and inevitable plunge.

He always has singers, bandmates. He always had dates and partners in high school, and after. Always with someone or getting over someone, or trying to ask someone out.

Everyone except me.

Because I'm his friend.

We'll always be good friends . . . Nothing more.

I swallow hard.

It's not his fault I have these feelings. Not his fault he doesn't reciprocate them. But leaving Fern Falls couldn't have come at a better time.

"How are you doing?" Whitney asks.

That one question makes any last shred of composure slip. I slump against a cabinet door and barely manage to keep standing. "Besides being totally humiliated on a very public scale? Fine. Dandy. Doing great." She doesn't need to know about the added horror of everything going on with my dad. I don't know how to process that myself yet, let alone tell anyone else.

Whitney rubs the strap of her purple tank top between her fingers. "Been there," she replies.

My brows pinch together. "What do you mean?"

She pulls at her short braid. Her neon-pink nails pop against the blue dye. "I haven't told anyone in Fern Falls this, but I was engaged before."

I try to school my features. Whitney has only lived in town for a few years, but from the moment she arrived, she was all in. She walked into Peak Perk one day, ordered a double-shot vanilla latte, and asked about job openings. I pointed her to the community board on the café wall, and she's worked at the teahouse called Forest Fairy's and then the Reed Family Tree Farm ever since. Come to think of it, whenever questions about her past or family come up, she tends to change the topic. I know that she moved here from the East Coast, and now I know this secret.

"As you can see"—she holds up her left hand—"still single."

"Whit, I'm so sorry."

"I'm not," she says, chin perking high. "But you can imagine the mortification I felt when I left him at the altar."

I wince. "That must have been extremely hard. You are very brave."

She grips my shoulder gently, briefly. "So are you, Ben."

I breathe deep. "What did you do after that?" Maybe she can give me some advice.

She snorts. "I moved away. Which is not a helpful solution for you."

Miraculously, I laugh. "No, but it's tempting."

"You don't mean that."

I toe a pile of sawdust with my boot. "I know. Mostly."

She smiles softly. "But your grandma's birthday celebration will be good for you."

I nod. "Space will be good." Good for letting Adam go and trying to sort out the C&D. Not so great for my meddling family hassling me about my love life, especially now that they have probably watched it crash and burn on TV. But that's a worry for tomorrow. "Is there anything else you need for covering the bakery?"

She shakes her head. "What I need is for you to please go drink some water. Get the best sleep you can."

My whole body sags. All I can do is nod.

She pulls me into a warm hug.

"Thank you for being such a good friend." Even my voice sounds tired.

"You make it easy, Ben." She pulls back and fixes me with a gentle stare. "It's going to be okay. You're going to get through this. But first, take this time to enjoy yourself, okay? Let loose a little. Or a lot. I won't judge."

I grimace. Things can't get much more loose after today. "What do you mean?"

She laughs and ruffles my hair with her fingers. I fight the urge to comb it back out with mine.

"You don't have to be perfect all the time. I think letting yourself enjoy something spontaneous or like, I don't know, wearing a regular T-shirt like this more often will do you good. See what the summer brings, yeah? Let yourself enjoy it. You deserve to go for what you want in a way that feels wonderful to you. You deserve wonderful things, Ben."

I stand tall and barely manage to keep it together as she leaves.

Once her silhouette blends into the dark night, I slump against the beat-up nightstand, bracing myself with one arm.

Maybe she's right. Something like hope tingles through me. Maybe some summertime space in Maywell Bay will bring a new perspective, like Grandma's house always used to during my childhood.

As I reach to unplug my palm sander, my phone buzzes.

Again. Again.

It must be Mom calling for the millionth time. I'm sure she saw the live taping, and I shouldn't make her worry. I'll let her know I'm okay and we'll talk tomorrow. I can get my thoughts together during the drive down.

When I pull my cell out of my pocket, there is a text from Mom along with her missed calls, but more notifications flash across my screen.

I swear to god I'm going to delete Instagram.

One look at the app has me wanting to smash my phone.

@JakeGibbonsMusicManagement tagged you in a post

I gulp past nausea as I pull up the image.

It's a photo of Dad and me. I'm a toddler in it, my little hands gripping a cinnamon roll, mess all over my fingers, face, toothy grin. Dad sits beside me at the dining table, leaning to get into the frame, a platter of pastries before him. His dark hair is slicked back, contrasting with his pale skin. He wears a white button-up shirt and a tight smile like he always did.

The caption reads:

I taught my son Ben how to make his famous cinnamon rolls. Even though he's taken credit for my recipe, I'm still so proud of him.

He tagged Delish Dollars Studios.

It's not a school portrait on Missing flyers, but tell that to my nervous system. A thousand needles prick my skin.

He posted this an hour ago, after I left that voicemail stating that his C&D was an empty threat. Great, I basically caused this. He knew that the C&D was a failure, so now he's trying to tear me down through the very thing that built my business up: social media.

And it's not just about the bakery for him. He references me, his son. He's made this personal.

I hunch forward, throw a hand over my mouth.

What did I ever do to deserve this? Can't he stay out of my life like he always has?

The photo has a thousand likes and half as many comments, mostly stating how despicable it is that I didn't give credit where credit is due.

Another notification pops up: *@DelishDollarsStudios sent you a message.*

I go to my DMs, phone shaking in my hands.

The studio's official account sends me a link to my father's post and writes: *Ben. We've been trying to reach you all evening. We need to meet on this. Sunday morning at ten work for you?*

I type back, grip slipping. *Yes. Talk to you then.*

No sooner do I hit send than I receive a link for a Zoom call. I slam my phone down atop the nightstand.

Whitney's words ring in my ears. *You deserve to go for what you want . . . You deserve wonderful things.* If I deserve wonderful things, I should stop fucking everything up.

Chapter 4

Cresting the bridge into Maywell Bay makes me hum the melody to "Over the river and through the woods, to grandmother's house we go," except I'm out of the woods, and greeted by the most charming Pacific Coast beach town. This bridge forks off from the highway like a portal to a new world—exactly what I need. On either side of the bridge spans Maywell Harbor. A sparkling cerulean blue surrounded by private docks of houses that resemble whatever whimsy their owners desire. Some are miniature renditions of castles with tower rooms off the roof, topped with spires and weather vanes. Others are modern behemoths, walls of copper and stainless-steel reflecting the water at the edge of their lawns. Interspersed are one-story bungalows that haven't seen a coat of paint since this town was founded in the 1930s, shake siding weathered to grayish whites, light blues, and peaches.

Windows down, fresh ocean air grazes my cheeks, warming my skin. Sunshine and saltwater. I breathe it in, and the change of atmosphere is enough to barely loosen the C&D and Adam Reed holds on my chest.

My phone rings through my Subaru's Bluetooth. *Mom Cell* displays across the screen on my dash. I fiddle with my controls and it picks up.

"Mom—"

"Ben. Are you okay? After the filming?"

A pang of guilt hits my gut. I should have called her back last night. "I'm okay. I promise." I need her to think I really am all right. I can't worry her. I have to focus on getting through this and getting Dad to drop the C&D.

She sighs. "Okay. I'm glad to hear it. Are you seeing Jessica soon?"

I nod as if she can see me. "I have a virtual therapy appointment for this week."

"Good, good. I'm running into town for Grandma, but I'm glad I caught you. I can't wait to see you."

"Me too, Mom."

She hangs up as I exit the bridge near a row of wooden storefronts in different shades of the rainbow, made pastel by the ocean air. There's a psychic, a cupcake shop, and a select-your-own king crab restaurant, patio studded with yellow umbrellas.

This was the backdrop of my childhood summers for as long as I can remember. I rode my surface-rusted teal beach cruiser down these tight streets, dared the harbor lights to glow before I was ready to return to Grandma's house. I wasn't so nervous about life here, with the salty air making my hair unmanageable, bare feet covered in sand, cheeks baring new freckles.

I didn't have to think about Dad here, and all the mistakes I made before he left. I had space from the memories of him, from being no more to my neighbors than the kid who was lost in the woods, then lost his father. Space from the push and pull of my feelings for Adam and the extra-awkward version of myself I was around him—still am.

And it wasn't just me who was a little different in Maywell Bay. Driving over that bridge always made Mom's shoulders lower. She'd wear her hair loose all season so the sun bleached it platinum, and she'd laugh louder than the crash of the waves for the three months we'd stay every year.

The shops give way to palm trees and sand-swept sidewalks as I near the coast. If I keep straight, I could drive onto the beach. The sun is still at its early-afternoon high, and the typical morning fog has almost dissipated, so between the quieter residential rows of beachfront homes, the infinite blue ocean winks its welcome.

My jaw unclenches as I roll my shoulders. Away from rushing cars, Maywell Bay sings louder. Seals bark from the harbor behind me, and gulls mew overhead as I turn onto Sea Crest Drive. The breeze flaps through sky-high palm trees, fronds clapping. Far waves hush in and out.

A few things on Grandma's street are different. The triplex that was once on my left is now one massive home, old shingles replaced with smooth white stucco. Above the double glass doors is a hand-carved wooden sign that says, MIMI'S AND PAPA'S DREAM BY THE SEA.

There are of course, the ever-present frames of scaffolding on any given home, three on this street. Because of the corrosive properties of salty air, painting (among other upkeeps) is a constant task.

The plants are thriving, as always. Succulents are the landscape of choice, and they grow as wide and tall as small trees and large bushes.

Not much has changed, and in many ways, neither have I.

I'm still afraid of messing everything up with the bakery, still enraged at my father, and still heartbroken over Adam Reed. My stupid heart wants to leap with the knowledge that he came by the café to look for me yesterday. But then, he hasn't texted or called, so there's that gut punch that my heart needs to stay in check.

Even thinking about the filming, Adam, Dad's social media post, and the comments and Delish Dollars Studios message it spurred makes any beach-induced relaxation lapse back into muscle-tightening. I grip my steering wheel as I pull off to the right, into a narrow parking space along the curb, tires crunching sand.

Windows up, engine off, I sit still. Maybe I can gather my thoughts like the shells I used to find on this beach. Always finding things here, as opposed to the lost things of home.

You have two weeks to get your shit together.

Two weeks to get over Adam for good because pining for the rest of your life over someone who doesn't reciprocate your feelings is not a healthy way to live.

Two weeks to figure everything out with Dad and start to prepare for the Bake-Off in San Francisco, as long as they still want you to compete after the Zoom call tomorrow morning.

Two weeks to return to Fern Falls as a new Ben, a better Ben.

Outside the car window, the ocean peeks out beside Grandma's house, from beyond the sprawling back courtyard. The deep blue contrasts with the pale sky. The wide openness of the horizon makes me smile. For the first time in a long time, even with these obstacles, growth feels possible.

In a few minutes, I'll have an unobstructed view from my room in Grandma's not-so-humble home. I just have to make it through all the *hello*s and *how are you*s before I can head straight to my old summertime retreat. I can fake a smile for a few minutes.

As I step out of my little red Subaru, voices drift from the upwards of fifty windows visible from this side of the house alone. The foyer could fit one hundred family members. How many are crammed into each nook and cranny of this ginormous place?

I heave a sigh and drag my bag from the back seat. It's always a wonder how little I need to come here. Even summer nights in Fern Falls are chilly. In Maywell Bay, there is still the dampness from the sea, but the humidity tends to keep things warm after dark. It's a nice reprieve to be warm all the time.

I shut the car door and turn toward the driveway. There's no denying the beauty of Grandma's home. Although, beauty is a flat descriptor. The mansion is grand and glamorous and honestly? Excessive. Before me, a cobblestone drive winds its way around a fountain large enough to hold four life-sized statues of bare-chested merfolk, each spraying water from their mouths. Behind the feature is one twenty-foot-wide staircase that leads to the main entrance. The double doors are large enough to be standard for the Plaza hotel, and each bright magenta side is carved with a floral pattern. The house itself is a sand-colored stone conglomerate the size of four standard suburban homes pieced together. Fluorescent-pink begonias and dark green ivy trail each window, balcony, and column.

Since I haven't been back in about a year, when Grandma returned from the hospital after her stroke, I thought the property might appear smaller somehow, but no. I still can't view it all in one glance, or five.

"Ben!"

Tiny golden-brown arms grab my leg and, fully unprepared, I trip back against my car, canvas bag swinging.

I pat a little head of curly black hair, and when two big brown eyes shine up, I can't help but smile.

"Matthew! Wow, you've gotten big. How old are you now?"

"This many!" Matthew steps back, his chest puffed out, as he holds up four tiny fingers.

I smile and hold my hand out, which he promptly high-fives.

Laughter sounds as his parent rounds the side of their car. Their smile is bright against their rich brown skin, glossy black braids hanging to their waist.

"Ben, wow! It's so good to see you!" My cousin's spouse folds me into a hug. They smell like coconut and summertime.

"Janet," I say, pulling back. "You too. How long has it been?"

"Gosh, three years, I think?"

"This many!" Matthew says proudly, holding up as many fingers.

Three years without seeing this little guy. "He remembers me?"

Janet gives me an apologetic smile. "I told him you're his daddy's cousin as we walked over. He's so excited to be around family. Jason's been working so much lately."

"How's he doing?"

When we were young, my older cousin Jason would coax me into performing rambunctious renditions of old musicals after big family holiday meals, ones Dad no longer attended. Reciting lines from *The Music Man* or *My Fair Lady* was the most I'd talk the whole visit. He'd wink at me after my monologues, like he held some kind of victory in getting me to participate. Warmth rushed through me because I was able to be the center of attention in a way that comforted me. Speaking up with a script, so I couldn't mess up, falter. Fail. Since then, Jason has taken his theatrical skills and become a world-renowned nature cinematographer, traveling the planet to capture majestic sights, while amassing millions of online fans from posting his gorgeous images.

Janet's smile pulls tight. "Trying to get through these next few months. He's been on some bigger productions lately. Really hoping he can break away to be here, but he's in South America filming for Nat Geo, and hiatus isn't for another month."

A burly older man in red swim trunks and a neon-yellow tank top approaches, carrying a suitcase on each shoulder. He's suntanned and white-haired, and ready for a *Baywatch*-themed party. Which, knowing Grandma, is probably just what she has planned for her birthday. "Let's hope Jase makes it," Uncle Tim says. "I have to beat him in our kayak race for the third year in a row."

"Grandpa!" Matthew cheers, wrapping himself around his leg.

Janet laughs. "You go so hard on him, Tim."

He smirks, sun glinting off his sporty sunglasses. "Eh, what's a little father-son competition?"

"Or a lot," Janet says, chuckling, taking Matthew's hand.

Uncle Tim places the bags at his sides and lunges forward

without warning, gripping me in his bare arms. My nose buries into a hairy bicep, but it's still so good to see him and get a hearty, Parrish-style hug.

I haven't spent real time with Uncle Tim since he last visited Fern Falls a handful of Christmases ago. Janet and Jason were on an island babymoon, and Uncle Tim spent the holidays with Mom and me. It was just like when he visited when I was young, after Dad left. Back then he came and took me sledding and snow fort building, did all the mountain traditions with me that Dad was never interested in like he was interested in work. We made sugar cookies with Mom and decorated the tree. We set up a tent that overtook our living room, and had an indoor camping movie night with *While You Were Sleeping* playing on loop until I fell asleep.

I couldn't ask for a better uncle, David Hasselhoff's doppelganger, and all.

He pulls away, gripping my shoulders. "Great to see you, buddy. Glad you could pull away from the bakery to be here."

I smile as he grabs the bags. "So good to see you too, Uncle Tim."

The front door bursts open and a small, stalwart old lady steps out. "Y'all gonna jabber out here all day, or are you coming inside to hug me before I die?"

Matthew gasps. "No!" He runs to her. "No dying. No zeros!"

"Hey, Mom!" Uncle Tim yells, scaling the steps in his flip-flops, two at a time.

Janet follows behind and I'm next. As I walk up the steps, my bag somehow gains twenty pounds. I want to leave the events of yesterday behind, but they edge in, especially now, seeing Grandma. I have to fix this situation with Dad and Delish Dollars Studios. She wanted me to be in this competition. I can't let her down.

She looks amazing. Her hair is the same bright red. She says she never dyes it. No one else dares say otherwise.

Her maroon Lululemon pants match her Nikes, and complement her deep purple hi-low sweater. She has better fashion sense than most people my age.

Uncle Tim engulfs her in a hug, then hauls the bags inside. Janet says their hellos with Matthew, then goes through the doors, where a chorus of greetings echoes.

Grandma props her hands on her slim hips, eyes me with what some would say a twinkle and what I would call sass. Then, she breaks out into a huge bright smile, red lipstick popping against her warm white skin. "Who is this strapping man and what did he do with my grandson?"

I laugh and ascend the final step, setting down my duffel bag. "I missed you, Grandma."

She gathers me into a hug, and I breathe in her rose perfume. It takes me back to beach days and tea parties and oatmeal cookies for us and sugar water for the hummingbird feeder. Guilt stabs my center. I should have visited sooner and more often.

She pulls back. "I missed you, too. And it's G-ma now."

"Ah, right." I raise a hand. "And so it shall be forevermore."

She pinches my cheek but frowns. "You look tired, pale. How is your love life? Come on, I'll show you to your place."

Before I know what's happening, she takes one bright purple AirPod out of her ear then pops it into mine, and Frank Sinatra serenades my eardrum as I grab my bag.

There are at least twenty things from that one moment that make me need a long nap or a long cry, but that's just Gran— G-ma: overbearing, spectacular, invasive, loving. "Great, thanks," I say over Sinatra's crooning of "I've Got the World on a String." "Great" covers all bases. I should be used to my family's meddling ways by now, but without a steady partner to put all questions of my dating life to rest, each time it comes up only grates on me.

Instead of heading inside where my sunrise-colored room

awaits, spa tub with an ocean view, she leads me around the side of the house.

"Don't you want me to stay in my regular room?" Please? I brought bath bombs.

I picture the stark white, overstuffed comforter, the marine-blue sea out the expansive windows. Massage jets of bubbling bliss.

"We needed the interior space for the littles. You're not a little anymore, are you?"

I bark out a laugh. "Last I checked, no."

Although, I could throw a tantrum about all the shit going on if I put my mind to it.

I sigh as the song says, "*What a world, man this is the life.*"

Shut up, Frank. No need to rub it in.

We round the hibiscus bushes and stone-lined succulent gardens.

The massive courtyard is full of vendors hanging lights and setting up tables and temporary structures like something out of the movie *Sabrina* circa 1995. My mom loves that movie. I love Harrison Ford. There's a giant sparkling aquamarine pool in the center of the space, and a platform is being erected over it with lights mounted beneath and trussing above.

"This is going to be some party, huh?" I ask.

"Oh, hunny," Grandma says with a smirk, "these are going to be two weeks you will never forget."

I breathe in deeply. I don't know how I'm going to sort out this Dad issue with endless parties happening. I'm going to have to try and work my way around Grandma and Mom whenever I can. I'll try to call him again. Worst case, I'll have to drive an hour to Studio City and surprise him at his office. I stumble on a stray electrical cord.

Grandma strolls through the courtyard like a character from *Bridgerton*, and doesn't look back as she steps in time to the Sinatra song. "Your mom left a few minutes ago to gather supplies in town. My book club has a big craft fair on the pier before my final party, and she's preparing everything for our booth." She spares me a glance, matching purple AirPod in her left ear. "She'll be home soon, lovie. She's looking forward to seeing you."

"I can't wait to see her," I reply, trying to keep any unease from my tone.

Did they watch the recording of the show yesterday? What do they know so far? What don't they know? How disappointed are they? I don't want to bring it up in case G-ma is still in ignorant bliss. I don't want to put a damper on this happy time for her. After everything she's been through with her stroke and recovery, she more than deserves to celebrate. Not that celebrating should be earned, but I want this to be a carefree time for her after too many months of the opposite. It was so scary when Mom and I got the call from the hospital. She'd fallen at home and a member of her book club was there and called the ambulance. She had a faster-than-expected recovery, surpassing milestones in physical therapy sooner than doctors expected. I helped Mom move her essentials down here when she first moved in, and seeing Grandma with all her spunk back now gives me so much joy. I'm so glad Mom has been here to give her support. I've missed them both so much.

My racing thoughts skid to a halt when we approach the brand-new building at the other end of the courtyard, the side closest to the ocean.

The small guesthouse is painted a soft shade of lavender. A waist-high white gated fence encloses a small yard before it, and in the center of the cobblestones is a fountain. The mermaid in this one is smaller than the ones out front, and holds a giant conch shell over her flowing hair.

Grandma opens the gate. I pull the earbuds from my ear and relinquish it back to her. "I didn't know you had this built. Wasn't there an outdoor kitchen here before? When did you have this guest home done?" I ask, my voice sounding far away. I didn't expect this change. I've missed so much more than I thought.

She holds the gate open. "This past year. A few months after your last visit, I decided I wanted to throw this big birthday celebration, so I had this built to prepare for all the family coming. I want my home overrun with people I love. What's the point in having all this stuff and space if I'm not going to share it?"

We head toward the guest cottage door, which is a deep fairy-tale purple. Succulents circle the base of the fountain, and no space of the lavender siding is untouched by morning glory vines; they spill into planters brimming with lavender bushes and yellow roses.

"Don't just gawk," G-ma orders as she pushes the front door open. "Go in."

We step over a turquoise mat that says DREAMERS WELCOME.

I place my bag on a blue mosaic-tiled bench near the entry, and take in the space. It's a cozy little cottage. To the right is a simple white kitchen save for the bright yellow countertop.

Straight ahead are sliding doors that lead to a small patio, then out to the wide-open beach, the shimmering sea beyond. On either side of the slider are two open doors that match the purple of the front and must lead to bedrooms. Facing the kitchen is a living room that looks more like a plant nursery. There's a TV in the corner, draped with vines. A coffee table and a velvet green sofa is camouflaged among fiddle leaf figs and dracaenas. The leaf-papered accent wall behind the couch is covered in pothos vines and Spanish moss, all planted in gold mounted pots.

Last time I was here, she took me on a tour of her new plants in the main house. She spent days teaching me what their names were (scientific and given), and what water schedule they preferred (Brenda the monstera was a guzzler). I'm glad to see her passion for plants has only grown. Literally.

"G-ma, this is adorable."

She nods matter-of-factly, then turns to me, pulling in her lips.

Her thinking face. I take a deep breath, bracing. She must have seen Dad's post. She doesn't have Instagram, and neither does Mom, but what else could she be thinking this hard about?

"Listen." She places her hand on my arm. "I know the show was rough on you. I saw it in your eyes as soon as that host brought up Adam. They had no right. But you did amazing. And you and that Reed boy will figure things out in your own time. Maybe sooner than you think." That sass in her eyes twinkles. "I'm so proud of you."

I grip the hem of my sleeve, twist the button. Guilt is a tangible stone in my gut. If only she knew that Dad is trying to take the recipe away and that I'm right back where I was years ago: trying to save our business. I should be grateful that she is fixating on my romantic life so that I have more time to solve the C&D issue.

My nails dig into my palms. "I think what I need is to let Adam go, G-ma."

She tilts her head to one side. "Have you even told him how you feel?"

My cheeks heat and I examine my loafers. "No."

She scoops her head beneath mine to catch my gaze. "Why not?"

We both straighten.

Because I'll lose whatever part of him I do have. I'll break our friendship. I'll be faced with his rejection every day. Because I'm terrified. "I haven't found the right moment."

She narrows her eyes and crosses her arms. "You've known that boy since you were eight years old. You think you're gonna find the time yet?"

She's not wrong.

I met Adam the first winter that my dad was gone. Mom was always the one to make Christmas magical in our home, but that year neither of us had the heart. There were still cookies and snow, but no Santa or carrots for the reindeer. There were the whispers when my teachers thought I couldn't hear, sad glances from my classmates' parents. There were casseroles. So. Many. Casseroles. I wasn't Ben anymore. I was the kid who got lost in the woods, the kid whose dad left him behind. Maybe that's not really how my neighbors viewed me, but there was the before and the after.

The thing that gutted me most was that there weren't activities I missed doing with him, no traditions he broke by leaving. There was a void, the house was more quiet without his business phone calls, Mom and I didn't have to whisper while he worked anymore, but there also weren't specific traditions that made me miss him. How could someone be your parent, be in your life for so long, then be gone without a trace?

He left on a Saturday. It took him four minutes to disappear. I counted the Mississippis until his black sedan shrank away, fit behind my reaching hand, then vanished beyond the trees. I wanted to chop them all down. I could have, Mom taught me how. We always picked out the perfect one for Christmas every year in the forest behind our home.

That year Mom didn't have the energy to harvest our own tree, so we visited the Reed Family Tree Farm. This tall kid stood behind the red kiosk. His shaggy dark hair peeked out from the bottom of his blue beanie, and he wore an oversized green plaid coat. "How can I help you?" He sounded so confident about the offer, like he could grant us anything, he was sure of it.

I wanted to cry because an almost nine-year-old couldn't say things to strangers like, "Can you bring my dad back?" So, I puffed out my chest, raised my chin, and said, "I'd like an ax, please."

He paused, but didn't squint or twist his brows into a question mark. He nodded and reached beneath the counter. Then, he rose with a red-handled ax.

"Thanks," I said, taking it in my hands. Its weight steadied my stance in the snow.

Mom stayed by the car, and the boy came with me. He didn't say a thing as I searched for the perfect tree, didn't whisper or exchange sad looks with any passersby. He studied the pines.

When I finally swung the ax, he said, "Good pick."

I thwacked the trunk until my arms, back, fingers, even my teeth hurt.

He didn't offer to help, like he already knew what my answer would be. He turned his back and let me swing until I was done. Until the tree fell and the tears stopped.

Then, he held out his hand and I returned the ax.

He rested the arm of it over his shoulder and trailed me as I dragged the tree down the hill, assisting with his free hand every so often. After I paid him, he helped me wrap the tree and mount it to the roof of Mom's car.

She started the engine. His breath fogged in the air. "Thank you," I said.

He smiled. "I think you're in class with my sister Rachel. I'm her big brother, Adam." He held out his hand. "It's nice to meet you."

His grip was firm, like he meant it.

Unable to reply with nothing more than my name, I nodded, then left.

As Mom drove and the forest blurred by, I didn't picture the girl in my class or the words *big brother*, it was just Adam. It was always Adam. The first person who didn't treat me like I was broken.

After everything, the thought of telling him how I feel and being rejected is too much. I couldn't stand having him look at me like he did yesterday ever again. Like he felt sorry for me.

I sigh. "It's not that easy to tell him how I feel, G-ma."

She raises a perfectly penciled brow. "It ain't that hard, either."

I huff a small laugh and side-eye the plush sofa. I could lie down there for five hundred years. Sleep and sleep and never have to face Adam or social media or a camera again.

She claps her hands in a *well, that's that* sort of way. "You make yourself cozy. Rest up and get ready for tonight."

"Tonight?"

She nods. "Our first themed bash. The closets in each bedroom are stocked with costumes."

I nearly swallow my tongue. "Costumes?"

"You know it." She circles her fist in the air like she's on a mechanical bull, which will probably be a featured attraction at this party, knowing her.

When I was growing up, Grandma's celebrations weren't just the talk of the town, they were in the Maywell County newspaper. Over the years, her events grew so extravagant that people off the guest list would buy tickets, and she started using her birthdays to raise funds for charity. No theme was off the table, and guests went all out in rented costumes.

I eye a bedroom door warily. Hopefully, I'll find a way to make a button-up, slacks, and oxfords look like cosplay.

The front door squeaks open. "Oh, by the way." She pauses on the front porch, reaches into the side pocket of her leggings, then tosses me a white tube.

I fumble the slick plastic in my hands. Then, I nearly fall to the floor as I turn it over and read the label. "G-ma, is this . . ."

She waves a hand flippantly. "Yes. Lube. For masturbating. Or other activities. With partners."

My mouth falls open. Permanently.

"Don't look so shocked, Ben. I've been around the block. You have angst in your pants and it's making you do the horny dance. Get it out. It's good for you. Why do you think I gave you a whole guesthouse to yourself? Feel free to invite someone to stay the night. The best way to get over that Reed boy is to get under someone else. Or on top. Hell, any direction. You're creative." She pops in her second AirPod then exits, casually closing the door behind her like this is a conversation grandmothers have with adult grandsons on the regular.

I cannot move because I am dead. I am literally dead and in a dimension of hell where my eighty-year-old grandmother just told me to jack off, among other things.

Conniving fathers and TV show catastrophes are on pause because I can only imagine what spiked and collared outfits await me in the closet, and I'm gonna need a goddamn nap.

Chapter 5

The itinerary posted to the closet door of the Teal Room (the bedroom I chose over the alternative Yellow Room) allocated three different costumes for each Saturday of my stay and specifically stated, No Substitutions. So, here I am, hiding behind the mermaid fountain out front of the guest cottage in buckled boots, leather pants with a matching jacket, flouncy beige blouse, and a giant black brimmed hat with an equally giant purple feather sticking out of the top. Pretty sure this outfit should transform your average pedestrian into a hot pirate, but the pants sag at my ass and the late-evening fog rolling off the water makes everything inside the leather a sticky, itchy horror show.

From beyond the fence of the cottage, I can hardly make out the courtyard due to the amount of people here. The guest list must have a lot more than Parrishes on it, or G-ma sold hundreds of tickets for charity. There are glimpses of the aqua pool, now mostly covered by a stage that's illuminated by purple lights affixed to overhead trussing. On the stage, actors in full pirate

garb duel with actual swords. The crowd clusters at extravagant buffet tables that line the perimeter of the courtyard. Even
from here, the carving stations and ice sculptures are visible,
and a bar with a neon magenta sign that reads THE TREASURE
CHEST has a wall-height backdrop of glittering bottles draped
with jeweled garland. A live band beyond where I can see plays
a blend of sea shanties and classic rock, and my restless thirty-
minute nap was grossly insufficient. If my grandmother wasn't
walking toward me right now, I'd take my sweaty ass right back
inside to spend quality time with my bath bombs.

"Shiver me timbers, if it isn't my handsome grandson," she
yells above the racket.

She wears a flowy crimson blouse with a purple-striped,
tattered-looking miniskirt and knee-high boots. Her red hair is
curled up beneath a floppy hat with a red feather.

Before I dare complain about my costume, she pulls me into
an ironclad hug. Eighty has nothing on her.

"Happy birthday," I force out through her vise grip. "It's a
full house. Did you open this party for charity tickets?"

"Not tonight," she says as she pulls back, allowing me the
courtesy of breathing. "I know there aren't many guests your
age, but I want you to feel comfortable partying as hard as you
like. Fern Falls is a small town. You go ahead and let off some
steam in Maywell Bay." She sweeps her arm across the scene as
if unveiling the land of milk and honey.

I cough on salty air. "Aren't most of these people my relatives?"

"No, no." She waves a hand, gold coin bracelets jangling. "I
invited neighbors, townsfolk, my book club, so choose widely
and wisely!" She gives a hearty laugh. "It'll be hookup rou-
lette."

I answer with a wheeze. If the Parrish bloodline could take
a five-second break from forcing people into awkward dating
situations, that would be fantastic. I guess this is what I de-

serve after meddling in my friends' love lives myself. But hey, Rachel and Morgan might not be married if it weren't for me getting Morgan back to Fern Falls with a tricky fundraiser proposal. Dammit. Maybe I should listen to Grandma and dance with someone tonight. Couldn't be worse than when I brought a summer crush to the Parrish block party the summer after high school. He was a lifeguard and endured very thorough interviews from each and every one of my relatives. After being given a Costco-sized box of condoms from my grandmother, I would have had to drown in front of lifeguard tower four just to see him again.

There was Charlotte Crane, a cute surfer girl I spent time with here, and she was wonderful. We raced our bikes through the harbor streets and she made me feel brave those last couple summers of high school. But in the end, she wasn't Adam.

My two-week commitment to get over him is starting off with a bang.

Grandma pats me on the backside, cranking up the heat in my face by a million degrees. Then, she hops off, talking to every person who crosses her path—at least twenty-five by the time she's a couple feet away.

Breathing as deeply as my leather jacket allows, I exit the shelter of the garden gate and plunge headfirst into the crowd. Okay, I skirt my way around the edge, and hide my face beneath the brim of my hat. At this angle, there are infinite boot buckles occasionally interrupted by stilettos and fishnets. The fresh ocean air is no match for the concentration of cologne and smoke of all kinds, with not-so-faint notes of stagnant tidepool.

I can make it through this. I survived worse yesterday, right? I'll take a quick lap to find Mom and say an overdue hello. I'm sure she's here somewhere. Then, I'll slip back into the cottage and get serious about self-care, a.k.a.: meditation app, then earplugs, eye mask, and sweet, sweet sleep.

I'll get to that sliver of space over there and—

"Benjamin James Parrish?" sounds a high-pitched voice.

I freeze, then slowly angle my head up. The rising brim of my hat reveals a rosy-cheeked pinkishly pale face I haven't seen in at least five years.

The middle-aged woman before me is decked out in a purple velvet cape and corset, high-waisted leather pants, and lace-up thigh-high stiletto boots. A purple bandana is tied around the top of her head, bright blond hair spilling down her back.

"Oh my stars! I knew it was you!"

She crushes me to her heavily perfumed bosom.

"Hi, Cousin Betty," I say, voice muffled. I have not even been here half a day, and I'm one hundred percent sure I have reached my overbearing hug quota.

Between Grandma's six ex-husbands, I have a movie-theater's worth of cousins who are not actually cousins, but who can't be labeled anything else, so cousin it is.

She pulls back, fixing me with bright blue eyes. "I saw you on TV, and that's great, Ben. That's just great. You have my number, right?"

"I don't think—"

"Because let me tell you, I have been acting up a storm in my local theater troupe, just played Lumiere in *Beauty and the Beast*, got so much praise, sold out the show—you have my number?" She reaches into a sequined clutch and retrieves her cell phone.

I don't even try to respond because in a breath she's off again.

"I'd love to be in touch with your agent. Brought my head-shots, always gotta keep those on you in the biz, they're back in the house, and I'll go get—"

Someone yells and she looks past my shoulder and waves vigorously. "Roxanne! Look who I found!"

I duck beneath the brim of my hat. I'm really starting to like this hat.

"Sure is!" Her blond hair sways as she nods. "And he's gonna get me an agent!"

I snap my head up. "It's been nice catching up, Betty. I'll see you around."

"Wait," she says, tugging my arm. "You have to come with us." She gently turns me toward the direction of the pool where a giant group of not-really-cousins is clustered around the sword-fight stage. They wave and yell my name, calling me over.

I would rather fling myself into the Pacific than make more small talk or navigate agent conversations for an agent I don't have.

I wave back, then face Betty. "I'm going to try and find my mom, but I'll catch up with you later." As in another five years.

Betty sticks out her bottom lip in a bright pink pout. "Okay, but don't be too long. Those sword pirates are hot stuff. One of them has been eyeing me all night. Gonna give him some acting tips, if you know what I mean." She elbows me and snorts.

"Sounds like a great night for you. Enjoy." Before she can reply, I dive into the crowd, which is more preferable than continuing this conversation.

No more slow-going. I push my way to the outskirts, scanning the faces for Mom— *Oof.* A sharp pain hits my thigh, or rather, I hit the edge of a buffet table. Rubbing the ache, I take in the display before me. A burgundy drape is covered in gold platters, overflowing with enough bounty from the sea to make one question if this whole pirate theme is an elaborate ruse for king crabs to take over the land. And, bingo: The source of stagnant tide pool has been located.

"Whatcha want?" asks the large muscular man behind the table with a red beard and the mannerism of a butcher. Rough. Murdery.

Hot?

I shake my head. Don't let G-ma get into your brain. Don't. Do. It.

There are lobster tails and shrimp piled into a pyramid formation and platters of fish—I gulp—with their heads still on. Their beady little eyes peer up, daring me to make a pick.

"I'm, um, good for now, thanks," I squeak, wiping my palms on my pants, which does nothing but slather the leather with sweat.

The man grunts and stares over my head, rubbing his pale knuckles into his red beard.

My eye catches on a tray of sapphire-blue cocktails at the end of the table. Between the crowd, the discomfort of these clothes, and the attention of my fish-head audience, I could use a drink. I grab a glass and swig. Something cold and pineapple-y slides down my throat.

A fist slams down on the table, and I nearly jump into the arms (legs?) of a giant crab, clear plastic cup falling to the ground.

"I'll take crabs," a guest with sweaty pale skin slurs with the confidence of an eighteenth-century royal. "And not the contagious kind." He snorts, swaying slightly.

The Butcher of the Sea glares at the man, nostrils flaring.

Taking my chance to slip away, I edge the crowd on the shore side, gulping at the breeze, that shot doing nothing but making me slightly dizzy. From this angle, a different platform is in clear view. It towers over the sprawling lawn at the edge of the courtyard and is shaped like a giant ship. Somehow, a multitiered stage was made to look like a vessel from *Pirates of the Caribbean*. The drummer, keyboardist, singer, bassist, and guitarist are spread out in a straight line, the only way they could all fit on the narrow deck. Each band member is shrouded in a thin blue-hued fog. A loud boom makes me startle. Sparks fire from a faux cannon, further obscuring the band in clouds of smoke.

I take this moment to accept that my grandmother married and divorced some very rich men, made wise investments, and here is the culmination of that legacy: a pyrotechnic pirate ship and zombie crabs.

She's always been this way, though, above and beyond, squeezing every last drop out of life. Growing up, family holidays were full-blown soirees with DJs and bands, chocolate fountains and champagne towers (matching juice ones for the kid table). Birthdays were always like this, although this one really takes the birthday cake. Even though I was too young to remember him, she never loved anyone like my grandfather. Years after Mom's dad died, each of Grandma's divorces were cause for weeks-long trips to Palm Springs.

After my parents split, Grandma came up to our home with a whole decorating crew ready to "breathe new life into the place." That was when Mom revamped the front room. The space that used to be Dad's office transformed into Mountain-top Mystic.

After the renovation was complete, Mom's witchy friends who now own Tea and Tarot in Fern Falls came over and performed a cleansing ceremony.

While Mom waved a bundle of herbs and smoke formed trails in the air like sheer ribbons, Grandma held my face in her hands and said, "Listen here, sweet child. Whatever gives you joy in this world, that is what you do. That is what you deserve. Every good and wonderful thing." She put her arm around my shoulders and pointed to Mom, who smiled bigger than I'd ever seen and whispered in my ear, "We love you, we love you, we love you." Then, she placed a kiss on my head and told me to go to sleep because the adults were gonna drink some potions.

Grandma stayed with us for six months while Mom started up the naturals shop to keep us afloat. And how do I repay everything they've done for me? Here I am, a grown man, with one legacy: Makes Mistakes. I can't even be trusted with my own family business. I wish I would have slowed down with the bakery's online presence, taken more time to consider how going on a national TV show could impact things, and how my father would react to it all. I was the one who pushed for this, always so invested in ideas that I don't think them through, like how I plunged into taking over the bakery only to fail on my own, threw my whole heart into an unrequited crush, ran into the forest.

"Ben?"

A soft voice pulls me out of my thoughts, and I turn to find my mom smiling over.

The sight of her sends a wave of calm through me, soothing the storm.

That breezy Mom of Summertime has become her permanent state: white-blond hair long and loose, skin tanned as much as our European roots allow. There's an ease to the set of her gray-blue eyes, they match her flowy dress. Even the fine lines around her mouth and between her brows are relaxed.

"Mom." All my muscles unwind as I stride over and hug her.

"Oh, sweetie. I have missed you. It's so good to see you." When we part, her eyes shimmer.

"I missed you, too," I say. Something sharpens her relaxed demeanor and she chews the inside of her cheek. "Is everything all right?"

She gives a tight smile. "I have so much to talk to you about. Are you free for breakfast tomorrow?"

I nod. My hat slides forward, and I push it back into place. "Of course. Is this about the show? I'm sorry I didn't call back last night, but I'm glad we got to speak this afternoon." Does she know about Dad? Did she see his post?

"Partly, yes. I want to make sure you're okay. You were amazing on the show, though, I want you to know that. I'm so proud of you, Ben."

My shoulders relax. Her words are such a relief to hear, but something's not right. There's an edge to her tone.

Her eyes dart around. "I need to go pay the vendors, but I'll make sure to track you down tomorrow morning."

"Okay. I'll see you then."

"I love you." She gives me a quick hug then she's off, pulling a small stack of white envelopes from a pocket in her dress.

I exhale a tight breath. Whatever our talk tomorrow brings, I'll make it right. I won't let my mistakes or my father ruin what I have left of my family.

I need to get lost in the noise, so I make my way up through the crowd. It's not a loud power tool, but it'll work. People shout and music blares as I push toward the ship-stage. My pants stick to my skin, tugging at leg hairs with each stride, but I don't care. I need the volume.

At the front row, bodies crunch in tight and the collective heat makes it hard to get a cool breath, but I inch through until I'm eye level with the deck of the ship.

There's a break in the fog and I lock eyes with the leather-clad guitarist.

My blood runs colder than Davy Jones' Locker.

I rub my glasses. The fog must be skewing my vision.

But, no.

Those eyes are a deep, luscious brown—and blown as wide as mine.

Standing in front of me, free of all auto grease and the pine tree setting I'm used to seeing him in, where I've only ever seen him, where he should be now, is Adam Fucking Reed. In a giant red pirate hat.

His twisted expression makes it seem like *he's* the one who's surprised to find me at my own grandmother's eightieth birthday party.

I turn on my heel so fast my hips will regret it in the morning. "I'm out," I proclaim.

"No shit, Parrish. We've known you're queer for years," Uncle Tim says, materializing beside me as a towering version of Disney's cartoon Smee, complete with a striped shirt, blue shorts, and red cap.

"No, that's not—"

He smiles encouragingly. "You've brought your partners to the summer block parties."

I give Mom's only sibling a blank stare.

He beams. "But shout it out, baby! Loud and proud!" He raises a red cup and swigs.

I move past Uncle Tim, presently known as The Most Annoying Ally.

The music shifts into something less guitar-heavy as I flee, pushing through the crowd.

"Ben!"

I don't need to turn. I'd know that voice anywhere.

He must have jumped off the stage and is now chasing after me. That's the only way he could be keeping pace. I should slow down. And say what? Sorry yesterday was so awkward, but you didn't need to come all this way to pity me. You could have pity-texted. I cannot see that look in his eyes again. My brokenness reflected in his regret. The way he turned and entered The Stacks. I can't ever see that again, even if it means I must run from him.

I've never been thankful to be smashed between complete strangers until now.

There is one mission: Say a quick good night to Grandma so she doesn't come hunting for me, then hunker down in the guesthouse like it's the zombie crab apocalypse.

"Ben!" Adam's voice is muffled, but every damn part of my body is so attuned to him that it's like he's yelling in my ear. Curse the universe for knowing I am so desperate for this man that I can't even descend the mountains to escape him.

I near the sword-fight stage and duck my head to hide from The Cousins when Grandma's laugh spikes from a side courtyard. Glancing back, I find Adam's red hat bobbing not too far behind, then I pull a quick right past a tall hedge.

Grandma and her friends are nestled among climbing vines and low-hanging tree branches. Every person is draped upon oversized patio furniture. A pitcher of whatever purple drink fills their glasses sits on the coffee table between them.

The smell of pot might get me high.

I hustle in, breathing into the crook of my elbow to keep my eyes from watering.

"Grandson the Favorite," Grandma calls, rising from a chaise lounge and swaying a bit. "I love Jason, and I'm proud of all the nature shows he makes, but he's not here now, is he?" She winks.

All her pirate costume–clad friends cheer, raising their drinks. She pulls me into another Ironman hug and slaps a wet kiss on my cheek. "Welcome to Book Club!"

A few members reach forward and refill their glasses, no novels in sight.

"What are you reading?" I ask in a rush.

"Tonight's not for reading," says a person with deep brown skin and bright red hair, laughing.

Tonight's also not for running back into Adam Reed. I have to make this fast, get out of here before he locates me in this pirate festival.

Grandma squints. "What's wrong my dear? You look like you've seen a ghost."

Yes, a very hot ghost who looks like Captain Killian Jones.

I gulp hard. "There's someone here I didn't expect to see," I admit for some reason. I'm probably getting a secondhand high.

"That's not the look of a haunted man, that's the look of love," says someone with bronze skin and pink hair.

Grandma nods and rubs her chin like a spiritual advisor. "Ah, yes. The two looks can be easily confused."

"You need some of this," says another member, raising their glass.

G-ma retrieves the pitcher from the table and holds it up between us. "My Healing Heartbreak Tea," she says reverently, as if it's an ancient rune carved by the sands of time.

"Your what?" I ask.

She lifts the pitcher. Moonlight sparkles off the violet concoction within the glass orb. "A cocktail strong enough to make you forget . . ." She closes her eyes. "Well, shit. I forgot."

In the span of two seconds, a drink is poured and shoved into my hand.

The smell makes my eyes water. This might be cough syrup.

"Ben." Adam's voice sounds at my back.

I freeze, clutch my glass.

G-ma and the book club face the opening in the hedge.

This can't be happening.

I turn slowly, and despite my rapid-fire wishing, I am not granted my plea.

Adam stands at the mouth of the garden.

He removes his hat and nods at Grandma like we're in the goddamn seventeenth century. "Ma'am."

I drain my entire cocktail.

Chapter 6

The last of the paint thinner fires down my throat, and I barely keep from breathing flames.

When I open my eyes, Adam Reed still stands beside the tall boxwood hedge before me. He's blurrier, but there, in all his Colin O'Donoghue glory.

"Look," he says, wringing his hat in his hands, hair messy, cheeks flushed, "I know it must be weird, me following you here, but I—"

"Weird?" I blurt. "Weird would be my grandmother carrying mints in her purse instead of edibles. This is not weird. This is *horrific*." I vaguely register a person refilling my glass. "This is you not even giving me a goddamn minute to breathe, leave town with my tail between my legs, and try to recover from making a complete fool of myself on live TV. Can you not let me get over you? For once?" I choke-gag-sputter, swipe my mouth. Never have I spoken that way to Adam. Or anyone.

Jesus Fucking Christ. What a way to formally admit my feelings to my lifelong crush.

My mortification has transformed me into a word-puke monster. But I'd rather be prickly than pitied.

The book club gasps as I pull in my lips and bite down hard before more vile stuff pours out. Grandma hands a glass of this shit to Adam. I pound at least half of my refreshed drink. Between the shot from earlier and the rate of my current quenching, things are more spinny than I'd like.

Adam's face is panicked, blotchy, eyes wide and kinda desperate. Every ounce of Reed chill gone. "Ben, I didn't realize, I—"

Grandma points to his glass. "I'd consider taking a sip before speaking."

He sets his hat down on a nearby chaise and takes an audible whiff of his drink. His eyes go glassy. "Oh my god. What is in this?" he asks, decorum slipping.

"All the answers you'll ever need," Grandma says like some oracle visiting us from the past.

"I already had a beer, I just wanted to talk to Ben—"

"Your call," Grandma says. Her tone is so ominous goose bumps rise along my arms.

He pauses, considering, shrugs like *what the hell*, then gulps it down.

After a held-breath second, he clicks his tongue and gives his head a shake, the drink probably setting fire to his throat like it did to mine.

Everything beneath the surface of my skin is burned raw.

When he gets his breath back, he sets his glass on the ground then says, "I came here to apologize."

His voice is raspy. Fuck. It's sexy. I hate it. It's gross.

My arms go slack. Oh, right. Glass. I tighten my grip at the last second before my cup crashes to the ground. "Apologize for what?" I ask. Casually. Coolly. Very put-together-y.

"First of all"—he runs a hand through his hair—"for barging into your TV moment and making it horribly awkward. Second, for running away after that. Third, for chasing you down just now like a creep. Fourth—"

"You couldn't have said this in a text?" I blurt, pressing my fingers to my lips a beat too late.

"Not when I told him my party band needed a guitarist," Grandma hollers.

My glare cuts to her. Betrayed by my own flesh and blood. "You invited him?"

She tilts her head, smiling. "I remember his talent from when I would visit you in Fern Falls, and was so pleased to see him play during the live taping. The band needed a guitarist in a pinch or else they had to cancel. No way am I letting all these old neighborhood folks sleep during my celebration weeks. Adam saved my party."

I choke on a fresh wave of herbal smoke. "He isn't staying the whole time, is he?"

"Of course," she responds.

I glare at Adam.

His face matches his discarded red hat, but I don't give a shit, and this drink is making sure I don't hide it one bit. "You couldn't have texted? Given me a heads-up?"

He shoves his hands into his front pockets.

Don't stare at his front pockets, dammit.

"I didn't know if you had my number blocked." He huffs a breath. "Kidding. Kinda. I wouldn't blame you if you did. But I had to talk to you." His expression is pained.

"Again," I grit out. "A conversation easily had via remote means."

He comes closer until he stands right before me. My head might float off.

"Ben. I'm sorry." His voice is soft. "I know you're upset now, that you were really upset yesterday. I don't want to make it worse, I just had to talk to you in person. I'm so sorry."

There it is, the pity. I can't fucking take it. He must need to return to Fern Falls before the end of two weeks. Doesn't he have bandmates waiting there, warming his bed? "What about the auto shop? Don't you have cars to mechanic? Do you have precisely a two-week surplus of profit or something?"

He smiles. "Old Rusty is covering for me. Said he could give retirement a hiatus if I give his grandson guitar lessons."

I narrow my eyes. "So you do have a two-week surplus of profit." They don't call him Old Rusty for nothing, and "retiree" is a loose term for a fifty-five-year-old man who takes odd jobs and fiddles with cars just enough to keep them from falling apart. Barely.

Adam gazes at me with his lashes lowered. "It was a fair trade to come and spend the time with you."

I sway, falter, tilt to the side. He steadies me with his hand on my arm, because of course he does. His touch is not warm or comforting. It does not send a shiver down my entire left side. I do not like it at all.

"Okay," Grandma says, taking my glass. "The first time with the tea is always a short one. Let's get you two to bed, shall we?" G-ma and the Book Club, which sounds like the name of a blues band or drag show, wrangles Adam and me into the mass of them. We all stumble through the crowd like a conga line from hell until Adam and I are coughed out in front of the purple cottage and nudged through the garden gate.

A slurred "Really? He's staying with me?" slips from my mouth. I'm answered by a wink from my grandmother as Adam opens the front door and we tumble inside.

Once the door shuts and the outside noise muffles, he runs a hand through his hair. "I promise I'll give you space," he says, talking to the floor.

Moon rays filter through the sliding doors on the far wall, casting the light hardwood in silver.

I toss my hat down, then lumber to the kitchen and press my back into the counter to stay as steady as possible. I snort. I hated the way his apology felt like pity, but he did come all the way here, and that's . . . really fucking hot. Because what if I'm sick of space? Sick of worrying and caring too much but not being able to show it, always being too scared to show how much I care. "What if I want you closer?"

Adam's head shoots up and his eyes lock on mine.

Shit. I take it I said that aloud. I swallow hard.

"That's what you want?" He walks forward slowly, hands pushing into his pockets.

I nod.

He eyes me cautiously. "Tell me when to stop, then?"

I tilt my head to the side and glare at him. How dare this fucking man. Just when I was determined to get over him, set on it, ready to convert to an Adam-free lifestyle, he shows up with the audacity to be sexier than ever.

I shift to try and hide how much this turns me on, but that "tea" won't let me do anything with grace, and I slip along the edge of the counter.

Adam lunges forward with his arm outstretched, then stops and straightens as I catch myself.

"Are you okay?" he asks, voice tight.

I grip the surface to play it off like I was leaning. Blame it on a lifetime commitment to *While You Were Sleeping*. "I'm cool," I grit through clenched teeth, my libido making every muscle ache for contact with him.

He holds my gaze. "Do um . . . you want me to stay put?" His throat bobs. "Do you want me to stop?"

"Please," I huff, gulping a breath.

He nods sharply and turns toward the living room.

"Don't," I blurt. "Please don't, is what I meant." I stride forward. "Don't stop."

He turns for me as I near him, and whether it's my tea-riddled lack of depth perception or my brain catching up too slowly, I jerk to a halt and barely keep from slamming my nose into his mouth.

His goddamn mouth is right. There.

Neon lights dance through the front blinds, highlighting his skin in a fluorescent rainbow like a one-man Pride parade.

His lashes fan out across his cheeks as he stares down at my lips.

"Why are you here, Adam?" I hold my breath.

He exhales. "I had a whole speech planned, but it's fuzzy now." He shakes his head. "I fucked up during that recording, and I had to talk to you, see you. I couldn't let you go."

I am wholly grateful that he didn't text me that. My ears memorize the exact cadence, pitch, tone of his voice.

My fingers ache to touch him, but I wasn't invited. Yet. I'm adopting a growth mind-set.

His breaths are sharp.

In. Out.

Hot against my lips.

In—Out.

I could feast on the scent of him. Bake it into infinite recipes. Savory, sweet. Perfect.

"You've had a lot to drink," he rasps.

My eyelids flutter open. "You have, too." My voice comes out rough.

His lips near mine. "So, this is a bad idea."

Our thighs make contact and I hiss in air as a shock of pleasure shoots through me. He's going to feel . . . how hard I want him. "Terrible," I scratch out. "The worst."

"But you want to," he whispers. It's not a question.

Let him feel me. All of me. I can't hide it anymore, and I'm grateful. I'm so tired of hiding. "You know I do."

His hands grip my hips and I might pass the fuck out.

"Me too." He crushes his lips to mine.

My heart is no longer on that roller coaster, it's flying off the tracks in free fall.

I gasp, pushing my lips to his, my fingers to his chest, up his neck, the cut of his jaw, curves of his ears, grip the roots of his hair.

This is what it's like to kiss Adam Reed.

I could knead this man like dough in my hands for hours on end. He's firm all over, and with each touch—he moans. "Ben."

My name on his lips, my lips on his lips.

I offer my tongue, and he ushers me in greedily, devouring. Wanting. It's there. It's right there. He wants me. He must, to be kissing me like this.

His mouth is hot, his tongue a lick of fire, and I want more, I want it all. I want to burn.

His fingers brush my cheeks, beneath the rims of my fogged-up glasses, calluses scraping my stubble. Every cell in my body is alight.

He reaches beneath my leather coat, then works the laces of my thin blouse with deft fingers until he touches my bare skin. I push my tongue against his. More. Please. Now.

His hands plunge down and clutch my hips, drilling me against him.

The hard length of him presses against my own need, and I grind in response until he's backed up against the couch. Face hot, I glance down at the welcoming cushions, then back up at him, lick my lips.

His chest rises and falls against mine. He pinches his brows together, then places his hand on my shoulder and whispers, "We should . . ." A muscle flinches in his jaw. "Slow down. I don't want to give you the wrong idea."

I stumble back and steady myself against the counter as the room takes a spin. "The wrong idea?"

He nods, rubbing the back of his neck. "That this is what I came here for."

My stomach swoops. I might be sick.

Of course.

Right. Because why would he want to hook up with me?

A pity fuck. That's what this was—would have been.

I try to catch my breath as Adam slumps onto the couch. He searches my face, eyes pleading. "I'm sorry if I gave you the wrong impression. We've always been friends, and I'm sorry if you thought I just wanted—"

"Don't worry about it." I won't let him say that he feels bad for leading me on. I can't hear him apologize for kissing me.

I will not be pitied in my own grandmother's fairy-tale wet dream of a cottage wearing saggy leather pirate pants. "I'm going to bed," I say, before I might actually be sick in front of him and lose any last shred of pride.

I beeline toward the Teal Room and catch one last glimpse of Adam as his head falls into his hands. I slam my door.

If he regrets our kiss that much, then so do I.

Flinging my wasted body onto the bed, I break into rasping sobs.

I grip the silk teal pillowcase and hold on tight as the room swirls.

Forget tonight. Forget the high of the hope I had moments ago. That drunken kiss won't mean a thing tomorrow because hopefully I'm too far gone to remember it. Come on, Heartbreak Tea. Forget, forget, forget.

Chapter 7

No amount of painkillers could cure this headache. The fit I awoke from can't count as sleep; the memory I wish the tea stole played on loop in my mind all night long.

Adam's perfect mouth on mine, hands in my hair, orchestrating pleasure from every part of me like a love-starved symphony. I kissed the man I've dreamed of kissing for all my aware-of-kissing-years—then, boom. Gone.

I don't want to give you the wrong idea. We've always been friends.

I'm nothing to him but a regret now. He came all the way here to let me down easy. Why did he feel the need to kiss me? And like that? Make me believe he actually wanted me. Am I so pathetic that he couldn't be honest with me from the start?

I'm going to stay in bed all day. The whole two weeks. With my messy hair and bad breath and hangover spins. No more parties. I can Zoom with Grandma. I can—

Wait. Zoom. Shit. Fuck. What day is it?

I scramble for my glasses on the nightstand and my fingers

brush the bottle of grandma-gifted lube. "Ah, no." I wrench my hand back like it was bitten.

After putting my glasses on, I reach into the back pocket of these damn leather pants that I didn't even strip off, and pull out my phone.

It's Sunday. I have a Zoom call with Delish Dollars Studios in— Jesus Christ. One minute.

I might have time to brush my hair.

I bolt upright—clutch my head. The darkness behind my eyelids morphs into the teacup ride at Disneyland.

My phone shrieks with the Zoom ringtone.

I scootch back until I'm propped up against the headboard, run my fingers through my hair, adjust my glasses.

This is as good as it's gonna get, so I take a deep breath and answer.

My face fills the screen as the call loads and, oh my god. I have sleep crust beneath my puffy eyes, dried drool on my cheek, and overgrown stubble.

With this disheveled leather jacket, I look like a blond Tommy Lee with glasses. So, nothing like Tommy Lee. More like a geeky groupie who can't handle one party thrown by his grandmother.

I wipe my face just as Delish Dollars' video pops on.

"Mr. Parrish," a man with white skin, brown hair slicked to the side, and a gray suit jacket addresses me without shifting his focus from the surface of his giant mahogany desk. "My name is John Sawyer, and I am Director of Public Relations for the Delish Dollars Studio Network."

The Instagram situation is so bad that I am speaking one-on-one with a top TV executive. Cool, cool. "Hello," I croak.

His expression startles when he takes in the screen, then he returns his attention to his desk.

Good for him. I would also like to not look at my face in the corner of my screen right now.

"Mr. Parrish, have you checked your social media pages since Friday?"

And willingly throw myself further down a self-loathing spiral? "I have not."

He clears his throat. "As of ten minutes ago, there were roughly one hundred thousand likes and fifty thousand comments on a post from the account of Jake Gibbons Music Management claiming to be your father, and that you stole his recipe that you are competing with in *Take the Cake National*. Is this correct?"

My heart shoots into my throat. "No."

The man eyes me. "Jake Gibbons is not your father?"

"No, yes, he is."

He raises a brow. "This does not look good. The public is turning on you, and they're the ones whose votes matter in the Bake-Off finale, and whose views matter for the network's ratings. There is even a BoycottBen hashtag circulating in response to the post."

I swallow hard. "What do you want me to do?"

He folds his hands atop his desk. "Ideally, that Instagram post needs to come down."

I could make like a Disney Channel sitcom and sneak into Dad's office while incognito, steal his cell phone, and permanently delete his Instagram account. Perfect. Totally plausible. I bite my cheek. I can't let Delish Dollars Studios find out that the situation is a whole lot worse than an Instagram post alone. I glance at my duffel bag in the corner. The C&D letter is tucked inside the front pocket.

If some bad press is making the network question their investment in me, I doubt they'd touch the recipe with a ten-foot whisk if they knew about the cease and desist. "I can try to have the post taken down," I rasp, mouth dry.

He frowns. "You'll have to do better than that, or we'll be forced to disqualify you from the Bake-Off. It's a family-friendly show, and promoting this father-son discord will be terrible for ratings and our advertisers."

My stomach aches. "Is there anything else I can do?" I could bring out Mom's cookbook, show that the recipe is ours, but no one is going to care about a handwritten recipe unless I can prove the date and time, and that it was after Dad left. But then I'd also have to prove when he left, and that we didn't create the cookbook recently. So, that won't work. And reporting him on the app won't do a thing. This is a mess.

"There may be one thing," the man says.

I lean forward.

"Before your father made his post, there was a lot of sympathy on Twitter around your interaction with—" He references a piece of paper on his desk. "Adam Reed."

My hand turns slick and I adjust my grip on the phone. "What does he have to do with anything?"

"Viewers had empathy for your rejection, which is why the network is going to all this trouble, why they're giving you a chance instead of wiping their hands of this family conflict. There seems to be a very vocal sector of social media that wants to see you and Adam together. Badam, they are calling it."

Every muscle within me tenses. Pitied by the whole country. Just like the news when I was a kid. Badam? What the hell? I force a deep breath.

"If you can get photos with Mr. Reed for social media, show you two together, reconciling, that may bring the public around and overshadow this issue with your father. Fix the bad PR with good PR."

I shake my head. It's nearly ten thirty in the morning, and based off the disaster that was last night, Adam must be long gone back to Fern Falls. Plus, there's no way I'd ask him to do this for me even if he was still here. The thought of begging him to spend time with me, take photos with me, makes me want to crawl beneath the comforter and never leave. "I don't know if I can," I croak out.

"Then Delish Dollars Studios doesn't know if we can continue with this partnership, and we will need to recoup our losses."

I blink hard. "You will make me pay for being disqualified from the final competition?"

He taps a pen on his desk. "A month ago, you signed a contract stating that the recipe you entered into this competition was your own. That contract clearly states that falsified information will result in legal consequences." He shifts in his chair. "Making you pay for the production costs of your montage episode and the added costs of production delays while we locate an alternate competitor is generous."

I'm drowning in a sea of teal sheets. I can't catch my breath. "How much? Will it cost?"

"Approximately one hundred thousand dollars," he replies like we're talking about splitting lunch.

I clutch my stomach. I can't ask Grandma for money to save the business, not again. If they kick me off the show, I'll have to confess everything to both her and Mom. God, Mom. She trusted me to pull this off. My ears ring.

"Mr. Parrish?" the man says, his voice underwater. "You have two weeks to turn this around with better PR, as we discussed. My assistant will send you a Zoom link for a call two Sundays from now, and we'll come to a decision then."

Before I can respond, his screen goes blank and *the host has ended the meeting* pops up.

I lower the phone and slide down the bed until silk teal pillows frame my view. Hexagon-shaped mirrors are laid like tiles across the whole ceiling.

There I am, floating above the bed, a buckled boot in one mirror, a leather-clad arm in another, the top of my greasy hair reflected straight above.

How did I get here? Before filming, everything was fine. Life was quiet and orderly and comfortable. Safe and predictable.

I want to go home. I want to return to my bakery and make

my cinnamon rolls for the people I love in Fern Falls. I want to deliver them to the inn and wave hello to neighbors on my way, and smell the pine wafting through the air, warm sunshine trickling down through the branches.

I want to go back to my garage and fix things and be alone. Alone was fine. Alone was great.

My phone rings. Mom's name fills the screen.

I gasp in a breath and pick up.

"Ben?" she says with spunk like she's on her second cup of coffee and wasn't stupid enough to drink too much last night, kiss an unrequited crush, fall into a legal lockdown with a major TV network. "You there, sweet pea?"

"Here," I say. "Hi."

"I'll be there in ten minutes so we can head to brunch. Sorry I'm later, my morning meditation ran long."

Right. She wants to get breakfast today. She has something she wants to talk to me about. I could sink through the mattress from exhaustion.

I can't let her down. Gotta pick my total-failure-of-a-son battles. "Great," I say, trying my best not to sound like burnt toast personified. "I'll see you in ten."

She says goodbye and hangs up.

I rise from the bed slowly and creak open the bedroom door, peering out like there's a monster in the house.

The couch is empty. In fact, it looks like it was never slept on. Adam already left. He must have waited until he sobered up then drove home last night. He's probably back in his auto shop right now.

Stepping out, I glance into the kitchen, and the coast is clear. The patio to my right is empty. The bedroom door across from mine is closed, and no noise comes from behind it.

Maybe he slept in there. Maybe he is still sleeping and didn't leave at all.

My stubborn heart leaps at the thought. When will I learn what's best for me? I need to let him go.

I close my bedroom door and head toward my private bathroom beside the closet. At least I can finally be rid of this cursed pirate costume. I'm ready to burn it as a sacrificial offering to the zombie crabs along with the rest of my entire fucked-up life.

Chapter 8

"I cannot believe these biceps on you."

It's been twenty minutes since Mom and I left Grandma's property to walk into town, and it's the hundredth time she has commented on how much I've grown, like I'm still pubescent or something.

It's not like I measure my arms. Maybe I have bulked up from baking more? Sanding nightstands down to stumps? The short sleeves of my blue polo aren't tight though, and she's biased. "Mom, it's just been a while since we've seen each other in person."

"I know. My baby." She pulls me into a side hug and the top of her head meets my chin. "It's so good to have you here."

I squeeze her shoulder. "It's good to see you." I want to memorize her smile before I ruin her life with the news of how horribly I have failed with the bakery, the show, everything.

We return to our regular stride, and my loafers pad along the weathered planks of the boardwalk. The sand is spotted with late morning beachgoers, and silhouettes of surfers bob on the horizon.

Being here is a balm of comfort I desperately need. My problems aren't gone, not in the least, but there is something about the seaside that puts hardships on a brief pause.

Closer to the water, small dots of sandpipers skitter along the edge of the tide.

When I was young, I loved boogie boarding in the white water until my arms ached so badly I couldn't paddle anymore. Ocean water would drain from my ears and nose long after I returned to our beach towels, and salt crusted my hair as it dried. Mom read romance novels beneath her umbrella as I burritoed myself in a towel and buried my legs in the sun-warmed sand until I fell fast asleep.

Maybe Dad would have liked those beach days with us. Mom and I didn't spend summers here until he left. Before then, we only came for winter holiday weekends, when it was too cold to go in the water or enjoy the beach without wearing coats.

During those visits, he'd use the closer proximity to LA as an excuse to take meetings with artists and potential clients and partners, so the time he did spend with us was minimal, and usually centered around the dinner table. At least that was an improvement from home.

I once read a study in one of Mom's magazines that families who eat dinner together have lower separation rates. So, when we were all home, no matter what, I'd make sure we ate the last meal of the day side by side. If I brought my sandwich into his home office and asked Mom to bring her tarot cards, we were together, and there was food, so everything would be okay.

The day he left, I stood in the street and remembered that we ate apart the night before. I'd fallen asleep in front of the TV, and didn't have a chance to bring my Lunchables onto the patio, where they were fighting.

After he left, I would eat dinner early, and with Mom, glued to her side. I couldn't sleep well for months because each time I closed my eyes, there was my Lunchables tray on the coffee table, then his sedan disappearing through the trees. My brain added Mom's car following him, and then I'd be left there, standing barefoot in the gravel with my stupid crackers and die-cut lunch meat and artificially colored cheese, and no one left at all.

I slept in Mom's bed for months. Every little noise woke me up, and each one made me check her pillow, panicking that she might be gone, too.

My therapist helped me work through a lot of that, and so did Mom. Her steadiness, her calm, intuitive, reassuring presence.

She was always there. Always.

Just like she is now.

Maywell Bay is usually my respite from bad memories, but everything seems bad lately.

Mom smiles and light glistens off her oversized sunglasses. In the distance, children laugh while burying each other's legs in sand. One young girl frees her lower half, and lunges for her friends, arms outstretched, yelling, "Feed me brains!"

Despite everything, I chuckle. This right here isn't bad at all.

"Here we go, the restaurant's this way." Mom points to the right where two parallel rows of wooden buildings jut off from the start of the sand.

The boardwalk winds us up to the charming street where I used to get ice cream.

"Cone and Go is still here," I say, taking in the turquoise building with a pass-through window and pink awning above it. I would run up from the beach and grab two cones with one dollar.

Mom smiles. "Yep, right on the corner. I'll take you to get a double mint chip, but you have to eat all your breakfast first."

We laugh, and my steps lighten the farther we head up Main Street. There's Great Triton's Trinkets, a beachy gift store no wider than a large minivan filled with rainbow-painted sea stars and sand dollars, crocheted shell-collecting bags, and postcards of the Maywell Bay coastline.

We pass a trendy, airy space filled with plants, candles, and handmade pottery.

A vintage store plays Blondie from a boom box by the hot-pink front door.

Baskets of flowers hang from streetlamps. Succulents border every shop. The soft breeze scents the warm salty air with freshly baked bread. A couple of tourists wearing matching TAKE ME AWAY TO MAYWELL BAY T-shirts walk by holding hands as gulls swoop overhead. There's a quiet hum of relaxed busyness as shopkeepers greet customers. It all creates a feeling that something wonderfully unexpected is just around the corner; the feeling of summertime. Something I haven't felt in way too long.

"You'd think you've never seen this place before," Mom says, smiling over.

"It's changed a bit."

She nods. "A bit of change can be good. When Grandma started getting better, we visited this street with her friends, her knitting club, her book club, and I realized how much I missed Maywell Bay, the warmth of it, in so many ways. The wonderful memories from my childhood, and yours."

I step over a small mound of windblown sand. "I can see that. It's comforting being back, knowing that some good things stay good."

"Yeah," she says, smiling. "There are new places, too, that are just as good." She ushers me toward a little white wooden building that faces the water. There's a yellow awning above a red Dutch door.

A broad-framed light-skinned woman leans over the lower half of the door and waves, long red hair swaying. "Laura! Come on in! We've got your table ready!"

Mom beams and shifts her sunglasses to rest atop her head. "Tina, good to see you. Thank you."

"You're a regular, huh?" I ask.

She loops her arm through mine. "C'mon, you're gonna love this place."

The woman ducks inside and chats with someone at a host stand as Mom pulls me forward. CHARLIE'S BEACH HUT is painted in blue on the top half of the door, and we enter into a whitewashed, wood-paneled space that smells like bacon. So much bacon. A cross breeze passes through the open windows, wafting the scent beneath my nose. My stomach grumbles. We squeeze between tightly placed tables, crowded with guests who talk and laugh while Colbie Caillat sings about her toes from the overhead speakers. There's an open spot by a window, and as we approach, I notice a Post-it on the floral-patterned tablecloth that says *Reserved for Laura*. We slide into the booth and Mom studies her plastic-covered menu. I examine the media beneath the glass tabletop. There's a KEEP OUR OCEANS CLEAN sticker with Surfrider Foundation's website at the bottom of a wave, a business card for Lucky Larry's, which must be a plumber due to the clip art image of a smiling toilet, a kid's menu with crayon marks everywhere but inside the lines of dolphins and sea stars.

A collection of old license plates is displayed above the burlap window valance. Weathered shutters frame a perfect view of the ocean. The sky is clear enough that the Maywell Islands are visible, three small land formations that mark the horizon. They are protected bird sanctuaries only accessible to scientists and professors.

What would it be like to bring Adam to a little café like this, even as friends? Would he love it like I do? What would we talk about? There's so much I want to ask him, to know about his life. In many ways, my giant crush has held me back from any kind of relationship with him. Yes, we were closer when we were young, hanging out with Rachel and Morgan, attending school events, hiking on weekends, heading to the Fern Falls Peak swimming hole, all as a group. But then there was that time we went camping alone, and my feelings for him hit me like a lightning bolt. They've choked me up around him ever since.

Until last night.

Ugh.

"What are you having?" Mom asks in a breezy tone.

I lift my menu, like I was studying it all along, and not trying to solve my love life woes by staring at the horizon like a sailor of olde. "What do you suggest?"

"Hey, folks," a friendly voice sounds, accompanied by two glasses of water being placed on the table. "Are we ready to order?"

I smile at the petite Black woman with a long dark braid trailing down her back, a streak of hot pink woven through. Her smile is as bright as ever, and that same golden "C" charm hangs around her neck. Recognition fills me with joy. "Charlotte?"

My teenage sometimes more-than-friend, Charlotte Crane, who'd race me on our beach cruisers, who drew me out of my shell the last couple summers of high school, blinks back.

"Oh my god, Ben?" Her face breaks out into a brilliant smile.

I stand and am instantly swept into a classic Charlie hug. Warm, welcoming, all-consuming.

Her familiar scent of jasmine and sea salt flashes snapshots of my last full summer in Maywell Bay.

Coconut rum and pouring rain, soaking sand beneath a bamboo shade.

Charlie's fingers traced up my arm. I leaned in. Maybe, all I needed to forget Adam was to give myself over to someone new. Someone kind and gorgeous who wanted this, wanted me.

Her lips were sweet and her kiss was open and honest, laying all her intentions bare.

But she wasn't the one I wanted back, not like that, not romantically. Not like I wanted Adam.

I'll never forget the hurt in her eyes when I pulled away, how it sliced through me.

I clear my throat, halting the images. "How are you doing?"

She smiles, and there's no trace of the pain from that senior year summer. "Good, I own this place." She glances at Mom. "So glad you brought him in, Laura."

Mom beams.

"That's amazing!" I say. "I have a café up in Fern Falls now. Nice to see you, fellow foodie."

She chuckles. "I knew you'd find your way, Ben. You've always been so talented. How long are you in town for?" Her deep brown eyes sparkle.

If she only knew I was still so lost. Still stuck and afraid. Before Charlie, my teenage summers were spent on small flings with beachgoers and tourists and that one international student who worked at the ice cream shop. Always surface dates and short kisses, people who wouldn't be here long-term. Always with some sort of hope that Adam and I might get together come fall.

Sometimes, I'd sit on the beach and think of him, wondering what he was up to. Who his summer fling was that year. Would he notice my fresh tan, my sun-bleached hair? Maybe that would be the year I'd catch his eye.

But each fall I'd come home, and he'd be with someone new, but never for long, and I couldn't understand. The way he looked at me sometimes, like if we finally ripped past the facade of everything we didn't say, we could have something real, important.

But it's the speaking up that's the scariest.

It's running down the gravel drive and watching a sedan disappear scary.

Praying it was just another work trip scary.

Especially after last night, I wish I could get him out of my head.

I swallow. "I'm in town for a couple weeks, for my grandmother's family birthday reunion."

"Ah, Grandma Parrish and her famous parties." She grins.

"You should come by next Saturday, Charlie," Mom interjects.

"Yeah," I add. "It'd be great to catch up." Maybe it'd help me get over Adam if I danced with Charlie for a bit, hung out like we used to.

"That would be amazing, thank you! My girlfriend has been begging me to take a break from the restaurant. Would it be okay if I brought her?"

"Of course," Mom says.

I smile. Good for them. And best for me to not jump into anything, redirecting my pain like I did as a teen.

"Thank you." She smiles. "Your brunch is on the house. You want your regular, Laura?"

Mom nods. "Times two, please. Thank you, that's so kind of you."

"Thanks, Charlie. So good to see you."

"You too, Ben." She pats the table and turns, walking toward two double doors at the back of the restaurant.

Sliding back into my seat, I eye my mother as she busies herself with a napkin. "Mom."

"Hmm?" She doesn't look up.

"Did you bring me here so I could meet Charlie again?"

She sighs. "I didn't know she has a girlfriend."

I shake my head. A Parrish must always meddle. "I promise I'm okay. I'm good. You don't need to set me up."

"I just worry about you up in Fern Falls, alone. And the recording . . . I know that must have broken your heart when Adam walked away. You've held a torch for him for so long."

My stomach clenches. If only I'd known on Friday to prepare for the pain of kissing him and being rejected afterwards. "I am not alone," I say as much to myself as to her. "I have the best friends. I have a whole community. What about you? Do you have a community here?" I'd like to not discuss my crash-and-burn romantic life anymore, and I really do want to know about her new life here, in Maywell Bay.

Her face brightens. "I joined a local club for divorcees. We meet here every Wednesday."

Whenever Mom refers to herself as a divorcee, I get a tightness in my chest. It's been so long since my parents split. I want her to be happy. But maybe she is? Singledom can be a joy. "So, was a matchmaking attempt the reason why you brought me here? Is that what you wanted to talk to me about?"

She shakes her head, not laughing like I thought she would. "I want to talk to you about Grandma."

Worry knots my center. "Is she healthy?"

"Oh, yes, sorry. Nothing like that," Mom says, shaking her head.

I sigh with relief.

Lines paint her forehead. "I need to talk to you about her finances."

I shift in my seat. "Okay." I never thought this was a concern for Grandma, but the look on Mom's face says I was wrong.

"With all the family coming in, your grandmother asked me to take over the planning for the party. I've been hiring vendors and dealing with her bank, and it looks like, well—" She takes a sip of water. "To be frank, it looks like your grandmother is in major financial distress."

I reach for my own cup. My hand shakes as I lift it to my lips. I accepted Grandma's funding for the bakery when she helped me out. Could that have contributed to her hardships? A stone sinks in my gut. I set my glass down without drinking. "How bad is it?"

She doesn't look up. "After the party, we need to start liquidating some of her estate in order to build her account back up. And with the backlog of hospital bills that keep coming in, she may still lose the house she loves so much."

I slump against the yellow pleather seat. G-ma was so happy yesterday, talking about the legacy of her home, for her family. "What do we do? She cannot lose the house. It'll break her." It'll break all of us.

"Please promise me you won't say anything to her, Ben. She deserves to celebrate this milestone birthday, especially after fighting so hard to make a full recovery from her stroke." She reaches over and grasps my hand. "I know I had my worries, but thank you for doing the TV show. I'm sorry I was so scared about the media, and our history with your father. You were right to not let that hold us back. Keep doing what you're doing for our business. It's our biggest hope to make all of this right for your grandmother."

My mouth goes dry as she puts her hands in her lap and stares down.

I need to up the timeline on visiting my father in order to get that Instagram post taken down and appease Delish Dollars Studios. Plan B is getting good press with Adam, but after last night, it's safe to say that any hope for Badam is as crumpled as my pirate costume on the Teal Room floor.

Anxiety grips me. I have a bumpy two weeks ahead if I'm going to turn everything around.

But if G-ma can fight for her health, I can fight to help her finances. I can at least try. If I fail, I face disqualification from the show, and digging us an extra hundred thousand dollars into the hole.

I no longer have an appetite.

"Hey, folks, here we are." The redhead who welcomed us into the restaurant places two heaping plates before us, followed by steaming mugs of coffee.

A personal buffet of shredded hash browns, scrambled eggs, bacon, and sliced avocado beckons, and I can't stomach any of it.

"Enjoy, you kids," says the server.

"Thank you, Tina." Mom starts to dig in, but I can only stare at the vast expanse of sea beyond the window.

The solutions I need aren't on a plate, and I have a sickening feeling I may not be able to fix anything at all.

Chapter 9

Mom stays in town to pick up more supplies for the craft fair she is helping Grandma with next week, so I race-walk back. There's no time to waste. Approaching the courtyard to Grandma's house, I pull out my phone and search for Jake Gibbons Music Management. Google confirms that his office in Studio City is about an hour away from Maywell Bay. I should be able to slip away tomorrow afternoon. For now though, I could use a nap. Or a second shower. Or just a minute alone in the cottage to get my thoughts together.

I pocket my phone and enter the back courtyard—freeze. There, along the side of the house, is Adam's truck. A teal '77 Chevy Silverado with ADAM'S AUTO inscribed on the driver's door.

He didn't go back to Fern Falls, which means he must have been in the second bedroom this morning. Since I wasn't able to eat much at breakfast, I could use some coffee and food from Grandma's kitchen. That's why I head to the main house. Avoiding Adam in the cottage has nothing to do with it.

The courtyard bustles with workers, cleaning up the carnage

from last night. People haul tables and chairs while dodging discarded cups, feathered boas, and an array of scattered sandals. Some guests are either sunbathing on chaise lounges or passed out on the grass in pirate costumes, wide-brimmed hats low, covering their eyes from the late morning sun. G-ma sure knows how to throw a rager, which is something I shouldn't feel comfortable saying about my grandmother.

I round the front of the house where five box trucks labeled with HARRY'S RENTALS span the driveway and people in coveralls load up trussing and tables and lights.

A pair of workers pass, revealing the front fountain. Right in front of a spouting merfolk stands Adam. He is in running shorts and sneakers and nothing else.

My heart plummets through my loafers. I swerve and hide behind a truck, peeking around the side.

A silver-haired lady in a hot-pink sweat suit stands beside him holding a small terracotta planter. They both hunch over, peering at the potted succulent like it's a newly discovered species. At least, Adam does. The woman eyes his abs.

"I'm not too familiar with coastal vegetation," he says, rubbing his chin, "but I think it might be overwatered." He straightens. "Maybe cut back when the humidity is higher?"

"Are you sure?" the lady asks.

So, Adam is now the gardening expert of Sea Crest Drive. It's easy to see why when he takes the pot and lifts it over his head, those chiseled abs and arms on full display.

My stomach swoops.

How does he have the audacity to look this good? The traitorous sun hits the side of his profile as he rotates the container, examining the bottom.

There are three other neighbors in their front yards. The two that water plants turn and stare at Adam so hard that they now soak their driveways.

"Mom!" shrieks a teen as her cell phone is sprayed with rogue hose water.

Adam hands the pot back. "Yeah, I think that's the issue. The bottom soil is soggy."

The lady mumbles a thank-you and grabs her plant.

"Of course," Adam says. Then, he makes his way up the drive.

Shit. He's headed straight toward me.

Two workers pass by, carrying a long piece of trussing between them.

I duck beneath the metal. I can walk half-bent to the side of the house, no problem.

The workers turn faster than I anticipated, and I pivot too late. My loafer catches on a cobblestone, and I fly forward.

"Ben," Adam calls, panicked.

Instead of slamming into stone, my palms land flat against his bare chest.

My breath catches as he holds me, brings us both upright, and drinks me in with his intense gaze, firm hands on my back.

"Hey, Parrish." His voice is husky. "You okay?"

"Good, I'm good," I sputter, finding my footing and backing up. "I'm glad you could offer your gardening expertise to the neighborhood."

I smooth the front of my polo and wince. Why did I say that? Now he'll know I was watching him.

He runs a hand through his hair, mussing it into every direction. "I think your grandma told her friends I used to operate a tree farm? That was the third person to stop me during my quick run. I don't know why they are asking me for advice on succulents. You'd think they'd know not to overwater? There's already enough moisture in the air."

I chuckle. "Yeah, moisture. That'll do it." This man has no idea how gorgeous he is. Dammit, that makes him more gorgeous.

His lips tilt up at the corner. Tentative, testing. Everything that happened last night is a void between us, a conversation I don't know the way to yet, or if I ever will.

The worst part is that I want to kiss him again.

I inhale sharply, rub my arms. "Welp, I should be getting back to . . ." I jut my thumb toward the house as if someone expects me. He doesn't need to know that someone is an espresso machine.

He nods. "Oh, yeah, yeah. I should go clean up."

Do not think about him cleaning up.

My throat tightens. Our gazes lock. His eyes sparkle in the sun. There are gold rings around his pupils that fan out into the dark brown of his irises.

"Ben?"

"Sorry, what?"

He fidgets with a black bracelet on his wrist. "I wanted to talk to you about last night. I want to—"

"So glad to see you both out here!" Grandma's voice cuts through the courtyard.

Adam's attention shifts past me and I turn to find her heading our way, long purple duster flowing in her wake.

Impeccable timing, G-ma. I've never been more thankful to be interrupted.

Her face is alight and panic stabs my ribs. I have to fix things with the TV show. I have to make sure she doesn't lose everything.

She reaches us and grazes each of our arms. Her fingers are covered in gold rings. "I need you to run an errand for me."

"I can go alone," I volunteer. I need space to unspool my thoughts. Or take a cold shower.

"No." G-ma shakes her head. "Both of you need to go. Big errand. Lots of stuff to haul."

Adam eyes me sheepishly.

I am an asshole for clearly wanting to get away from him. "Do you have more rehearsing to do?" Please say you do.

He shakes his head. "We practiced early, finished at eleven."

My shoulders fall.

"Adam," Grandma says, turning to him. "You should stay

here," she coos. "I've been dying to show you all of Ben's child-hood photo albums."

"I'll go get my keys," I say, flying across the courtyard.

"I'll text you the address," she hollers.

Adam trails me as I stride to the guesthouse faster than necessary.

Chapter 10

The address G-ma texted belongs to a costume shop in Culver City, Los Angeles, about an hour south of Maywell Bay.

LA is alive with vivid colors and frantic horns. Passing food trucks scent the air with teriyaki and simmering beef. Gone is the calmer pace of the central coast beaches, the sprawling orchards farther inland. The heart of the city beats a frantic rhythm as people rush from excitement or stress or both.

I keep the windows down, blast classic rock, and don't say a word to Adam. It's best that way, because the longer we drive, the closer we get to LA, and the more I worry I might be sick from the realization that I won't have tonight to prepare to see my father.

The street we park on is a twenty-five-minute drive to Studio City, where Dad's office is. Ready or not, my *Take the Cake National* to-do list is getting checked off. Today.

Nerves swarm my stomach at the thought of driving to my father's office building.

We enter the costume shop, and I settle into a red velvet chair and try to catch my breath as Adam is pulled behind long yellow curtains by a bubbly tailor.

When he reemerges, Adam does nothing to help my frazzled state. I push my hands into the front pockets of my beige shorts and press back against the chair.

Never in a million years did I think an errand for my grandmother would have me sitting among pink feather boas and sequined yards of fabric before a half-naked Adam Reed.

This is torture.

Of course G-ma would put me in a situation where I'm forced to ogle my lifelong crush. The gifted bottle of lube was an omen.

"One more pin, there we go," the tailor, a voluptuous woman with platinum hair and suntanned skin, says as she tacks the hem of Adam's pant leg, lingering at his ankle a little too long.

The woman rises, hands on hips, studying her work. Up and down.

I shift in my chair. She is clearly checking him out.

There are three mirrors angled in front of Adam so he's everywhere. Infinite Adams down a row of reflections, shirtless and blushing in ass-tight leather pants.

I clear my throat, unable to tear my gaze from the dimples on his lower back. "Who is he supposed to be again?" I ask groggily.

The tailor side-eyes me like *how could you not know.* "Sandy. From *Grease.*"

"Ah." I cross my arms and nod. Leather pants. Got it.

Adam fidgets and twists to study his ass in the mirror. It's fair he should have a turn. "So, um, do these have a zipper?" he asks. "Because how am I supposed to piss if I can't—"

The tailor reaches up and loops a stretchy black top around his neck. "You don't." She winks.

He blushes.

This is my whole life. Watching other people flirt with Adam.

Of course he didn't want to kiss me. Why choose me when people throw themselves all over him?

It's not just this tailor, it's his ever-cycling slew of bandmates who drape their arms across his shoulders, kiss his cheeks. It's the groupies that follow him into The Stacks every weekend and stay late after he plays. It's the people who get more than too many oil changes at the auto shop and stand nearby to observe as he works.

I don't blame them one bit. Adam is charming and talented and kind. He once saved our entire homecoming football half-time from ruin by playing a jazzy rendition of "Get Low," lifting everyone's spirits after Snow Hill crushed Fern Falls. He keeps the streets plowed when the town can't keep up in the winter. I've seen him clearing roads at four a.m. when I've arrived early at the bakery. When his family's tree farm was struggling, he kept it afloat with his profits from his auto shop. Morgan told me that when she worked on the farm's fundraiser. No one asks him to help, but he does, and without needing recognition.

Adam is magnetic and good and apparently knows how to garden. I am a horny, terrified mess of a man who may tank his family business and his grandmother's estate in one fell swoop. If I were Adam, I wouldn't want to make out with me either.

He pulls the shirt on. It barely stretches over his nipples.

The tailor busies herself with the back of the top until the fabric is stretched so tightly that it might tear.

I cross my arms and dig my nails into my biceps because while I was focused on the pants, Adam's torso was over there doing that arrow-muscle thing on the sides. What are they called? Obliques? The name should be officially changed to o-fuck-me-nows.

Maybe, seeing Adam in skintight pants is my very particular brand of gay.

Leather-clad Adam is my newfound sexual identity.

Between those running shorts and these leather pants, it's painfully clear that his physique has changed a lot since those group hikes to the swimming hole. I'm seriously gonna have to step outside.

He sighs. "I know your grandma wants the band on top of a Cadillac for her *Grease*-themed party, I just expected to be a Pink Lady instead of the star of the show."

He places his hand on his hip as he sticks it out, and it takes everything in me not to fixate on that curve, the way his fingertips make indentations in his skin.

He . . . held my hand once. The first time we went camping in the woods, after he was dumped via text. The origin trip that became our group's annual campout started with just us. Adam and me, fourteen and sixteen, throwing bottles at the fire and being rowdy in the woods. The first snowfall came that night. When I awoke, the tent was caved in and every part of me was freezing—except my hand that Adam, fast-asleep Adam, held in his own.

What kind of fool keeps a crush for all these years because of a damn morning when he held my hand?

It's time to let go.

I give him my best friendly smile. "Sandy Candy could be your stage name," I suggest. Great. Thanks, brain, for pulling through with some excellent vocabulary here.

He eyes the mirror. "I don't hate it. Missing the red nail polish, though."

"That can be arranged. I'm sure Grandma has every shade." That's fine. I would say the same thing to Morgan or any friend. Manicures are a great platonic activity.

The tailor produces a leather jacket and holds it against Adam, assessing. "This will fit. We'll need you out of those now, so I can finish alterations and have all this delivered in time for Saturday." She turns to me. "Your grandmother has me on a tight deadline, and I still have the drummer coming in for a Rizzo fitting."

The tailor hustles out of the dressing room, and it's my cue to do the same. "I'll just let you . . ."

"Could you lend me a hand?" Adam points at the buttons on

the back of the top, and his muscles strain against the fabric. "I need some help breaking free."

I suck in a breath. "Yeah, sure. Okay." I carefully tread the maroon carpeting, praying I don't trip over my own loafers like I already did once today.

I reach Adam and pause, fingers hovering over the shirt. His shoulders rise as he inhales.

If I wait too long I'll look like a creep, so I tackle the first button.

My fingers graze his back. He's warm. His skin is soft, which sends a jolt of surprise through my arm. What? Did I think that working on cars all day would give him tree bark for skin? My palms grow damp.

A quick glance up has me meeting his eyes in the mirror. They're darker than normal, hooded. He grips his hips so tightly all his knuckles are pale.

I snap my attention back to the buttons, which does nothing to help my sweaty palms situation.

I free the other buttons in a hurry and step back like I barely managed to not fall off a cliff. Accurate.

Adam clears his throat and wiggles out of the top. "Sorry to keep making you get close to me, Parrish."

My cheeks flush hot. "What?"

"I just . . ." Adam rubs the back of his neck. "I'm sorry about last night. I shouldn't have—"

"Stop. Please?" The words fly from my mouth.

He clears his throat. Nods.

"You don't owe me anything, not even an explanation," I say, voice firm.

He tilts his head. "That's not what I—"

I hold out my hand. "Let's agree to not bring up last night?"

He pulls in his lips and his brow creases as he stares at my hand.

My throat grows thick and everything in me screams to pull back, but I won't. I can be strong. "I don't want to lose you as a friend." My voice is thin, but the words are true. It hurts to crush the hope of being with him romantically, but I'd break if I lost his friendship.

An emotion I can't quite place crosses his features—sadness? Fear? It's gone as quickly as it appeared. Then, he nods sharply and shakes my hand, one quick motion, but he doesn't let go. He holds tight, and my whole body clings to the warmth of his grasp. He catches my gaze. "You'll never lose me, Ben."

I tighten my grip as electricity jolts through me.

Friends don't linger in heated stares or electrocute each other. In a daze, I withdraw my hand and back out of the dressing room. "Good luck with the pants," I call before closing the door behind me.

Catching my breath, I take in the area. The charming shopping area juts off the main street, free of excess traffic, allowing people the space to walk around. Couples stroll hand in hand. There's a cute boba shop on the corner, an Italian eatery with a tree-shaded patio, and the most adorable romance bookstore painted in pink whose name is an ode to classic bodice-rippers. I'll have to come back with Mom one day so we can both browse the shelves.

It's a regular day in the world, but for the new hope blooming in my chest.

I'm so grateful to have Adam in my life, whatever that looks like. My feelings made me afraid of true friendship with him for so long, afraid of being hurt. I fixated so hard on telling him how I feel that I pulled back from having any relationship with him at all. It will be good to spend time with him again, to talk honestly.

Even if the electricity in his presence is one-sided, I can handle that if it means we get to talk, share, laugh together. It'll hurt like it's always hurt to see him with partners, but I want him to be happy. I want to be in his life, and I want him to be in mine. Eventually, I'll find a romantic love that is right for me. I fill my lungs with pizza-scented air. This is a new chapter.

The door swings open and Adam exits, back in his jeans and black T-shirt. "Ready to head back?" he asks.

My stomach drops. I was so distracted with the new dynamic between us that I forgot all about what awaits me. "Actually, would you mind if we make a stop first?" I ask before I can change my mind.

Adam puts on his sunglasses. "Tell me about it, stud."

I snort-laugh. "C'mon, Sandy Candy."

Then, we get into my red Subaru. Leave it to Adam to make me laugh during this dreaded situation. Despite how afraid I am to see my dad and confront him about the C&D and Instagram post, it'll be good to have a friend with me.

I start the engine and back out as a stab of longing for more than friendship with Adam pierces my heart. That pain will fade over time, and I can bear it. I can.

Chapter 11

"There is an orgy in my mouth." Adam swipes a napkin across his chin and closes the to-go tray in his lap, discarded food wrappings inside.

On our drive into Studio City, we stopped by a red, white, and green food truck called Tacos Palacios. I ordered the asada quesadilla while he went for the birria tacos. Now, parked in front of my dad's office building, I couldn't be more grateful for Adam's top-notch food critique granting some much-needed levity.

I snort and clean hot sauce from my fingers with a wet wipe, then package it all up, too. "That is quite the image," I reply, laughing, and not a little awkwardly because imagining anything sexual regarding Adam's mouth is so far beyond the friend zone, I've hit zero gravity.

He reaches over and takes my container, stacks it on his. "I've had great tacos, but those made every one of my taste buds orgasm at once."

Adam talking dirty about food—this is great, this is fine. I grab my cup from the console and take a sip of handmade horchata. It's cinnamon-sweet, smooth, and ice-cold. Cool down, Parrish.

"When was the last time you were in the LA area, besides today?" Adam asks, tucking our recyclables at his feet and settling back into his seat.

"About ten years ago." I place my drink back in the cup holder and try not to fixate on the painful memory of when I last tried to visit my dad.

He takes in the passing view of traffic out the windshield. "Yeah, I think it's been about that long for me, a little less. I visited my sister when she went to art school."

That's right. Rachel lived in LA for a while. "Was it nearby?"

He nods. "Not too far." His voice is quiet, pensive. He grasps his hands together in his lap, studies them. "The last time I was here, my dad called to tell me my mom had moved out. Rachel and I were at a small indie concert so I didn't get his voicemail until midnight." His voice grows soft. "I couldn't reach him, so Rach and I drove home that night. Found him passed out drunk, all Mom's stuff was gone."

Emotion punches me in the gut. Rachel came home early from art school to help her dad through rehab after her mom left for Florida, for good. Until Rachel returned, Adam handled everything on his own from starting up his auto shop and running the tree farm. He didn't play music at The Stacks very much during that time. I saw him infrequently as I was busy with running the bakery, but I made it a point to save the best cinnamon rolls for him.

Even though he was older when his mom left, absent parents is something we have in common. It's comforting to know I'm not alone, but I wish he didn't know how this felt, too. The ripping loss of a parent leaving. The endless questions with no comforting answers.

"Sorry, that was TMI," he says, not looking up.

"No, not at all. Thank you for sharing that." My muscles tense. "I'm actually here to see my dad."

His arm stiffens, but that's the only sign of surprise he reveals.

He's never asked me questions about my dad leaving, but he knows, like all of Fern Falls knows.

"Is there anything I can do?" he asks, shifting his attention over.

My face is reflected in his sunglasses; worry lines frame my eyes.

I hadn't considered if there was anything anyone could do to help me. His offer makes the knot in my chest loosen the slightest bit. "I know I didn't give you much of a choice, since I'm driving and all, but thank you for being here. That already helps more than you know."

His lips twist to the side like he's biting his cheek. "I hope it's not weird that I'm here, in general. I know I crashed your grandma's party and—"

"I'm happy you're here, Adam. We haven't been able to spend time like this in years. It's really nice." Sunlight warms my face.

He smiles wide, summoning that dimple. "I like being with you."

There's a flash of movement in my peripheral, and I find Adam's hand on the console between us, fingers outstretched.

He pulls back as soon as I notice.

I want to grab his hand and never let go.

But having him here with me, him wanting to be here with me, fills me with strength.

I clear my throat and face Dad's office building directly outside my window.

The concrete-block exterior is the same as I remember, and it brings me right back to when I was last here.

It was a couple months after I earned my driver's license. I got the car keys and a Saturday with the sedan while Mom was on a yoga retreat, and I went to see Dad on my own. I wouldn't have to hurt Mom by bringing him up, or risk her feeling uncomfortable with the visit, worrying to let me go alone. It could just be a trip between me and Dad. The first thing we could share apart from the sporadic cards, emails, phone calls, FaceTimes.

A week before, I gave him a call and he agreed to meet me at his office.

It took over five hours to get there from Fern Falls, and I spent every minute fighting the urge to turn around, that warning feeling in my gut. I convinced myself that everything would be fine. We'd grab lunch, walk and talk. We'd end the day being re-bonded despite the fact that it had been the first time we'd seen each other in years.

I parked outside the concrete building and after a half hour, finally talked myself into going inside. He said he'd be here, what was I so nervous about? Once through the doors, I'd never felt so small. The slate walls reached so high I had to angle my head back to see the top of the staircase, the ceiling, the massive water feature that spanned the height of the wall, complete with hanging ferns and vines.

"Can I help you?" said the receptionist without looking up from her phone screen.

"Is Jake Gibbons here?" my voice echoed.

"Is he expecting you?" She peered closer at her screen and smoothed a stray strand of her blond hair.

"Yes."

She turned to her laptop and clicked around. "He's out of the country."

That couldn't be right. "Are you sure?" There had to be a mistake. I spoke to him yesterday.

She glared up. "He got a last-minute call this morning from a touring artist. Had to fly out."

The phone rang and she picked it up. "Jake Gibbons Music Management."

That was it.

He wasn't there. He didn't even tell me so we could reschedule, and didn't care about the time I'd spent driving down.

I wasn't thought of at all, just like the night I got lost in the woods when he was home.

I drove to Grandma's that night after leaving Studio City. She called Mom as I cried and made up a cover story, said I'd driven down to see her. The next day, she took me antiquing in town, and that's when I got the idea to decorate with old objects, things thought of as broken, forgotten. My trip to see Dad was our secret.

This is the first time I've thought of it since.

I don't know what's going to happen when I enter that office. It could be like last time, a total dismissal. Or, based on the fact that he sent a C&D then followed up with an Instagram post after my voicemail, it could be demoralizing. I don't know the man anymore. I don't know how he'll treat me . . . and I don't want Adam to see me break down. The light, friendly conversation we've had today has been a comfort. I don't want to lose that because he feels sorry for me, I can't.

"Do you mind waiting?" My voice is thin.

"Of course not." He removes his sunglasses and smiles softly. "I'll be right here."

A sense of calm washes over me. "Thank you." I sigh and exit the car, leaving the keys with him.

The double glass doors labeled with a white looping JGMM makes me want to sink beneath the sidewalk, but knowing Adam will be here when this is over helps my feet move forward. I won't be alone.

With a deep breath, I push through the doors, startle when they slam behind me.

A sense of unease creeps across my skin as I take in the space. The once-polished stone walls are now worn and chipped. There's a boarded-up hole in the lobby where the fountain was. The wall of plants is nothing but cracked plastic pots. There's a faint odor of stagnant water.

A phone rings, and I turn toward a slightly ajar office door along the side wall.

"Jake Gibbons Music Management." A few deep grunts. "Wrong number." The phone slams.

Chills skitter down my spine.

It's raspier and more tired-sounding, void of the force and drive he used to have, but it's Dad's voice.

The sound of it is like an ominous sky before a fierce storm. I should turn and leave, return to the safety of the car with Adam. My muscles wind up into fight-or-flight mode. That's what my therapist calls the start of my anxiety attacks. What was I thinking of trying to do this without meeting with her first? What was I thinking of coming here at all? I take a deep breath. Grandma could lose everything if I lose my spot on the baking show, the chance of taking our company national and saving our reputation along with it.

A reputation that wouldn't need repair if it weren't for this man.

I roll my shoulders and push back against the urge to grip my churning gut and curl into a fetal position.

My steps echo off the tile, but there's no response from his office.

I pause at the door, hand poised above the laminate wood surface. I should knock.

Why? He didn't give me a single courtesy with the C&D letter, the Instagram post, flying out of the country when we had plans to visit; never calling me afterwards to apologize. Why should I treat him any differently?

I push the door open.

My face tingles and I have this strange sense of disappearing, floating out of my skin.

Dad hunches over the desk. He's smaller than I remember. His navy suit is tailored to perfection, pressed and spotless. If someone saw him in the street, they'd think his office was in a pricey high-rise. His lean arm braces him up, while his free hand clutches his salt-and-pepper hair that sticks out extra-spiky, like he used gel and didn't plan on messing it up.

I should say something, but all I can do is stare. The ceiling panels are brown and water-stained. The molding is peeling like a rundown doctor's office, and the framed posters on the walls are of unrecognizable bands, their styles outdated.

He slams the desk with his fist and I jump, bumping into the door.

His head snaps up.

I freeze, hand on the metal doorknob.

His dark brows shoot up toward his hairline, then arrow together. "Ben?" His voice is high, eyes wide and bloodshot.

That expression . . . the same image from eighteen years ago flashes in my mind. His stricken stare, lit up by flashlight beams as strong people in orange jackets carried me up my driveway. Mom cried and pulled me into her arms, while he stood still and silent. I knew then that I'd broken something that couldn't be fixed.

With the way he stares now, that's more true than ever.

I clear my throat. "Yeah. Hi." Regret gnaws at me. *Yeah* and *hi* are the first words I've said to my father in years.

He scans the room and his face reddens. "I—what are you doing here?"

I shift my stance. I wasn't anticipating a warm welcome, but this isn't even tepid. Ignoring the pinch of disappointment in my throat, I reach into the pocket of my shorts, retrieving the C&D letter I grabbed from my duffel bag before I left Grandma's. "We need to talk about this." I hold out the paper, but he doesn't move. "You could have spoken to me before sending it, or after my voicemail, or your Instagram post," I say, voice shaky.

He walks over and takes the envelope, scowls. "I don't know what this is."

I cross my arms and press against a burning sensation in my diaphragm. "Maybe opening it will jog your memory."

He takes the letter out and studies it, pressing his free fingers to his mouth. He fixes that same stricken expression on me. "I've never seen this. I didn't send it." His tone doesn't waver.

I glare, deadpan. "Is the name on the envelope, the letter-head, not your company?"

He clutches the paper as his other hand falls to his side. "No, it is, but this is all Phillip's doing."

I squint at him. Maybe he named his conscience Phillip.

"My PR manager." He returns to the desk and sets the paper down, grips the edge of the surface. His knuckles whiten. "Phillip runs our social media, sends out correspondence. Jesus." He hangs his head.

Now that I think about it, the signature on the C&D was signed as the company name. This doesn't make sense. "Why would your PR manager create a fraudulent document? Did Phillip also post the photo of us on Instagram?"

Dad spreads his arms. On a bookshelf behind his desk, there's a photo of us. The same one from his Instagram post of the two of us eating cinnamon rolls. A hollow pit forms in my core. Has he had that photo up all these years? Do I matter to him?

He slumps into his black desk chair. "If you can't tell by look-ing around, my business is barely hanging on. We haven't had any major clients in years. I've seen how successful you've been online, with the bakery, and I told Phil to take some pointers from your Instagram. I mentioned that I made cinnamon rolls with you. I guess he took things a bit far."

I shove my hands into my pockets. He could be telling the truth, or this could be some elaborate story. For what, though? To save face? He let me down so long ago, he shouldn't care what I think now. His intentions don't matter. The only thing that matters is getting this taken care of. "Now that you know what your PR manager did, you can drop the C&D and take down the IG post."

He steeples his hands, pressing the tips of his fingers to his lips.

"Dad, please. You haven't been involved in years. You don't want to take over the bakery. What good does this do you?"

He glares at his desk. "Yesterday, Phillip told me that our social accounts are doing better than ever, and that it's already generating calls from the press and new band leads. We have a meeting with a potential client tonight."

"Are you saying you won't delete the post? You know it's Mom's recipe." My tone is acrid.

He snaps his gaze to me. "I have to look out for myself, Ben. And so do you. That's at least one thing I can teach you."

Heat flares through me. "I don't need you to teach me. My entire life, this is the only thing I have ever asked of you. Let the C&D go. Delete the post. I'm only asking you to do the right and honest thing."

His eyes glaze over. "You don't understand. This social media attention is our last chance. I can't let it go. Not unless you can find me the next breakout band."

This cannot be how it ends. I cannot fail here, fail my grandmother and Mom. My arms tingle and my palms sweat, but I stand still. "I won't leave until you delete that post."

Dad grips the armrests of his chair and gives a cold laugh. "This is ironic, all these years later. You know, things would have been much different, Ben. I wouldn't be in this position if . . ." He shakes his head. "Never mind."

"What? If what? Say it." My fists curl in defense. I know what he's thinking. That night I got lost in the woods was the same night he had a major call with a huge up-and-coming artist. It was between him and another manager. That's why he told me to play outside, so I wouldn't make noise in the house during his call. Because of me, he lost the meeting, the client, and the illustrious career that artist went on to have. Then, the DCFS article was the nail in the coffin. He blames all his failures on me.

"If I would have had more support from your mom when we were together—"

My head jerks back. "What does Mom have to do with this?"

He gives another cold laugh, shakes his head. "You know I met your mom at a party in a Malibu mansion? She was gorgeous and at the cusp of an acting career. We had a whole plan, the two of us. To travel and work hard, party harder, achieve our goals side by side." He straightens in his chair. "But Laura changes with the wind. I never wanted to live in Fern Falls. That was all her, when she got into nature and herbalism. I thought we'd live up there for a few months tops. Then, she got pregnant."

There's no questioning his meaning. My very existence ruined his career, and I drove in the stake when I ran into the woods and spurred those headlines. My body numbs, like the shock of falling into ice water. In a haze, I turn to leave. Pause. "Did you ever get the letters I sent you? When I was younger?" I ask, peering over my shoulder.

He squints, pulls in his lips. "I travel a lot, Ben. Things don't always make it across my desk."

I give my head a hard shake, swallow. "There was no deer, you know," I whisper at his office door.

"What?"

I grip the doorknob. "There was no deer that led me into the woods."

His chair squeaks. "I don't know what you mean."

I huff a dry laugh. He doesn't even know what I told the reporters back then. "When did you notice I was gone?" The doorknob slickens in my grip.

"Don't dig this up." His tone is cold, distant.

I glare back. He holds his cell phone, taps on the screen. Of course he buried the details of that night. Meanwhile, every moment has eaten at me like an undead parasite. "Answer me. You owe me that much."

He flinches, then meets my gaze. "When your mom returned from her gem convention and asked where you were."

The room shrinks, narrows down to his empty stare. I knew it, but hearing it? My insides hollow out, disappear. All I wanted was to see if he would come find me. All I wanted was to know if he loved me. Finally, I see my father for who he is: a lonely, self-centered narcissist. "You're a coward."

He returns his attention to his cell phone. "Something I realized that night they pulled you from the woods," he says, voice monotone, "was that I wasn't meant to be a parent."

I dig my nails into my palm. Harder. I will not cry in front of him. I will not let him have my tears. "I hoped you could at least be a decent human being, and even that was too much." Without a backward look, I exit and slam his door shut.

It would have been better if he wasn't here at all, like before.

My heart pounds in my ears as I pass by the empty reception desk, float my way through the tomb of a lobby, and emerge back into the Los Angeles sun.

Despite the heat, my limbs are cold. I reach my car and brace both hands on the door, gasp for breath.

"Ben. Hey, are you okay?" Adam's voice is beside me. I didn't hear him exit the car.

I shake my head.

"Is it okay to touch you?"

Why is he . . . I nod.

He presses firmly against my lower back. The full surface of Adam's hand is warm and grounding. I focus on that spot of contact and my elbows unlock, shoulders loosen.

I turn into him, his arm slides around my waist. I search his face, and his brows crease with concern.

A sob wrenches from my chest.

His arms tighten around me, pull me to him.

I cover my face with my hands, sink into his warmth, and cry.

"It'll be okay," he whispers, gently swaying us back and forth, holding me close, holding me tight, holding me. "You're not alone."

Those words mean more to me than he'll ever know.

We stand like this until the noise of traffic sounds again, the feeling is back in my legs, and my tears give way to a bone-deep exhaustion.

He rubs my shoulders and leans back slightly, peering down. "Do you smell a coffee shop nearby?" he asks.

I take a deep breath, fill my lungs, and cough, pressing my hand to my nose. "It smells like fresh asphalt and charred grease."

He laughs, soft and low. "You took a deep breath, though. That's what matters."

My lips tilt into a small smile.

"There's an art gallery across the street." His voice is slow, melodic. "I looked at their window display from the car. Wild-flowers and fireflies. Lit up lanterns. Canopies of trees. Real fairy-tale shit."

I peer over my shoulder and find PORTAL PAINTINGS embla-zoned on a wooden sign against a concrete facade. He's right. The art in the window could be in a storybook. It reminds me of home, our mountain.

"Let's get out of here," I say, turning to him.

His arms relax at his sides. "Would you like me to drive?"

My whole body sighs. "Please."

He nods then loops an arm through mine and walks me to the passenger side, leans over, opens the door, holds it for me.

Ninety-nine percent of me does not want to let go of him. I meet the warmth of his brown eyes. They crease at the corners as he smiles softly. This is what it feels like to be taken care of, cared for. The one percent of me that knows we can only be friends makes me release his arm and settle into my seat.

He gently closes my door, rounds the hood.

When he gets behind the wheel, his scent fills the cab. Pine. Musk.

I breathe it in deep, close my eyes.

"Let's go home," he says. Then, he starts the car and we roll into the street, leaving this place behind.

I know the home he means is the guest cottage in Maywell Bay, but having him here with me feels like a piece of Fern Falls. He feels like home, and that isn't just enough, it's everything.

Chapter 12

"I'm gonna keep my camera off, okay?"

My therapist doesn't need to see me huddled in a fetal position between these teal bedsheets, and I haven't showered in a few days. Is today Friday? I don't want to smile a hello, or turn on a light.

Putting my phone on speaker, I set it on the mattress beside me.

"More than fine." Jessica's voice is steady and soothing, like it always is. "I'm glad we had this appointment set up. Go ahead and start wherever you'd like."

Jessica has golden-brown hair and skin and the warmest smile. I picture her in her Fern Falls office, a little pine cabin in the center of town. She always has nature scapes playing in her waiting room, and there's a tabletop fountain in the corner. Her therapy room is a bright, sunny yellow. Mom first brought me to see her when I was nine, and she's been the biggest support ever since.

"Adam has been bringing me meals." My voice is tired.

"Reed?"

I nod. Oh, right. She can't see me. "Yes." I've told her about him over the years, but I don't want to share about our drunken kiss. That's too much to unpack alongside the visit with my father.

I thought I'd be fine after seeing Dad last Sunday. I tried to be okay. I watched fireworks over the harbor for the Fourth of July, and went to a movie night in Grandma's home theater with all the cousins. I watched Adam rehearse with the band and help Mom make suncatchers for the upcoming craft fair, all while compulsively checking social media, hoping my father took the post down.

He didn't.

For the past few days, here I've been, unable to get out of bed except for survival essentials. I'm too tired. Everything hurts.

When the depression hit bone, I asked Adam if he could tell my mom and grandma that I was sick, and requested that no one visit.

I can't handle seeing them right now. I can barely handle masking in text messages, replying to Mom that I'll be okay, I just need some rest. In person, I'd break down and spill everything about Dad, Delish Dollars Studios, and Grandma's finances. The whole birthday celebration and all G-ma's joy would be ruined.

"So, you're getting meals?" Jessica asks.

I blink. I haven't spoken in too long. "Grandma's soup, mostly." When I made the appointment after the filming, I let Jessica know I'd be in Maywell Bay, at my grandmother's house.

"And you're taking your anxiety meds? Eating?"

"Yes." Adam brings me scrambled eggs and toast, too. Sandwiches, fruit, water. Asks if there's anything I want or need. I haven't eaten much, but I have eaten.

"Are you talking to Adam or anyone else?"

I shift my head on the pillow. "Does through the door count?"

He asks how I'm doing when he leaves my meal trays outside my bedroom, and knocks gently in between. Today he wrote *not as good as those tacos, but don't tell your grandma* on the napkin beside my soup bowl. I spot the napkin on my nightstand and crack a small smile.

"Any kind of communication counts," she says.

I pull the turquoise comforter to my face and press the soft cotton against my cheek. I have to talk about seeing my dad. I clutch the fabric tight. "I don't think I can say it out loud."

"If you need me to just be here, I'm here."

I close my eyes and sigh in relief.

Not everyone in the US is fortunate enough to have mental health or therapy included in their insurance, or to have health insurance at all. I hate this system. Things would be so much harder without my therapist.

I could sit in silence for the whole appointment, but I have to try to talk this out. People are waiting for me. I want to feel better. I want to see Adam play guitar on a Cadillac in his leather pants.

"I saw my dad." My voice cracks.

She is silent for a beat. "Do you want to tell me about that?"

I open my mouth to speak, then close it. Hot tears slide into my hairline, onto the pillowcase.

"I'm here, Ben. Talk when you're ready."

I gasp for breath. Again. Fill my lungs, deep and slow. "It was awful."

I share everything about the show, the C&D, the post, the entire conversation at his office, skirting around the Adam parts.

Jessica listens to all of it. "How do you feel right now?" she asks.

I swallow hard. "Like I can't see straight, or make sense of anything. Is it normal to feel like I've been possessed or overtaken? I'd done so much healing, and after one conversation, it's like I haven't moved past my pain at all. I'm mad. I'm frustrated.

I'm tired. There's a mountain on my chest." These sheets are going to be stained with salt.

There's a rustling sound like she's shifting in her seat.

"Of course that is normal, Ben. All your feelings are valid. Healing is a journey, and you have come so far. You're reaching out and asking for what you need. You're taking care of yourself by eating and drinking and resting."

"Yeah," I say, voice small. I am doing those things, unlike other times in the past when I didn't. That's progress.

"The thing about trauma," she says, "is that our bodies can hold on to it. So, when a triggering event happens, and the meeting with your father was indeed triggering, your body can feel like the original events are happening all over again, in that moment and beyond. And there's the added trauma of the gaslighting and narcissism your brain is sifting through from the conversation with your dad. You went into the meeting openly and honestly, and he responded with emotional manipulation and abuse. You see that treatment for what it is, and that is also growth, Ben."

I let out a deep sigh and swipe the back of my hand across my eyes. "What can I do?" I ask groggily.

"Take care of yourself, as you are. And it sounds like you have a lot of people around you who love you and wouldn't want you to go through this on your own. Your mom, grandma, Adam. Don't be afraid to lean on them. Be patient and gentle with yourself. You're not alone."

I'm not alone. That's what Adam told me after I saw my dad. I don't know if I can open up to my mom and grandma without making everything worse, I can't even think that far ahead, but I could talk to Adam.

The front door to the cottage creaks, closes.

There's the tapping of cabinets in the kitchen, the clanking of dishes and silverware.

"Thank you, Jessica," I say, sitting myself up against the headboard.

"I'm just a text or phone call away," she says. "Do you want to set up another appointment now, or do you want to reach out if you need to?"

I roll my shoulders, feeling stronger already. I don't have to do this by myself. "I'll reach out when I'm ready."

"You're doing great, Ben."

I smile. "Thank you."

We say goodbye and I hang up and place my cell on my night-stand, my bare feet on the floor.

I stand on shaky legs and stretch. Streaks of light leak into my room, and I head over to the window and open the blinds, squinting against the late afternoon sun.

A quiet knock sounds on my door. "Ben? I'm going to leave some lunch here for you. Are you doing okay?"

Instead of answering right away, I walk to the door. The floor is already starting to warm where the sunrays hit. I pass the closet mirror and take in my blue plaid pajama pants, the pink sleep shirt my mom gave me last Christmas that says You Bake Me So Happy. My beard is getting its lucky break, and my hair went through a car wash. I . . . have a feeling that Adam won't care. We're just friends, anyway. Hopefully, he doesn't mind how I smell either. Ugh.

I pull the door open and find him straightening after setting my meal tray on the floor.

His eyes widen briefly, then he sighs and his whole body seems to deflate. "How are you doing?" he asks, stepping for-ward, around the tray.

I offer a small smile. "I'm okay. I'll be okay."

"I've been worried about you." The light from the patio high-lights dark circles beneath his eyes. His facial hair is scruffy.

Has he been sleeping? "I'm sorry."

"No, please don't apologize." He reaches forward, grazing my arm with his fingers, then shoves his hand in his pocket. "It's good to see your face."

"Yours, too." I rub my arm, where he touched me. A flash of warmth reaches my chest.

He shifts on his feet. "Honestly, if you didn't come out of your room by tonight, I was going to come in and camp out on the floor."

I lean against the doorframe. A sense of light courses through me, clearing some fog. He meant it when he said I wasn't alone. I rub the hem of my shirt between my fingers. "Thank you so much for looking out for me and keeping me fed and hydrated."

"Of course. That's um . . ." He rubs the back of his neck. "That's what friends do, right?"

I bite the inside of my cheek, nod. "Right."

"Oh, I just remembered."

I search his face. "Yeah?"

"Your grandma has a group dinner reservation in town tonight. The whole family is attending, the band, everyone."

A twinge of worry hits me. Was Mom able to budget for that? I sag against the doorframe. I'm not ready to see so many people, answering questions about if I'm feeling better, masking how I really feel. I want to take a nap just thinking about it.

"I do have another option, if you want to get out for a bit, but need something more mellow," Adam says.

Relief makes me straighten. "Yeah?"

His chest rises and falls as he takes in a breath, exhales. "I was wondering, would you like to go somewhere with me, just the two of us? If you have the energy? It's not too far and I'm happy to drive."

I smile, comforted by the thought alone. "I'd really like that. After I shower."

He grins wide. "I'll freshen up and meet you in the living room."

"Okay, great. Be out in a bit." I close the door as Adam practically skips toward his room. Leaning against the wall, I try my hardest to push my internal butterflies down where they belong.

This is not a date.

He took care of me during one of the deepest depressive episodes I've had in years. He wore his worry all over his face.

He was going to camp out on my bedroom floor.
Shaking my head, I make my way to the bathroom.
I would have never let him sleep on my floor.
I would have offered to share the bed.
It's called manners.

Chapter 13

Clean-shaven Adam turns off the ignition and pulls up on the parking brake, soft evening light sheening off his leather jacket.

The scent of his aftershave, soap, cologne, deodorant, or whatever magical essence diffuses from his pores is just the right strength. Pine and musk are the perfect pairing, and the cab of his truck is a banquet. Five stars on Yelp.

I missed the smell of him when I was in my room. It's so reassuring to breathe easier again. It always gets better. Sometimes, when you least expect it.

I'm more myself in my gray pants, dark blue button-up paired with a pressed jean jacket, and brown suede lace-up ankle boots. Shaved and showered, I could take on the world. Or, at least be here, with Adam, which is a victory in itself. I am out of my bed, and outside. I'm doing great. "You were right," I say, unbuckling my seat belt. "The drive wasn't long at all. What did that take? Fifteen minutes?"

He nods. "Just a short distance up the canyon from your grandmother's house. Can't believe you haven't been here yet."

He faces the gravel lot, trees and greenery all around. Down the mountain, the steep road curves and disappears into the trees, a glimpse of ocean blue at the bottom. The sun slips closer to the sea, casting brilliant streaks of orange across the coastline of Maywell Bay. All my summers coming here, I never ventured up the canyon. I love that he found a new place in a town I know so well.

I love this, being with him, without the stress or pressure of exposing how I feel. I forgot how much comfort is in the simplicity of spending time with him.

"Ready to go in?" he asks, casting a tilt of his lips.

I'm hooked. That smile could reel me in anywhere, anytime. My friend has a very nice smile.

I follow his gaze out the windshield to a massive lodge carved into the canyon wall. The varnished logs gleam and café lights frame the mossy roof. There's a wide porch and elegant purple doors with a sign at the peak above that says MAYWELL CANYON ART FESTIVAL in a subtle gold font.

A cool sea breeze caresses my cheek as I exit the vehicle. "How did you hear of this place?" I call over to him.

Adam closes his door and joins me at the front of his truck. He's in black jeans with a white shirt beneath his jacket. His black boots shuffle, making indentations in the gravel.

Shoot. Was I checking him out?

I shift my attention to his eyes. They sparkle in the glowy light. That's great. Wonderful. My friend has very nice eyes.

"It's an art festival that Rachel took me to years back," he says, "but it's evolved over the years. I thought of it while you were recovering, and when I googled it on my phone, they had a whole new theme for the summer, so I had to bring you. I think you'll love it."

I smile, picturing Adam googling an art festival. My grin broadens because he googled it with the intention of bringing me . . . because I'll love it.

Calm down. This is not a date.

"Shall we?" Adam asks, motioning toward the entrance with a tilt of his head.

"We shall," I smirk, moving forward.

Our steps fall into stride, crunching the gravel in rhythm—a very non-date-like occurrence.

Other people trickle in from the parking lot, and we walk along to the tune of upbeat music lilting through the open purple doors, a happy melody grounded by a light bass, accented by joyful acoustic guitar runs.

We enter through the doors and a sense of wonder tingles down my arms. The entrance was a facade because there isn't a roof. The mini world we step into is canopied by the sunset sky, early stars winking down. The entire floor is covered with a thick layer of sawdust, creating paths that curve and wind through rows of whimsical art booths. Musicians play on a stage far up at the front, and every structure between us and them is accented with blossoming floral garlands, twinkling fairy lights, and vibrant hanging moss. A few children run by wearing pink flower crowns, sheer ribbons flowing in their wake. The air is scented with peaches and honey, and a banner spans the space above the steps that lead down into the exhibit space says: WELCOME TO MAYWELL COUNTY ART FESTIVAL'S MAGICAL SUMMER NIGHTS.

There are so many beautiful spaces, I can't decide what direction to head in.

"It's something else, huh? They have different themes for each season," Adam says, eyes aglow.

"It's breathtaking," I say, elated to share this with him. "Where should we start?"

His whole face lights up. "Follow me."

We skirt along the edges of the booths until the solid wooden wall becomes an entire window pane.

Adam stops and peers through the glass. His profile is framed by soft light. "This is the best part," he says, a smile playing on his lips.

"Best for first?" I say, stepping up beside him.

He tilts his head toward the scene before us. "You tell me."

I follow his gesture to find a lower-level room. Like the space we're in, the floor is covered in a compact layer of sawdust.

A furnace glows against the back wall as a glassblower in a brown leather apron turns a long metal rod within the flames. They step back and pull the rod out. At the end is a glowing orange orb. They then roll the rod along a metal table. It's fascinating and mesmerizing and I'm enchanted just watching it.

"Wait, I lied before, this is the best part," Adam says, leaning into me and pointing toward the shifting sphere of molten glass.

I glance at where our arms meet and smile, warmed from his touch. I love that he thinks everything about this place is the best.

The glassblower props the rod on a stand and blows into the end, spinning it constantly, as the orb expands into an illuminated planet.

"It really is the best," I say, taking him in. He is radiant with joy.

"C'mon." he gives my arm a quick and gentle tug like we're about to board his favorite amusement park ride.

I'd go to every overpriced, overcrowded place if it meant Adam would touch me like this. It's so familiar, so comfortable. I never want it to stop.

I follow him along the window, past a view of other glassblowers using different metal tools to mold glowing masses into all sorts of shapes.

The window ends, giving way to a cozy wooden alcove filled with shelves of glass figurines. They all sparkle in a multicolored rainbow beneath a low ceiling of string lights.

Adam's eyes brighten as he browses a wooden table display topped with at least a hundred tiny charms. There are trays of four-leaf clovers and red hearts priced lower than the more intricate sculptures like mini houses and the Eiffel Tower.

I move closer to him. "I'm really glad you brought me here."

He pauses as he takes me in. "Me too."

Turning back to the table, he picks up a small charm. "This one was made for you." He holds up a small glass cinnamon roll. It even has a thin layer of white on the top for the frosting.

"This is amazing." Do friends cry over glass cinnamon rolls? Yeah. I think they do.

He smiles softly. It's a little ridiculous how the lights form an ethereal haze at his back.

I turn my attention to the table to keep from melting at his feet. A little yellow guitar, like the one he has, catches my eye. I pick it up, hold it out to him. "This one's for you."

His eyes shimmer as he takes it in.

"May I buy this for you?" he asks, holding up the cinnamon roll.

Emotion swirls through me. This is what I want. Whatever part of Adam I can have. There will always be that tug of the loss of a romance with him, but this is good, it's worth it. I missed this. I nod and smile. "Only if I can buy this for you? As a friend?"

He smiles, but it doesn't reach his eyes or make his dimple appear. "Deal."

We pay for our figurine gifts at the front of the booth.

He offers me mine. I reach out, and our fingers meet. A delicious heat flows up my arm.

"Thank you," I say, voice soft.

He blinks, lets go. "Of course," he replies, examining the guitar I gifted him.

I ache from the loss of contact, however brief.

My cinnamon roll figurine is warmed from his touch, and I hold it tight, relishing the smooth glass.

His thumb pauses as it rubs over his guitar. "Thank you, Ben. I love it." He smiles, steps close. Our eyes lock. He searches mine.

I lick my lips, and his part.

My chin tilts upwards.

It would take nothing for me to fall into his kiss.

Which is why I have to move. Now.

"My turn," I say, planting my feet firmly on the ground.

He tilts his head in question, expression dazed. "What do you mean?"

"Follow me." My voice is a bit scratchy.

He smirks and tucks his tiny guitar into his jacket. "Yes, sir."

I don't miss the way that phrase sends a tingle of pleasure through my core. This friendship arrangement would be a lot easier if I wasn't so damn attracted to him, desperate for him, fantasizing about kissing him. Again.

Okay, move. Walk. I place my figurine in my pocket and lead him through the booths. We weave past jewelry vendors and an artist selling ceramic fairy figurines that Whitney, Rachel, and Morgan would love. I follow my nose until we stop before a wooden stand painted a bright shade of teal. "Found it," I proclaim.

"Debby's Baked Goods," Adam says, reading the sign across the top of the booth.

I nod. "Yep. The source of the peaches and honey."

He grins. "I knew it smelled amazing, but couldn't place the scent. You have talent, Parrish."

"Right there." I point to a display case where at least twenty tins of peach cobbler shimmer with drizzled honey.

A person with rich brown skin and short black hair peers over the case. "What may I get for you?"

I turn to Adam. "Do you want to share one with me?"

He clutches his chest like he's been wounded. "We'll take two, please," he says to the vendor, laughing.

They wink. "Don't let go of that one," they say, reaching into the case to retrieve our cobblers.

My face heats.

When I turn to Adam, his attention is already on me, a soft smile on his lips. "Want to go get a table? I'll get these."

He points to a dining area in front of the low stage. There

is quite a crowd, but off to the side, a couple vacates a wooden bench. "I'm on it."

I weave through the gathering and claim the seats, mission accomplished.

From where I sit, I can make out Adam as he pays, and this feels like . . . a date.

He walks toward me, two blue boxes stacked in his hands. He passes beneath one of the bordering fairy-lit trees, the soft glow warming his brown hair to auburn.

His grin tilts in that crooked way that makes his dimple appear, and my rebellious heart hammers.

As he takes a seat beside me on the bench, the musician on-stage shifts into a calm, sweet melody.

"So, what do you think of this place?" He asks, sliding me a blue box, topped with a bamboo fork.

I open the lid to reveal the cobbler. A waft of steam rises, filling my face with the mouthwatering scents of brown sugar, butter, honey, and perfectly ripe peaches. "It's one of the most gorgeous places I've ever been."

He beams and his chest rises like I paid him the biggest compliment. "I'm so glad I could bring you. The band has one more rehearsal tomorrow before the big *Grease*-themed party, but we took tonight off."

"Are you enjoying playing with them?" I ask, taking a bite of my dessert. I hope this imprints upon my taste buds.

"So much," he says around a mouthful. "They're a really great group. I'd love to introduce you."

He takes another bite of his cobbler and closes his eyes, lips wrapped around his fork.

I swallow hard. Watching Adam savor food is a special kind of torture.

His eyelids flutter open and he lowers his utensil.

I snap my gaze down. "I'd really like to meet the band." I take another bite. "Is the auto shop doing okay with you being gone?"

He hums, digging into his dish. "Old Rusty brought in his daughter to help him out. She's a new mechanic and looking to work at a shop. He thought this would be a great chance for her to get some experience." He looks up, twirling his fork. "It's great timing because I've been wanting to hire someone on."

"Really?" I shift on the bench.

"Yeah. It's so busy with just me, and I'd love more time to play music, discover more things I enjoy, things like this." He gestures between us.

My face warms. He's enjoying this. With me. "It's good you're taking more time for yourself. You deserve to escape when you need to."

His expression softens. "It's nice seeing this side of your life. I'm glad you had Maywell Bay growing up." He stares at his food. "I used to wish for that sometimes. An escape."

My throat grows thick. "What do you mean?"

His lips twist to the side but he doesn't look up. "I don't think it's any secret that my parents aren't the easiest people to deal with."

Rachel and Adam have been through a lot with their mom and dad. Last I checked in with Rach, Tanya was still along the Florida Coast somewhere, only sparing a passing phone call to share updates on her relationship statuses.

"Is your dad doing okay now, though? After finishing rehab?" Jim has been living in Snow Hill, Fern Falls' neighboring town, to be close to resources and AA meetings. "He's doing better, right?"

Adam nods. "Yeah, he is. But I'm always on pins and needles hoping he doesn't relapse. I think one day that worry will go away. Maybe. I don't know yet." His knee bounces.

"The worst part is that I'm happy for my mom that she left. If it weren't for Rachel, and for getting Dad into rehab, I would have left, too. But working on cars made sense. I could fix things in an engine even if I couldn't change anything in my life."

A lump forms in my throat imagining Adam leaving Fern

Falls. I picture his coffee orders and how he never veers from cinnamon rolls. How he drives over to Snow Hill every Tuesday to see Jim. He fixes auto parts, puts everything back into place, wants to fix things. Like me. Maybe Adam wants to feel safe because too much in life does not.

That's how I feel. "Have you talked with your mom?"

He shrugs. "She calls occasionally, but it's so quick and only surface conversation. I think she touches base to hit some quota to stave off the guilt of leaving. But she checked out long before she left."

I take a deep breath. I know exactly what he means. That's how each phone call with my father felt growing up. A to-do item checked off his list, a pat on his back, a quarter for the meter.

Adam toes the sawdust with his boot. "My dad, he loves big and loud, but he isn't particularly good at being responsible, so a lot of duties fell on me, and I think that's what led me to music, the escape of it, especially while Rachel was away at art school. That was the worst of my dad's spiral. He just wasn't himself anymore."

My stomach knots. I turn toward him. "Were you okay?"

He doesn't look up. "Honestly, no. He never hit me or anything like that, but there were times when he came close. When he was loud, but skipped the love part. He'd get up in my face and I had to leave the house. I went and played guitar in the barn or in town to drown it all out."

My blood boils that Jim would do that. A sour taste fills my mouth and I set my dessert aside. "Adam, I'm so sorry."

He puts his pastry box down. "You have nothing to apologize for. I'm sorry I spewed all of that. I don't usually talk about it, but I . . . feel so comfortable with you. I always have." His cheeks redden as he faces me.

I hold his gaze. "You can talk to me anytime."

His throat bobs. "You can talk to me, too, Ben. Whenever you need someone to listen."

My therapist was right. I'm not alone. I want to share everything about Dad, Delish Dollars Studios, and Grandma, but I don't know where to start. For now, it's so good listening to him, reconnecting. "I appreciate that," I say, placing my hand on the bench between us.

A comfortable silence settles, and we take in the crowd of patrons. An older couple heads to the open space at the base of the stage and sways to the music.

That's the future I want. Dancing on a Friday night beneath the stars with the love of my life.

I grip the bench. "What's next for you?" I ask, tone a bit timid, like I'm afraid of the answer . . . of him leaving Fern Falls.

He takes in the guitarist as they play a soft solo. "I don't know. Rachel is settled, Dad is better, Mom is gone. Maybe it's time to unpause my own life now." He examines his boots. "You know something I've never told anyone?"

I smile. "What?"

Pink rises high on his cheeks. "I've always wanted to try and pursue music in some sort of professional capacity." He laughs. "That's dumb."

I turn toward him. "It's not dumb at all."

His smile is appreciative. "It's just that when things at home were hardest, I'd take shelter in my room, outside in the trees, or in the barn, and I'd write songs. Sometimes, that was the only way I could express the big emotions I felt about what was happening with my family. It's how I coped for years. I put my hopes into those songs and all the comfort I wanted to feel, and I always thought that if I ever got the chance, I'd want to share them with others who are going through a hard time, too. Like maybe my songs could give people hope like they gave to me."

His voice is quiet when he finishes, but I hang on every word.

I inch closer. "That's beautiful. And brave. And I think your music is a gift, and of course it would comfort people if you shared it however makes you happiest."

His answering smile hits me right in the heart. "Thank you for saying that."

I tilt my head toward my shoulder. "I don't know much at all about pursuing a musical career. What would that look like for you? Where would it start?" I ask softly.

He fixes his gaze on me. "It starts with this summer. With you."

A thrill shoots through my fingers. "Me?"

He nods, expression serious. "Between work and making sure the tree farm was okay, and before that, trying to help my parents out, my dad, mostly, I've never been able to pursue what I really want. It's never been the right time." His eyes bore into mine.

I don't flinch. I embrace the high of this moment, the way my whole body might fly off this bench. A splinter digs into my finger. "What do you really want?"

He leans in and a soft glow highlights the strong arc of his brows, bridge of his nose, barely there freckles on the apples of his cheeks. The glint of his lips. "Ben, for a really long time I've wanted to tell you—"

A high-pitched squeal sounds directly into my ear.

Adam and I startle and face forward to find two teen girls standing before us, staring.

"Hi?" I say in a daze.

"You're them!" one of the girls squeaks, jumping up and down.

Adam and I meet eyes, dumbstruck.

"We're who?" Adam asks, turning back to the girls.

The second girl holds up her phone and squeals again. "You're Badam! From *Take the Cake National*!" She points to a photo on her screen. It's an image from the show taping on Friday. Adam and I stand on the patio of The Stacks, facing each other. I flinch to see the pain in my expression, and his.

My cheeks burn. I'd like to dig a hole beneath the sawdust and never come back out.

"Are you two together now?" the girls scream.

Adam eyes me, questioning.

I want to respect his wishes, to be friends. That's why he broke the kiss off the other night, why he walked away during the filming. I don't want to embarrass him. I also don't want to make him feel dismissed, like how I felt last time we were asked this in front of the cameras. I face the girls. "We're just out right now eating some dessert."

"Oh my *gahhhhd*! Can we get a picture?" They turn around with their phones in selfie mode.

Adam and I share a shrug, then lean across the bench.

"Get closer!" they yell.

We move in until we're all in the frame.

Adam's warmth tingles along the side of my neck as we press together, his pine and musk encapsulating me.

The girls take the photo, and run off, staring at the phone and exclaiming in high-pitched voices.

I don't move.

Neither does Adam.

I focus on the slight space between our thighs.

His hand is on his knee, and it would take nothing to inch my pinkie over and loop it around his, draw him in.

He angles toward me, eyes glinting. "So, Badam, huh?" He smirks.

I huff a laugh. "Just think. Could have been Bendam, and that sounds like a hemorrhoid cream, so."

Adam lets out a hearty laugh that makes me grin as wide as my face allows.

Our knees knock together and we lock eyes. Instead of flinching back, he presses his leg against mine, harder. I gasp.

A chorus of screams echoes from nearby.

I blink, breaking our trance, and follow the sound to find that the teens have multiplied and a larger group is headed our way.

"That's our cue," Adam says, voice tense.

Disappointment sinks me down, but I rise with him and we head back toward the entrance, picking up our pace as the teens track us.

He stays close by my side, and we emerge back through the entrance undisturbed.

It's not until we reach his truck that I realize . . . none of that bothered me—the media, the attention. It wasn't triggering. With Adam by my side, I was safe.

Chapter 14

"I'm sorry about all that," I say once Adam pulls onto the road.

He faces me in the dark cab, the soft glow of the dash highlights his cheek, a glimmer in his eye. "What are you sorry about?"

How do I apologize for people assuming we're a couple? I take in the scenery out the windshield. The ocean is a midnight blue beyond the slope of the canyon. "The photos. Did you feel uncomfortable?"

He smiles. "Is it weird that I think it's kind of cool that we have fans?"

My shoulders relax and I laugh. "I never expected something like that from a baking show, so it's definitely something." I keep waiting for the fear to set in, the fact that I'm recognized by strangers. I hated seeing the discomfort on our faces in the photo of that recording, but being with him now makes everything okay.

He shakes his head. "There are so many ways that I'm afraid

to be seen, as queer, as an artist, as someone struggling to make sense of their family, and their life, and the whole damn world." He glances over. "But I like being seen with you, and by you." His voice is soft, quiet.

My heart is in my throat. I can't tear my eyes away from him. Everything he said feels like it was pulled from my heart. And he likes being seen with me, by me. "I like that, too, Adam."

I want to say more, like how he makes me feel safe and cared for, how he's held me still throughout the chaos of the past days, how he holds every part of me. The content smile that tugs up the corners of his lips proves I said enough.

A car passes by on the opposite side of the road, headlights shining, lighting up Adam's fingers as they clutch the steering wheel.

His hand was so close to mine moments ago, back on the bench at the festival. Suddenly, I'm extra aware of space. There is less than a foot between us on this gray leather seat. His bedroom door in the cottage is twelve steps away from mine.

I grip my seat belt, squeeze hard.

"Did you feel uncomfortable?"

I take a deep breath. "I thought I would." I focus on the road as it levels out, the sparkling blue-black sea beyond the quiet highway.

"Do you want to talk about it?" Adam asks as we head toward the low lights of Maywell Bay.

The tires whir against the road as his question hangs there, an open invitation. My therapist's words echo in my mind. *Be patient and gentle with yourself. You're not alone.*

I exhale. There's a free-fall swing in my stomach, like I'm trusting Adam to catch me. "I didn't get to control the narrative when I got lost in the woods all those years ago. I was just the face on the flyers, on the news. Like being young meant I was unaffected by the hordes of reporters outside our house, or oblivious to the fear it caused my mom. She made me stay in my room when she discussed the social worker's visit with Dad, as if the door was some magic barrier that silenced their yelling. After seeing my dad yesterday, I realize why my mom tried to hide the article he published, didn't encourage visits with him. She was trying to protect me." A weight lifts from my shoulders.

Adam is quiet for a beat. "Do you want to talk about that? Seeing your dad?" His tone is gentle, reassuring despite the warp speed of my thoughts.

My throat thickens, but I force the words out. "It was exactly how I expected it to be." My voice is strained. "He's using the media from the baking show for his own gain, just like he used the media before, at the cost of my mom and me. At the cost of trying to repair any kind of relationship with us. He's a narcissistic opportunist, and seeing that firsthand? It's something else. The years I spent away from him were a blessing."

"Ben, I'm so sorry." His tone is sincere, not a hint of pity.

"I'll be okay." I focus on the road as we turn onto the bridge that always transports me to the haven of Grandma's street.

"Of course you'll be okay," Adam says. "You're the strongest person I know."

His expression is sincere, despite how I spewed my scariest thoughts. "You think I'm strong?"

"Of course I do." He eyes me like I said I hate the Ramones. "You are. Being vulnerable is brave." He pauses. "I'll never forget the first time we met."

I melt against the back of the seat.

A soft smile plays on his lips. "You walked onto my tree farm like you owned the place. This small kid, commanding an ax twice his size with a vengeance." He smirks. "Not gonna lie, you scared me a little."

I bark a laugh. "I did not scare you."

His brows shoot up. "You felled that tree and I didn't even assist with all my strength when we dragged it down the hill, wrapped it up, strapped it to your car."

I snort. "It was a long time ago. The details are fuzzy, I'm sure."

He pulls up along the curb out front of Grandma's house and shuts off the engine.

"Fine, don't believe me, but it wasn't just that. You've faced hard shit over the years." He worries the keys between his fingers. "When my dad called and told me my mom left, do you know what my first thought was?"

My breath hitches, hanging on his words. "What?"

He is a silhouette in the darkness, but his body shifts nearer. "I wanted to call you. Ask how to get through it. You're always seeing the best in others, Ben. You put so much good into the world despite the fucked-up shit people do. I needed you to tell me how to see the good when all I wanted to do was burn everything down."

His words grip me. I reach forward, press my palm on the seat between us. There's so much I want to ask, like how he could see me that way when I'm a raging pool of anxiety, how he thinks I have anything together. But one question races to the tip of my tongue. "Why didn't you call me back then?"

He lets out a puff of air. "I didn't deserve to. I've been a terrible friend to you."

His answer makes me jerk back. "No, you haven't. What are you talking about?" I clutch my knee, ground myself. How can he say that? His morning visits at the café are what keep me going most days, knowing I'll see his steady smile, his reassuring presence.

He tucks the keys into his pocket, runs a hand through his hair. "I haven't been honest with you."

I gulp. "About what? I don't want you to feel like you can't tell me things. I know we haven't talked like this in a while, but it's still you and me. I won't judge you."

He sucks in a hiss of air, nods. "I love being with you, Ben. I want you to know that."

I hold his stare. "I love being with you, too."

"I love talking with you." He moves closer.

I breathe against mounting pressure in my chest. "I love talking with you, too."

He reaches forward and rests his hand beside mine. "For a long time, probably since I first met you, I've always wanted to tell you—"

A bright flash lights up his face and I squint. "What the hell?" I hold up my hand against more bright bursts.

Images of flashlights in the dark woods bombard me. Strangers' voices calling my name. Strong arms picking me up off the forest floor.

"Ben," Adam calls. "Exit on my side." He guides me toward him, the grasp of his hand, grounding and secure.

We slide out of the driver's side, close the door behind us.

Adam tucks me beneath his arm as a reporter shoves a mic between us. "Ben! Can you tell us more about your father's involvement in your business?" I can't see their face.

Adam nudges the mic away and ducks his head over mine.

I clutch his jacket, hold him close, try to catch my breath.

"You don't have to say anything," Adam says into my ear. "We'll head right inside."

"Are you two together now?" comes another question, mic, flash of light.

"Adam, are you sorry for rejecting Ben?" They yell so loud, like they aren't right in our faces.

"Let's just get to the driveway," he says. "They can't come on private property."

We head toward the house, but they don't stop. At least five reporters crowd in next to me. I can't tell how many are on Adam's side or behind us.

His arm tightens around me as we near the front fountain.

One reporter nudges in and Adam trips to the side.

"Are you hurt?" I ask in a rush, gripping his waist to keep him upright.

"I'm fine," he says, but his eyes are wide.

Rage burns all fear from my veins, and I face the person who tripped him as they slink into the crowd, light blurring everything. "Get off our property," I yell at the gathering. "I'm not talking to any of you. You're wasting your time."

They all speak at once, in loud voices and frantic tones, and I can't make any of it out.

"Let's bolt inside," Adam says.

I check the house. Most of the windows are dark. That's right, the family is at a big dinner in town tonight. I take a deep breath. If we go in, we'll be stuck in there, waiting for the paparazzi to leave, and my family will be accosted when they return home.

A glimmer of hope and a little rebellion sparks through me. I face Adam. "I have an idea."

He tilts his head. "What?"

"Ready to run?" I ask.

His lip kicks up and his eyes brighten. "I am so game. I have always wanted to be in a high-speed chase without like murdering anyone or robbing a bank or—"

"Let's go," I say on a laugh, grabbing his hand and pulling him up toward the side of the house.

We knock together as we sprint as fast as we can through the side entrance.

Footfalls sound behind us, lights flash, people yell.

I slam the gate at our back, and grip an iron bar, panting.

Adam is at my side, breathing heavily. "Ben, I don't think they're going to stop."

He's right. Closer to the street, silhouettes sneak around the side, heading toward the beach access. "You think they'll come up through the courtyard?" I ask.

"I wouldn't put anything past them," he says, voice tight with concern.

"Okay," I say in a rush, scanning the space for any way out. The last thing I want to do is bring them right to our little cottage on the sand.

I spot an opening in a hedge and a smile curls my lips. "This way." I grab Adam's hand and pull him toward Grandma's garden. "I used to play hide-and-seek here with my cousins. They'll never find us."

We dash across the cobblestones and duck through wall-height jasmine and boxwood until we emerge onto the sandy beach access.

Adam pauses at my side as I check the start of the path, up near the street. Voices drift our way, but no one has made it here yet.

"Follow me." I tug him into a cypress grove that borders the far side of the beach. I drop his hand and raise a brow in challenge. "Ready to run?"

He answers with a smirk, and we're off.

The only sound is the crunch of leaves and grinding of compacted sand. I push past branches, against curling bark. Go, go, go. Run, run, run.

Like the night in the woods.

The thought of it punches my stomach.

I didn't run back then, not right away. At first, I nestled between some tight-knit trees and sat, ate a granola bar, and watched Dad through the side window of his home office.

I was never allowed in that room, and there were cool things on the walls. Posters and plaques, several framed drumheads covered in autographs.

He paced back and forth in front of the window, his voice drifted through the open screen. Lots of words that I didn't understand, but some that I did: "You are the best there is, and I'll bring you to the top," and lots of other nice things he never once said to me.

My legs started to ache when the sky turned gray, but I couldn't move, couldn't take my eyes off him.

By the time it grew dark, the hunger in my gut turned to anger.

Didn't he notice I wasn't inside? Didn't he want to eat dinner together, like I always made a point to do?

The whole world was blue-black but for the yellow rectangle of that window.

He must have thought I was in my room. That was all.

"Dad," I called.

No response.

I yelled his name again, louder.

His head jerked toward the window, phone against his ear.

He'd tell them to wait. He'd come outside to get me.

Instead, he returned to his conversation, pacing in front of the window again, hand on his hip.

"Dad!" That time, I didn't hold back. I threw every broken piece of rage into that scream.

He jumped, looked around. His features twisted in frustration.

Then, he closed his office window with a resounding bang.

I felt that sound like it had struck me in the chest.

Stunned, I sat still, staring at him as he continued to work, continued choosing whoever was on the phone over me.

That's when I ran.

I couldn't go back in the house. I couldn't be with someone who didn't want me around, who didn't want me.

All I hoped for was to hear my father's footsteps behind me, hear his voice call my name.

To be loved, to be cared for.

To be found.

My shoe catches on a fallen cypress branch and I lunge toward a tree, planting my palms on the brittle outer bark of the trunk.

"Found you," Adam calls, from several paces behind.

I shake my head, returning to the present. "What?" I ask loud enough so he can hear me.

He nears, panting. "You got so far ahead."

"What did you say?" I ask, catching my breath. "Before."

He braces his hands on his knees and angles his gaze up, moonlight sparking off his eyes. "I found you." He smiles, big and true.

I loose a breath from deep in my diaphragm, down to my core, down to my bones. My vision blurs at the edges.

Adam straightens. "Hey, are you okay?" His forehead creases in concern.

I shake my head.

He steps close. "What's wrong? What can I do?"

"I'm sorry, I—" The words wrench through me. "I can't do this."

He searches my face. "Okay. We can walk. Let's head back," he says, words rushed. "Do you want me to call your mom? Grandma?"

"Adam." I grab his hands and he sucks in air. His wrists pulse fast beneath my touch. My body flushes with heat. "I can't be friends with you."

He rips his focus from our hands, alarm flashes in his eyes. "What do you mean?"

The pain on his face is sharp enough to pierce. A knife to the heart would hurt less than what I need to say. "I can't settle for your friendship alone. Not when you say things that put me back together, and you don't even realize it because caring comes so naturally to you. When you lock eyes with me and all I want is to drown in your attention, all I crave is your touch." My voice cracks and I drop his hands.

He widens his stance. "Ben."

"Please. You don't need to say anything." I swipe the wetness from my cheeks as a gentle breeze blows the sage-like scent of Pacific cypress through the gap between us. The leaves and bark and sand blur as fresh tears gather in my lashes. "I ruined everything, I'm sorry. I tried to be okay with this. I don't want to lose you in my life, but I need space before I can be friends. Right now, I want you too much. I don't know how to not want you yet, and I don't want to make you uncomfortable while I learn how to want you less. I'm sorry." My voice is a whisper. I shove my hand in my pocket. My fingers rub against a small glass sphere. The cinnamon roll. I turn around and hide my face. I can't keep it together anymore. Everything snaps at once. I slump against the tree and let the tears fall.

His hand cups my shoulder, and I lean into his touch like a fool.

"Ben." His voice is pleading. "Please look at me."

My pulse pounds in my ears as I wipe my cheeks with the sleeve of my coat.

I turn and his hand slides down my arm, his touch burning through my jacket.

He is so close. Moonlight glints off his eyes. A tear glitters down his cheek.

I reach to catch it and he presses his hand to mine, leans into my touch.

My rapid heartbeat pulses his name. A-dam. A-dam. A-dam.

"I'm so very sorry," he says, breath warming my wrist.

"You have nothing to be sorry for," I say, voice raspy. "I know that you want to stay friends, and that's okay. It is. I respect it, and I'm sorry if I made you uncomfortable on Saturday night, when you first arrived. I came on too strong with the kiss. You didn't want that. I'm embarrassed. And really sorry."

His thick dark lashes brush back and forth across his cheeks as he scans my face.

I steel myself. I can take this. I've self-rejected for years. Why would this confirmation kill me? I clench my free fist. Wrench me free, then.

He exhales, shakes his head.

"Adam, it's okay. You don't owe me any—"

He lowers my hand, and grabs the other one, too. "I want to be more than friends with you, Ben."

Each word reaches through my chest and grips tight, each cell in my body electric and alive and starved.

He leans closer. "I tried to tell you with every look. Every interaction. Everything. And when I got the chance during the filming, I couldn't. Not like that. It was your time. I couldn't make it about me, what I wanted. I didn't realize then that you felt this, too. I didn't want to put that pressure on you."

I swallow hard, trying to process each word. I can't. "Please. You don't have to tell me something because you think I want to hear it. You don't have to want this. With me."

He moves in close, cups my face in his hands, and stares straight into my soul. "I have never not wanted you. Never."

If it weren't for his touch, I'd crumble.

I say with any voice I have left, "Why did you wait so long? To tell me?" Not that I have the right to ask. I only just told him how I feel. But that's why I need to know. I couldn't bear it if he was saying these things out of pity.

He drops his head, trails his hands down my arms, stops at my elbows. "Because the recent years have been a mess. I thought some day would come when I had my shit together enough to tell you how I feel. And when they asked me about us during the filming, my only wish was to put my arm around you and be able to say we were together." He shakes his head. "But I've missed every chance to make that happen, and I have no one to blame but myself. When you left, I worried I'd lost that chance for good." He takes my hands in his, threads our fingers together. "That's why I came here, to tell you how I feel. And then I feared that I fucked it all up by kissing you too fast too soon." Moonlight sparks off his eyes. His lips. "I tried to tell you at the art festival, then again in the truck before the cameras came."

I search his face, each worry line, and knead his fingers between mine. "Why did you pull away, when we kissed?" My voice is hoarse, raw.

He winces. "I just, I want to take this slow. My other relationships, if you can even call them that, were always fast, rushed, a distraction from whatever I didn't want to think about with my parents." He scans my face. "This is different, Ben. I didn't want you to think I only wanted something physical with you. I don't want to just hook up. I . . ." He makes a small laugh and shakes his head. "This is gonna sound silly."

"It won't." I rub my thumbs over his knuckles.

He holds my gaze. "I don't want to scare you off."

I swallow hard. "You won't. Please tell me." We've gone too long leaving everything unsaid. I want it all.

His chest rises. "I don't even just want to date you, I want to court you," he exhales the words in a rush. "I want to take my time getting to know each part of you, not just physically when we're ready, if you want that, but you. Everything. I've missed so much time with you. I don't want to miss you anymore."

His eyes are deep and drowning. All I want is right here.

But he can't possibly mean . . . "Do you know what courtship is?"

He bites his lip. "I do."

He can't understand. I've read my mom's entire historical romance shelf. "You know it means dating with the intention to . . . marry?"

He breathes deeply. "Ben. I'm not trying to overwhelm you, but dating you wouldn't be anything else to me. I want to call this what it is. I want to make my intentions clear because I've held back for far too long. Dating is too fragile." His expression darkens. "My feelings for you are not fragile."

My mouth is dry. My throat is dry. My entire body is a wasteland.

Say something. Anything. What? What words could there possibly be when every fantasy I've ever had, everything I've ever dreamed of hearing echoes in my ears?

Adam's cheeks redden. "You don't have to answer now. Or at all, truly. If you want to keep things as they are, I respect that, and we can move on from this conversation like it never happened. I needed you to know exactly how I feel about you, but you do not have to feel the same."

I pull his hands in so our chests meet. "No—" I catch my

breath. "I want that," I say, voice thick with emotion. "I would love to court you, Adam."

His eyes shimmer. "Really?"

"Yes," I rasp.

He gathers me close. I nuzzle into the crook of his neck, breathing him in. Adam. I clutch the back of his jacket, his body firm beneath my touch.

"I know it's not the eighteen hundreds, we don't have to call it courting or anything, I just know that simply dating you is not enough," he says softly, warm breath in my hair. "I don't know what I'm doing, but I'm all in, Ben."

"You're doing just fine, Reed," I say. "You're doing great." It's hard to get the words out when all I want to do is cry.

Never in a million years did I think this is how today would end.

I pull him in to me as tightly as I can. I need his heart to beat against mine.

A-dam. A-dam. A-dam.

Chapter 15

"What do you mean he just *showed up*?" Whitney shrieks over FaceTime, blue-tipped bob swinging at her shoulders.

My phone is propped on my nightstand while I browse the costume closet for tonight's assigned outfit. "I mean, he is here, playing guitar with the party band for the entire two weeks. It's okay. No need to get overexcited."

Call me the Energizer Bunny for all my excitement, but Whitney doesn't need to know that right now.

With Adam rehearsing for tonight's *Grease*-themed sock hop most of the day, I've had plenty of time to think about last night.

After the walk home, he held the door open for me, kissed my hand, and wished me sweet dreams. Said he'd always wanted to do all of that in that exact order.

Of course, I didn't sleep at all. His moonlit gaze was all I could see when I closed my eyes. His words playing over and over in my head: *My feelings for you are not fragile.*

My heart stutters.

"Ben! You can't just casually mention this and not expect

me to freak out. After what happened during the filming, then seeing your names break the internet, all of Fern Falls is losing their shit. Mayor Park is calling a town hall."

I snap my attention to the screen. "Whitney, oh my god."

"I'm fucking with you." She laughs.

I sigh. My nerves are going gaywire. "Whitney, please. This conversation has gotten way off track. I only have two questions."

"Okay," she says, leaning into the screen. "Call me your love guru, let's go."

"Is everything going okay at the bakery? Please tell me the paparazzi haven't descended upon Fern Falls, too."

She groans. "Oh my god, of course you would ask about the bakery at a time like this." She nods. "Yes. Everything is under control. Tanner brought in a second espresso machine from the bar's kitchen to handle the new tourists visiting because of the TV show, and he pulled in some of his off-shift employees to help with the crowds." She smiles softly. "He's, um, actually been really helpful."

Her words are such a relief.

I still have to appease Delish Dollars Studios with good PR before our Zoom call, and I don't think the paparazzi fiasco of last night is gonna do the trick. After checking Instagram this morning, not much has swayed the BoycottBen hashtaggers. I need to talk with Adam. I know he'd take photos with me, but this thing between us is so new, something I've wanted for so long. I don't want to share private moments with the intent of swaying online haters. If I post photos of us, it'll be because I want to share how I feel when I'm with him: overjoyed.

"What else?" she asks.

"Hm?"

"What was your second question?"

I blush so hard I press a hand to my cheek. "I need your help getting ready for tonight's party."

Her eyes widen. "Is this our early oughts romcom movie moment?"

I shake my head. "Whit, no. I don't want a full makeover. I just . . ." I pull out the hanger labeled with today's date: a white T-shirt and jeans. "You have such a great edgy style. How do I make this look cute?"

Something falls from the top shelf of the closet and I jump. A pink box is now on the floor, and at least ten packaged sex toys scatter across the hardwood. "G-ma," I whisper under my breath.

"What was that?" Whitney asks.

"Nothing," I reply, rehanging the clothes and shoving everything into the box and back into the closet. The last thing I need right now is her commentary on butt plugs.

Too distracted to notice the toy fiasco, she squeals and presses her hand to her chest. "It would be my greatest honor to help you, Benjamin."

I straighten, sighing with relief for multiple reasons. "Thank you."

She holds up a finger. "But since our relationship has now leveled up to a Nora Ephron–approved status, and I have been typecast as the main character's over-involved bestie, I'm going to need to know a few things first."

I laugh and wince simultaneously. "What do you need to know?"

"Are you and Adam sleeping together?"

"Whitney. Jesus." My face is on fire.

"Ben, this matters. I need to give you advice on what to wear under the jeans."

"We have not slept together." I retrieve the clothes, twist the fabric of the shirt in my hands.

"Oh my god."

I look up. "What?"

"You've kissed."

I close my eyes.

"I knew it! Are you dating?"

"I . . . think so." My voice is quiet.

She clicks her tongue. "What do you mean?"

"How is this important for the outfit?" I ask, eyeing her.

"These are my conditions," she quips with a raised finger. "If I don't have the full story, I cannot fairy-godmother. That's the rule."

I shake my head. Swallow hard. "He said he wants to court me."

I've never seen Whitney at a loss for words. Maybe the screen is frozen. "Whit?"

She blinks. "That is so romantic, I'm gonna puke."

I snort. "I'm not telling you anything ever again."

"Is this like some kind of kinky Bridgerton shit because that's hot."

I can't help but laugh. "He said dating me would be too fragile." I swallow hard. "And that his feelings for me are not fragile." Even as I say the words, they don't sink in. Last night was a fever dream.

Her eyes fling wide and she returns to a stunned state.

I huff. "Since you forced this out of me, how about a little help here? I can't call Morgan because this is her brother-in-law now. Please promise you won't tell anyone. I don't know how to handle this. He was practicing with the band all day, but I'll see him tonight, and I don't know how to act. I don't want to look like an idiot."

Whitney shakes her head, coming out of her stupor. "I can't say that I've been in this position, but I would advise you to roll with it. Be yourself, Ben. That's who he likes, who he kissed. Who he is motherfucking courting."

My neck flames. "Yeah?"

"Hell yeah. And you said tonight is *Grease* themed?" She paces back and forth in the bakery's kitchen.

I nod.

"Ben." She gets all up in the screen. "You have to wear the greaser shirt and jeans. Take a one-night break from starched linen shirts with buttons. Maybe dressing differently will help with this new phase you and Adam are in, get you feeling comfy with new things. Is there any leather in that closet?"

"More like, is there anything besides leather?"

"Okay, good. Let's get you sexed up so you can court Adam's ass right into the sheets."

I glare. "Goodbye, Whitney."

"Oh! And don't forget to masturbate before—"

I stab my forefinger at the red hang-up button on my cell's screen.

Jesus Christ.

I stare down at my loafers, now splattered with stubborn specs of sand.

Adam looked extremely hot in leather pants. If I could make him feel even a fraction of the want I did in that fitting room, maybe I won't be the only one flustered tonight.

I take a deep breath. If my muscles could relax the slightest bit. My gaze drifts to the bottle of lube on my nightstand table.

Whitney has a point.

I set the clothes on the bed and slowly approach the nightstand. Pick up the bottle.

You've got angst in your pants making you do the horny dance.

"Ah." I toss the tube in the waste bin by the door. I cannot and will not jack off with a gift from my grandmother. It's basic principles.

I lean against the doorframe. I have to get myself together.

With hardly any sleep and Adam . . . God. His bed is right there. I stare down his closed door. What do his sheets smell like? Would they smell like musk? Pine? Has he touched himself since he's been here? Has he touched himself thinking about me? Him touching me . . .

I halt. The pressure in my shorts is no longer something I can deny, and somehow, I've gravitated toward his door.

Okay, Jesus. I need to take care of this.

I retreat to my bathroom and turn on the shower.

Stripped in seconds, I'm beneath warm water and already working on giving myself a fraction of relief.

My feelings for you are not fragile.

Would his touch be fragile? Or would he be rough?

I think I'd like that. To feel his teeth, the scrape of them, shivering up my spine.

I push my free hand against the tile wall.

The moonlight in his eyes. How his expression shifted in so many ways. Gentle, caring, pleading, dark. Hungry.

My fingernails scrape across the grout.

What would I do to him in this cottage, this little space that is all ours? What would he do to me? Our time here is just beginning. There is so much. I would crawl on my bare knees for him. Push him against the headboard. Take him so deep—

Relief rips through me, hot and fast.

My chest heaves. I let the water run down my back, muscles unwinding.

Whatever happens tonight, whatever happens in this next phase with us, I'll try to accept it, not push it away or fear every new thing. The first step is tonight. I can focus on tonight.

There's a knock at the front door muffled by the running water.

Oh, shit. Please, for all that is holy, do not be my grandmother. I turn off the shower then towel dry and grab a robe from the door hook, wrap it around me, tie it.

"I'm coming," I yell as I exit my bedroom, making my way past the kitchen. I wince. Great choice of words seeing as I already did that. My brain is on a one-way track.

I open the door and am not greeted by a person, but a giant bouquet of red roses.

"Are you Ben Parrish?" the roses ask.

"I am."

"These are for you." The bouquet jolts forward, and I take it, wrapping my arm around the glass vase.

"Thank you," I say, peeking over the petals.

A petite person pulls the door shut.

I place the flowers on the coffee table and straighten. One dozen red roses. There's a note card at the top.

I pull it out, open it up. Press my fingers to my lips as I read.

Do you remember our first camping trip?

I swallow hard.

I woke up holding your hand. Each one of these roses is for each year that passed by afterwards when I wanted to take your hand in mine, but was too afraid to ask. AR

My whole heart is in my throat. I set down the card and count the flowers. One dozen. One for every year.

A tear falls down my cheek.

"What a gorgeous bouquet," Mom's voice sounds from the doorway.

I look up, swiping at my face.

"Why are you crying?" She strides in, voice worried.

I hand her the note.

She reads it. Presses her hand to her cheek. Reads again. When she looks up, her eyes shimmer. "Oh, honey," she says. "I do believe you are being wooed."

I smile, laugh. Adam would love to hear that. "Did you know about the flowers? See them being delivered?"

She shakes her head, handing the note back to me. "No, this is a wonderful surprise. I'm so happy for you."

I smile. "Thank you." I am happy for myself, too.

"I'm sorry to barge in on this moment, but I wanted to talk to you about the paparazzi from last night. The neighbors mentioned the fiasco to Grandma, and we saw some stragglers when we returned from dinner last night."

My stomach sinks. "Mom, I'm so sorry. It's so invasive. I'm trying to get rid of them, I—"

"No, Ben." She places a hand on my arm. "I want to make sure you are okay. I hope it's not triggering for you, the media attention, the whir of it all."

My shoulders relax at her words, her thoughtfulness. "It's

a bit triggering, yeah. But I am okay. I had a therapy appointment, and Adam is really helping me through."

She folds her hands together. "I'm so glad. Please know I'm here if you need me, I'm going to look into hiring security to keep the paparazzi at bay, because there are still some camped out by the gates."

Fear tightens my muscles. "Do we have the funds for that? You don't have to—"

"I'm your mother. I will always protect you, Ben. No matter how old you are."

I blink hard. There are things I want to protect her from. Like the knowledge that I met with Dad, or the fact that he is single-handedly trying to sabotage our business for his own gain. I can't share that with her. I don't want to give her more to worry about. "I love you, Mom."

She squeezes me. "I love you." She pulls back, nodding to the flowers, the note in my hand. "And it looks like Adam does, too."

My face heats.

She winks. "See you tonight."

Then, she heads out the door, closing it behind her.

I hold Adam's note to my chest.

If this is courting, I'll take it.

Chapter 16

How is it possible that this party is even more crowded than the first? Did we amass more relatives in the span of a day? People press in around the pool, and I worry someone might fall in. With so many dark leather jackets in one place, it's hard to tell where the party ends and the night sky begins.

I can't take more of Grandma's second cousin's kid's nephew's sisters-in-law. More names I'll forget at Christmas dinner. Or more cousin Bettys with invasive questions and pressure to bond just because we are related down the line.

I only want to be with Adam.

I stand on my side of the cottage's mermaid fountain. A pair of perky stone tits shields my face from the crowd, and most importantly, from the pink Cadillac in the center.

There's a fog machine, of course there is, and it shrouds the circular platform around the automobile so it looks like the band floats on a cloud with a car. It's pretty damn cool.

And Adam? A fucking dream. He's fully embracing the leather pants and crop top Sandy vibe as he strums to "Jailhouse Rock." He's also tied some Travolta in there with his expert hip swivels.

How am I going to make it through tonight without blatantly lusting all over him?

The scent of roses still clings to my skin.

I sigh and grip the edge of the fountain, damp and cool.

Clare West, give me strength. That's the mermaid's name now. Sounds old Hollywood-y, and I'll need some silver screen confidence to pull this off.

Time to channel my inner Olivia Newton-John.

The stiff jeans scratch my legs as I pass through the cottage courtyard, but not too badly. The black boots from the Teal Room closet are a little tight, but nothing my toes can't take. The tucked-in white T-shirt is way too snug, but maybe it gives an illusion of muscle, beneath my leather jacket.

I run a hand over my slicked-back hair, still stiff with product. Whitney sent me a YouTube video on how to style it into a pompadour and my hair feels like a Ken doll's. I left my glasses off and added a touch of eyeliner along my lashes. I don't think greasers wore eyeliner, but I wanted to drive this whole makeover thing home.

Stepping into the larger courtyard feels like a coming-out party. Where, um, no one notices me, but that's fine. I only care about one person witnessing my mini transformation.

"Ben! Oh my god, you are gor-geous!"

Guess I was wrong about the not-noticing.

I squint at a tall person with deep black skin, their lean muscular build accentuated by body glitter on their biceps. They stun in full Pink Lady drag, rocking a bubblegum-hued wig to match their satin jacket and miniskirt.

I don't understand how they know my name, but pride at my makeover success tingles through me. If a drag queen calls you gorgeous, it's never a lie.

"You don't remember me, do you?" They grin, bright teeth gleaming.

"Sorry, no? But you look amazing." I wish they could have given me make-up tips.

"Baby, I know I do." They wink and bounce the end of their wig. "I wasn't in drag the other night, but I have a show after this and thought I'd bring along the theme. How about now? Does this spark any memories?" they ask, holding a full glass to my nose.

The turpentine turns my stomach. It's G-ma's Healing Heartbreak tea. I wince. "Book Club, I'm guessing?"

They lower the glass and jut out their hip. "That was some telling-off you gave that hot pirate last Saturday." They nod toward the stage. "You're an icon in my book."

Oh god, the telling-off. It's fuzzy, but I'm sure I said things to Adam I'd never say without the tea. And the things we've said since then, well. Heat sizzles through me.

The music stalls and feedback sounds from the stage as the lead singer speaks up. "Glad to see everyone getting their kicks!" They wear a leather jacket and red bowler cap. "Thanks for coming out to celebrate Grandma Parrish's eightieth birthday. Can we give the legend a round of applause?"

I cheer along with everyone else.

"Let's dive into this *Grease*-themed dream, shall we? Sandy Candy, take it away!" They motion to Adam, and he launches into a guitar solo.

I cross my arms despite my straining shirt and jacket. I need pressure against my chest because my heart might burst. He used the name Sandy Candy. I smile. But even more, it's clear he's in his element. His head sways to the rhythm of his strumming, and a peaceful smile graces his lips while his whole face is aglow. He's never looked more loose and relaxed. This is different than when he plays at the bar in Fern Falls. He's away from everyone he knows, besides me, and the seaside air must be working its magic.

Like how I feel whenever I cross the bridge into Maywell Bay.

This is it. Playing guitar is Adam's escape, just like he said. His safe place. And I get to witness it.

With all his responsibilities on the tree farm growing up, with his mom and dad, and now the auto shop, he's never been able to leave Fern Falls without letting someone down. Music has always been his retreat. Maybe he's never prioritized what gives him joy.

"You want this?" my new friend in drag asks, holding the glass of Toxic Tea out to me.

I take a deep breath. Liquid courage may numb me for a moment, but no. I need to be lucid, fully aware of this new gravity between me and Adam. I shake my head. "Thanks, but I'll pass."

They smile. "Good for you. Go get him."

I grin back then plunge into the crowd, grateful for the spring their words put into my step.

I head toward the pink Cadillac like my boots are wheels on a track fueled solely by Adam's guitar music.

When I reach the edge of the stage, the crowd presses in and I proudly take my place as an Adam Reed groupie. I bite my lip. He's magnificent. Lights on his hair, shining down from the trussing, glowing him up in pinks, yellows, blues. His skin glistens from his effort, and his outfit—heeled boots, leather pants, crop top—would be approved for a Harry Styles fashion line.

Everyone around me knows he's hot shit. They scream and holler and swoon.

But then, Adam looks up, straight into my eyes, and smiles so big that spotlights glint off his white teeth.

I grin back like a fool and gladly accept my role as groupie manager, director, and president.

I suck at my bottom lip as his eyes scan me while he plays. My hair, jacket, jeans.

He cocks a brow like, *new look?*

I shrug. Smirk.

This is so easy, being with Adam.

His eyes grow dark and hooded while he holds my gaze. He forcefully strums that guitar like he might stroke other things, and he is *noticeably* checking. Me. Out. My throat's dry. I can't breathe. Has anyone died from too much sexually-charged attention? I'm about to be the first.

"Ben?"

I startle. Ben. Yes, I'm Ben.

Charlie, my old summertime friend, stands beside me, smiling. She's in a neon-orange top and poodle skirt with hot-pink eyeshadow that matches the streak in her long hair.

"Charlie! So glad you could pull away from the restaurant."

"Thank you for inviting me, this is incredible!"

Adam's guitar hits a high note.

"It really is." I smile. "Did you bring your girlfriend?"

She grins and nods toward the edge of the crowd where her partner waves, smiling. She has a short blond pixie cut, sun-kissed white skin, and wears high-waisted jeans with a hot-pink crop top that hugs her plus-sized curves.

I wave at her and turn back to Charlie, who is positively beaming.

"You two are adorable," I say.

"Thank you, she is truly the best. Not into big crowds, though. I'll go meet her in a bit, but I had to weasel in and say hi."

I don't have much time to chat with her now, and the way I left things between us that final summer gnaws at me. I try to run my fingers through my hair. Right. Too stiff. I pat my head instead. "Charlie, are we, um, good? We're good, right?"

She tilts her head. "You mean after your kiss-and-run of senior summer?"

My stomach drops. "Yeah. That." The courtyard ground is covered in pink glitter.

"Ben, look at me." Her voice is soft and kind.

I find her smiling and my shoulders relax.

"There aren't any hard feelings."

My limbs loosen. "Really?"

"I promise," she says. "We were young, still figuring things out. I wouldn't have met Stacey if we would have been a thing, never realized I'm gay."

My chest warms. "You're welcome, then. Gay is contagious, you know."

She snorts and hits my shoulder playfully.

"I'm so happy for you," I say, beaming.

"And I'm . . ." She shoots a look at Adam. "Really happy for you."

My whole body tingles. I follow her stare to the stage—to find Adam staring at me.

His lips are rolled in and white at the edges like he's biting down hard. The rest of the band has joined in on a sped-up version of "Heartbreak Hotel," and the strokes on his guitar are firm and fast. I stare back in a silent challenge. More of a challenge to myself. I won't look away. *We can do this, can't we? We can be us, together, in this new way.* Adam doesn't flinch. Like he's communicating through his stare, a firm and steady *YES.*

I pull at my collar. Is it hot? It's hot out here. The cool sea breeze is stifling.

Charlie elbows me. "That man looks at you like he wants to drown in you."

My face heats unbearably. "Please have some consideration for my fragile nerves."

My feelings for you are not fragile.

My body is on fire.

She lifts both hands in innocence. "Calling it like I see it. I'm sure you will survive, Ben." She laughs. "And on that note, I'm gonna track down Stace. The milkshake bar is calling my name." She pulls me into a hug and twists me around as she disappears through the crowd, so I'm facing Adam again.

He smiles sweetly, a twinkle in his eyes, like he saw me laughing and is in on the joke.

I grin back.

My phone buzzes.

I nearly whine aloud at having to break eye contact with

Adam as I pull it from my pocket. Hopefully, everything at the bakery is okay.

I check my screen, then freeze.

It's a text from Dad.

I want to fling my phone into the sea. Why the hell is he contacting me?

For a brief second, I hope he's writing to say he took the IG post down. Then, the sinking feeling in my gut reminds me that can't be true.

There's a video link from BuzzWhir News, and my nerves fire warning shots.

The thumbnail shows Adam, onstage, in his Sandy Candy apparel.

Dad: This is your friend, right? The one in all the photos with you?

I type back. My hands shake. **Stay the fuck away from Adam or I'll go to the press myself, tell my side of the story. Like you did all those years ago.**

I glance up.

Adam is radiant beneath the lights. This man who now sends me flowers, kisses my hand, walks me home. My friend for so many years. I will not let my father near him.

My phone pings with a new text.

Dad: If you get me an intro, I'll have Phillip delete the Instagram post and put up an image of congratulations to you. I'll stop tipping off the paparazzi. This kid has the talent I've been looking for. This could change everything for me.

The crowd freezes. The noise mutes. I take in Adam's expression and shove my phone into my jeans, burrow my hands into my jacket pockets.

Could he want that? To start a music career this way?

I wouldn't trust my father with his livelihood, his dreams. I won't let him near Adam.

I scan the crowd and find Grandma. She smiles and waves from the side gates where paparazzi press up against the bars, cameras flashing.

Mom is nearby, directing security.

My stomach drops. In no time, all of this could be gone for my grandmother. Everything she's built.

Mom catches my eye. She's so tired. Her face is tight. Nothing like it should be here, now.

I find Adam again.

There's a question in his eyes, like he sees all my thoughts splayed above my head. I clutch my arms, the most selfish thought on repeat: I don't want Dad to take Adam from me, even if this could be a dream come true. I just got him, and I don't want to lose him to music, to anything.

Chapter 17

The party dies down around midnight, and by dies down, I mean becomes a tolerable level of loud, manageable amount of crowded. The paparazzi have thinned out too, leaving only a few stragglers by the gates.

My stomach still hurts from Dad's texts, but I've coped by making no less than ten snack runs for Adam and the band. I don't know if they wanted ten Bitchin' Brisket Sliders each, but that's what they'll have after this round.

"Here ya go, honey," says a brunette woman with olive-toned skin dressed like a 1950s carhop in a pink and black blouse, full chiffon skirt, and white apron. Her name tag says DADDY-O DANI. She pushes a tray of sliders in red baskets and checkered papers across the retro bar.

"Thank you," I say, taking the food.

"Sure thing." She moves to the side to help another guest, revealing the full projector screen across the yard behind her. Red and teal classic cars park before it on the lawn. Corvettes,

Bel Airs, and Thunderbirds are crowded with guests watching *Beach Blanket Bingo.*

Gotta love G-ma and her commitment to a theme.

I turn and head to the stage, dodging another person in a carhop costume, except he's on roller skates.

Once I make it past slow-dancing couples, I'm at the front of the round platform where Adam and the band play. Placing the food tray on a pub table, I approach the edge of the stage. Adam slings his guitar to the side and the others keep a soft tune steady as he comes to me, squats down. "Hi," he says, voice sweet.

"Could you all use a real break this time?"

He squints out at the thinning crowd, then over at Grandma, who sits at a retro-styled milkshake bar, chatting closely with a friend. Very closely. They share a straw in their pink malt. "You think it's okay?" he asks.

I smirk. "I know the owner of this fine establishment, and she seems a bit distracted at the moment."

He smiles, then goes and talks to the lead singer.

The singer gives Adam a thumbs-up and speaks into the mic, "Okay, you cool cats, we're gonna take a short break and be right back."

Adam motions to join him onstage. I ascend the steps and stand beside the pink Cadillac. Being beneath the lights beside him is a whole new experience. I can understand why he likes it. The spotlights make everything beyond this small space fade away. This is different than the flashes of media cameras or beams cutting through dark trees. This is a choice. My chest inflates with pride. This is a harnessing of power.

"Are you having a good time?" he asks, setting down his guitar.

"Better now," I say, blinking away from the spotlights. I take his hand . . . that's a thing I do now.

He smiles at our laced fingers.

I catch his gaze. "Thank you for the roses. The note."

His lips tilt up.

I rub my thumb over his knuckles.

"You must be Adam's guy?" The lead singer approaches with a friendly smile and holds out his hand. "I'm Taylor, he/him." He has brown skin and dark hair beneath a red bowler cap.

"Hi, Taylor." I shake his hand. "I'm Ben, he/him. Yes, um, I'm Adam's guy." The proclamation makes my knees consider disappearing. What would it feel like to call him my boyfriend? How would he respond if I asked?

Adam squeezes my hand. When I look over, his eyes are wondrous, taking me in like I'm some sort of marvel.

Fireworks sizzle through me, heating my face.

He clears his throat. "That's Shyla she/her on the drums, Howie they/them on bass, and Ryan he/him on keyboard." They all wave respectively.

"Hi, Ben!" they say in staggered unison. "Nice to meet you," Taylor says, then returns to the group.

Turning into me, Adam pulls me close and runs his hands up the length of my arms. "I'm so glad you like the flowers."

I lean into his warmth.

"I love them," I say, clinging to his arms.

The light touch of piano keys sounds.

Adam smiles against my cheek. "Looks like we have an audience."

He pulls me even tighter and sways, turning me slowly to the melody.

There's a soft beat of brushes against drumheads, the gentle pluck of a bass.

I peek up to find each band member smiling over as Adam and I dance onstage.

I close my eyes and breathe him in. "You love this, don't you?"

He hums and the sound vibrates down my neck. "I could dance with you like this forever."

Forever. I push down the fear that creeps in. We have one week left in Maywell Bay, and then what? He doesn't seem happiest in Fern Falls, working at his auto shop. He seems alive here, onstage. The thought of letting him go so he can pursue his career makes me cling tight to him. "You love this, though. The music. Performing." I try to keep any concern from my tone. I want him to be happy, whatever that looks like for him. Even if it looks like introducing him to my father? No. That would only lead to heartache.

He pulls back, searches my face. "You sound worried. Is everything okay?"

I nod. "I just want to soak up this time with you."

He smiles softly. "You know, the band will be fine without me now that the crowd has died down. Want to do something, just the two of us?"

All my muscles relax. "I would love that."

He goes and wraps up with the band while I descend the stage.

"What would you like to do?" he asks when he reaches my side. He shrugs into a leather jacket and the plane of stomach displayed by his crop top . . . I shouldn't stare.

I snap my gaze up, scan the party, the moonlit beach beyond it. "Follow me."

He smiles. "Anywhere."

I lead him past a banquet table, lifting a bottle of chardonnay from a bucket of ice. Adam winks and takes two glasses. My stomach fizzes like I'm Sabrina finally heading to the solarium with Greg Kinnear.

We take a path along the side of our cottage until we reach the sand. There are decorative metal lanterns dotting the border of Grandma's property, reflecting gilded filigree upon the ground.

Before us, the coastline is a moon-muted canvas. Silvery sand stretches to the cypress grove. Farther up, the lights of Maywell Bay and the pier sparkle, casting wavering lines of gold across the rippling water. Then, it's wide-open midnight blue as far as the eye can see.

"This is so peaceful and gorgeous," Adam says. "I'll never get my fill of this place."

I smile over. "I want to enjoy it with you while we can."

He grins and holds up the glasses. "Want to toast to that?"

I point the bottle of wine toward the back patio of our cottage. Café lights span overhead creating a space made just for us. "How about there?"

"Perfect," he says. Soft light reflects off his leather jacket as he turns.

When we reach the deck, Adam sets our glasses in the center of the low, wooden patio table.

I lower onto a soft turquoise floor cushion. "Oh, thank god it's a twist-off," I say, opening the bottle.

"The universe smiles upon us." Adam laughs, taking a seat beside me.

I pour his glass, and sense his attention on me. My hand shakes as I fill my wine flute. Why am I nervous? It's just Adam. I swallow hard. It's Adam. And me. Alone for the first time since we confessed our feelings. What happens now? I'm used to the before, the bottomless wanting. Now that I have him, what if I mess everything up?

I set the bottle down harder than I mean to, and our glasses jostle. I clear my throat and raise my drink between us. "To us."

He lifts his glass and clinks it against mine. "To us. And to you, bringing all the romance."

Warmth swims through me. "Says the guy who sent me roses." And that note.

Adam blushes. "It wasn't too corny?"

"Are you kidding me?" I lean in close. "You're making my dreams come true."

He sets his glass down. Runs a hand through his hair. "Good." He peers over through his lashes. "Because if you couldn't tell by the whole courting-you thing, I love corny. But I also mean

every bit of it. I don't want to come off as insincere. I just . . .
I've never done this."

I tighten my grip on the stem of my glass. "This?"

He nods and grabs his drink, stares into it. "When I've dated
before, it was, I don't know. It was whatever. This matters." He
fixes his gaze on me. "This is you, Ben. I don't want to mess
this up."

My throat goes dry. "You are not going to mess this up."

He smiles softly. "I've held back for so long, I don't know
how to sort of siphon those feelings out now that I can share
them with you?"

I smack his arm playfully. "Listen, if anyone is gifting a six-
foot teddy bear, it's gonna be me."

Adam laughs, head tilted back. "Cheers to that," he says,
wiping his eyes.

I take a sip of chardonnay and it sings down my throat, crisp
and refreshing. Then, I stare into the wine. "I'm scared, too."
That I'll hold him back. That he'll leave. That this is temporary.
I look up, set my drink down. "But we can be brave together."

His eyes brighten.

My heart swells as I inch forward.

His breath hitches.

His lips are so close.

I want to lean in until nothing separates us, but the last time
we kissed, it wasn't the right time. "I want you," I exhale. "I
want so much at once. I don't know how to process it. I don't
know where to start."

The backs of his fingers graze my cheek and he closes in until
my only view is of his dark brown irises. "How about we start
right here?" He breathes against my mouth.

I tilt my head and nuzzle into his cheek, nestle my nose beside
his, against the softness of his skin and the scrape of his stubble.

Then, with one last sigh, I press my lips to his.

A single soft kiss that shoots straight to my center and bursts
into flame.

Adam clutches my arms and pulls me in tighter. His touch tingles through me. Quickly, he pulls back and taps my nose with his, smiles. That motion gives the command, and my last thread of hesitation cuts loose. I kiss him like a crashing wave. With my whole body. With a force that could make the earth's perfect patterns burst into something bright and blazing.

He moans against my lips and I part them wide, asking, begging, pulling him in. He sweeps his tongue across mine, staking his claim. The taste of him is bright and wine-sweet, grounding and rich as caramel, and something new, something that's just the two of us.

He growls low and deep and hungry and I melt, any trace of tension leaving my body. My hands scramble for purchase as they run wild down his back, nape of his neck, base of his spine, curves of his ears and jaw and shoulders.

His fingers dig into my sides as he pulls me on top of him. I straddle his hips, and hot bliss grips my core, shocking my senses to white noise.

"Ben," Adam rasps into my open mouth. "Ben."

I grip the roots of his hair and tilt his head up so he faces me. His eyes are glazed and dark and deep enough to drown in.

He smiles with swollen red lips, a wry grin that curls across his cheeks. "Hi," he whispers.

Warmth rushes through me and I smile back. "Hi."

I hold his face in my hands. This is good, the kind of good that makes my heart pound, blood rush, lungs burst. My something good.

I bend to his lips and kiss him with reverence, tender and slow, searching and learning his mouth like a language. His hands reach beneath my jacket, trail up my sides, trace my ribs, fingers over bones, and I know, with all my cracked-apart heart, this is it. This is all I want. Tonight, tomorrow, across days and months and years.

I trace the tips of my fingers along the sides of his neck, and with the very points of my thumbs, tilt Adam's face toward the stars.

His head falls back. Pressure and want and need builds to unbearable in my core. This most vulnerable part of him, right here, before me, offered.

I press my lips to the thin skin of Adam's throat like a prayer. He answers with a hitch of breath, goose bumps rise along his neck, beneath my touch.

I could kiss him for a thousand years and never want to stop.

He gasps, chest heaving. "Ben, hold on."

Concern grips me. "Are you okay?" I ask, voice thick.

Adam rests his forehead against mine. "I'm fine." His breaths warm my face. "Sorry."

I stroke his cheek. "No, I'm sorry. I got carried away. I should have asked. You said last night that you want to take it slow."

Adam takes my hand. His grip is shaky as he lifts my fingers to his lips. Kisses my knuckles.

I sigh as pleasure ripples through me.

"Ben," he breathes into my skin. "I've wanted you for so long, I'm worried I'll devour you in one bite. I've never craved this hard. I want to savor this, but my body is too hungry for you." A muscle flinches in his jaw. "Okay. Done with the food metaphors." He gives his head a quick shake, makes a sharp laugh.

My skin is on fire. I clutch the lapels of his coat. "You can have me now, as much as you want. You can have seconds, thirds. I'll be your midnight snack."

He hugs my waist and laughs sweetly. "I fucking adore you."

"I—" I bite the tip of my tongue.

He angles his gaze. "What?"

I shake my head. "No. I can't."

Adam raises a brow. "Do you have something you want to say, Parrish?" he smirks.

I inhale sharply. "No, it's dumb."

He bends so his ear is at my lips. "You can tell me anything you want. Right here. In our space, just us. And I love everything that goes on in that brilliant mind." His breath caresses my neck.

I swallow hard. "After you said you fucking adore me?" I get chills at saying *fuck* in Adam's ear.

"Mm-hmm." His murmur is deep, rumbling across my skin.

I lick my lips. "I wanted to say, you can fuck and adore me all you want."

He clutches my hips. "Jesus. Ben."

I wince. "Sorry. I'm not used to dirty talk."

He pulls me tighter against him. "Don't you dare apologize."

His eyes are piercing.

I've never felt more bold.

"Is that what you want?" he asks.

I roll my hips into his and it takes everything in me to not let my eyes roll back in my head. "I want everything," I grunt.

No sooner do I say the words that Adam presses his lips to my skin, paints kisses down my neck. Pulls my T-shirt aside, fingers grazing my collarbone, kisses me there.

I clench my thighs around his waist and the pressure is the best torture, but anxiety gnaws at me. I love this, kissing him, *obviously*, but what do I do next? How does he like being touched? How do I initiate? Are we ready for that? It's too soon.

I lean back. I don't know how to do this with Adam. God. How do I let go of my fears, loosen up? All the years of every thought, want, desire dams my brain.

Adam's brows crease. "Is everything okay?"

I take a deep breath. "I'm not sure."

He rubs his hands up and down my arms in reassuring strokes. "What can I do?"

My stomach drops. "I don't think I'm ready yet. For more than this, I mean."

"That's okay." His face is open, sincere. "It's more than okay."

I close my eyes, adjust in his lap, lean back on my heels. "My body is ready—" My lids fling open and I snort. "Oh my god, I did not just reference a meme during a serious conversation about sex."

Adam barks out a laugh.

My shoulders rise as I breathe in. "What I'm trying to say is that my brain isn't quite there yet. I want to be in the moment with you, but I keep anticipating what to do next."

He smiles. "I am glad you're telling me this."

"Really? It's not a total mood killer?"

Adam shifts and I slide off his lap. He brings his knees up beneath him. I pull mine in so I sit cross-legged.

He slowly shakes his head. "I want to murder whoever made you feel ashamed to speak your mind, your heart."

I let out a small laugh. "That is the sweetest thing anyone has ever said to me."

The corner of his mouth kicks up. He lifts his head, presses his knuckle beneath my jaw. "Hear me, okay?"

I swallow, nod. My chin rubs against his finger.

"Your feelings are valid and important no matter how they make me feel. Does that make sense?"

"I think so."

He runs his fingers up my jaw, cups the side of my face. "If for some reason you not being ready for sex were a mood killer for me, you would not be responsible for that. That would be my own issue, not stemming from you."

I nod. "Okay."

He traces the side of my neck. "And for the record, you sharing your needs, wants, and feelings is hot as hell. We don't have to have sex for me to be so fucking hot for you that I can't stand it. Intimacy is everything, however that feels best to you." He clutches my shoulder. "But again, you aren't responsible for my response. You don't need to act a certain way. I love you just being you."

My whole body melts. *I love you.* He said *I love you.* "Okay." That one word is all that my mouth can steal from my brain.

He smiles. "Good."

Then, he rises and holds his hand out to me. "Do you want to go watch reality TV on the velvet couch in our own personal jungle?"

I laugh, taking his hand. "Absolutely."

He hauls me up and we head toward the cottage.

I pull open the slider and let him go first.

He walks in, calling over his shoulder, "You think there are any leftovers in the fridge from this week, or should we order pizza? I think we need pizza for *The Courtship*. Or should we do *Temptation Island*? In that case, leftovers."

I laugh and take in the sight of him, illuminated by the light of the open refrigerator. His hair is mussed from my hands, lips swollen from my kisses. "Hey, Adam?"

"Yeah?" He pauses his scan of the fridge and locks eyes with me.

"I love you just being you, too."

He smiles and my heart could burst into a million tiny pieces, all belonging to Adam Reed.

Chapter 18

Morning light from the front window warms my face, making me blink awake.

Are you still watching? is frozen on the television screen, where we last left off in our reality TV marathon. *Temptation Island* led to *On the Plus Side*, then to *Ever After* and the empty pizza box splayed open across the coffee table.

And the head of tousled brown hair nuzzled on my shoulder, soft against my cheek. There's a throw blanket warming my lap that I didn't put there. Adam's arm crosses his torso. His fingers are entwined with mine. I have to stretch but I wouldn't move for days if it meant holding him.

How could I have gone all those years without this? His reassuring words and kindness. The healing he brings me. I never want to let this go. I never want to lose him.

That's terrifying.

I inhale sharply and he stirs.

His fingers tighten around mine. I squeeze back. I'm here.

He straightens against the back of the couch, and there are his thick lashes, full dark brows. Sleep lines crease beside his eyes, and they deepen as he smiles. "Morning," he says, dreamily.

"Good morning," I say back, heart in my throat. "How did you sleep?"

He scootches up and kisses my cheek. "Better than ever. Although, I'm sorry if I was a literal pain in your neck."

I laugh. "Not at all." I want him against me every night. Warmth pools in my center, along with a twinge of fear. Don't want this too much, too hard. He'll leave. I reach up, fingers shaky, and guide his lips to mine. We're here, now. I press into his kiss, sweet and smooth as honey, bringing every part of me to life, soothing every worry.

Adam tilts his head and gives a small laugh.

"What?" I ask, rubbing his arm.

"Don't make fun of me, but I have this fantasy . . ."

A thrill shoots through me. "Tell me."

"I have always wanted to make you coffee."

I laugh.

"Ah, no." He covers his face. "You can't make fun of me."

I hold up my hand. "I promise, I'm not."

He blushes. "It's just that at the bakery, you make coffee for me every morning, and I always fantasized about doing that for you . . ." He places a hand on my thigh. "After we woke up together."

I bite my lower lip.

I'd literally give up caffeine to wake up to him every morning.

I pull him close and kiss him hard.

After a while, he pulls back. "Okay. Let me go live my best fantasy life."

He stands and picks up the pizza box, putting it in the recycling bin beneath the kitchen sink before heading to the coffee maker on the far counter.

He reaches up into a cupboard and his retro Dashboard Confessional sleep shirt lifts, showcasing the dimples on his lower back, just above the waist of his gray sweatpants. He grabs two coffee cups.

I take a deep breath and study him as he scoops the grounds.

It's a moment I'll always remember and I don't want to miss it. The way the light highlights his profile as he works. He turns and catches my eye, winks as he grabs the mugs.

I blush, and he smiles victoriously, chuckling as he faces the counter again.

The sight of him pressing brew on the coffee machine, like an intimate morning routine we always share, like something permanent, does things to my heart that I don't know how to handle.

I want this, this feeling of stability and comfort with him.

Could we have this back in Fern Falls? Or, is this something I need to enjoy in the present, not put pressure on? There's this feeling I can't ignore, especially after seeing him play last night. Like Adam is just starting to explore everything he wants. His music, branching off from our hometown . . . Me.

The heavenly scent of hazelnut permeates the room, making me sigh.

I don't know if they all go together perfectly yet. His music may take him farther from Fern Falls at some point, and that's a place I don't want to leave for long. Despite the hard memories of my dad that are in my hometown, it's also the place that healed me. My bakery, my friends, I don't want to let those things go.

I clutch the blanket in my lap. I have to be braced for whatever our time beyond Maywell Bay looks like. I know Adam wants this for the long haul, and so do I. Of course I do.

But timing may have different ideas, and I push down the pinch of worry that sticks like a thorn in my heart.

Be here, now. That's what my therapist would say.

My phone buzzes atop the coffee table, and my stomach drops. Please don't be Dad following up about last night.

I reach over and pick up my cell like it's about to detonate.

The notification I find gives minimal relief.

It's an Instagram message from Delish Dollar Studios: *The fans are eating this up, ha, pun intended. Keep up the great work with this publicity, Ben. It'll be helpful for the finale!*

My heart stutters as the attached link loads. I've tried to avoid social media as much as possible, but maybe I need to see what we're dealing with after Dad wrote me.

The link leads me to a BuzzWhir article called BADAM IS BACK AGAIN. The opening image is of me, leaning back against a cypress tree as Adam kisses my hand. There are already hundreds of comments.

I slam my phone down on the couch, protection for Adam, for us, flaring hot in my veins.

I've wanted him for so long. I don't want to have to share these private moments with the public, have them invaded, stolen, used for publicity.

"Ben?" he asks, heading over with a coffee mug in each hand. "What's going on? Is everything all right?"

I shake my head. "I don't know how to handle the publicity surrounding our relationship." Saying *our relationship* out loud makes me swallow hard, butterflies jamming up my throat.

He settles onto the couch beside me. "Is this about our photo on the beach?"

I look up. "You saw that?"

He nods, brows pinched together. "Yeah. Yesterday before the party. I'm sorry I didn't say anything. At first, it made me excited to see us together. And then it felt invasive, and I wanted to protect you from that feeling, so I didn't say anything. I should have." He hands me a yellow mug that says TODAY'S GONNA BE THE TITS on it, and I can't help but crack a smile. Our palms meet, and his skin is coffee warmed and smooth, except for those guitar-string calluses that scrape across my fingers as he runs his over my knuckles.

The hot ceramic warms my hands. "What should we do about it?"

He sips from his purple mug. It has a pattern that could either be upside-down umbrellas or rows of boobs. "I was thinking, why don't we take the narrative into our own hands?"

"Like I wished I could have done as a kid."

He holds me in his deep, sensitive eyes. "Exactly."

"Okay," I say, taking a sip of my coffee. He apologized for not telling me about the photo, but I haven't been up front with him about all of this. And if more images are going to surface, he needs to know.

"Adam, I need to tell you something, too." I gulp. "A few things, actually."

He leans forward, cradling his mug in his hands. "Okay."

Jessica's words echo in my mind. *Be patient and gentle with yourself. You're not alone.*

I take a deep breath and tell him everything.

The C&D letter from my dad, and his defamatory post claiming I stole his recipe.

The pressure from Delish Dollars Studios to fix the bad publicity or get kicked off the show and pay for the losses and breach of contract.

The need for me to win the final competition so my business can thrive and I can help Grandma save her estate.

The one thing I leave out is that my dad wants to represent him. I can't bring myself to share that yet, to let my father have any hold here.

By the time I'm done, my coffee is cold, and I need a nap. I feel lighter, though, sharing the burden of it. Most of it, anyway. Hopefully, after my warning text, Jake Gibbons is gone for good.

Adam takes it all in. "You've been dealing with this all on your own?"

I nod. Exhaustion pulls me against the velvet sofa.

"I'm so glad you told me," he says, setting his cup on the table. Then, he picks up my cell phone and flashes a crooked smile. "So if Badam is what they want, let's give them some Badam, yeah?" He holds the phone out to me.

I take in a breath and smile, grabbing the device. The joy of having him by my side in every sense fills me with a newfound energy.

I hold up my phone on selfie mode and lean into Adam, placing a kiss at the edge of his lips. I capture the photo just as his cheek rises in a smile.

I pull back and look at the photo.

He nudges me. "We look really good together."

"We do." I grin.

I open Instagram and upload the photo with a caption of: *Brew with my beau.* Tag Adam. Post. Put my phone back on the table.

"I love it," he says, pulling me into a hug.

"Me too." I wrap my free hand around his back.

"How do you feel?" he asks.

I lean into his shoulder. "Is it bad to say that I think it's kinda cool? All this time we've skirted around our feelings, and now here we are for everyone to see, it's like we finally get to share how we feel in a big way. Thank you for helping me take control."

He places a kiss on my cheek.

I turn so the kiss moves to our lips. It's sweet and perfect and all our own in the privacy of this space. Our little cottage, where I'm getting to know this man like I've only ever dreamed of.

I reach toward the hem of his shirt, but stop short as an out-of-place sound reaches my ears. "Do you hear that?"

Adam scans the room. "No, I—"

Moans sound from outside the window. It is not the unpleasurable kind. And it is not alone.

"Yup, heard that," he says, face screwing up in confusion.

Another chorus of groans makes me shift to the edge of the couch and peer toward the window.

"I don't mean to alarm you, but is there a sex party in the courtyard?" Adam asks, grabbing his purple boob mug as he follows my gaze.

I snort. "I'm afraid to find out, and concerned that I can't immediately say no." I grab my coffee and pad toward the blinds as Adam strides to the door and pulls it open.

The look on his face says it all. "Ben." He waves me over. "If I have to see this, so do you."

I wince. "I don't know what you're looking at, but I already know that's fair."

When I join him at the door, I clutch my mug for dear life.

Grandma's book club, which I now suspect is some sort of senior citizen cult, is gathered in the main courtyard. They form a circle around the pool, backs on yoga mats, feet flat, as they do pelvic thrusts toward the sun, moaning with each gyration.

I need eyeball bleach.

Like, it's fine if my grandmother wants to practice some sort of sexual yoga religion with her friends, but do I need to witness this? No. I do not.

"Boys!" Grandma's voice calls out, winded. She waves from her purple mat, then stands up and leans back in a stretch.

"We've been spotted." I hold up my mug like a shield. "Go." I point toward the back patio. "Make it out while you can."

Adam's eyes sparkle with humor. "I'm not leaving you behind." He sips his coffee. "Plus, there is no way I'm missing this."

Before I can tell him to save himself, G-ma strides over, a violet sweatband in her bright red hair, and throws her arms around us.

"You two!" She pulls us in close, hot-pink sports bra inches from my face.

"Morning," I say, muffled.

She releases.

"You all get going early, huh?" Adam says with a hint of laughter in his tone.

I hold back a laugh.

"Carpe diem, my dears." She winks. "Greet the day with pelvic thrusts, that's what I always say."

This is the first time I've ever heard her use that expression, and I'd be thrilled to never hear it again.

"Actually," she says, crossing her arms, "morning sun thrusts are best done in the nude. Clears all kinds of bacteria, I'm telling you. Natural antibiotics."

Adam's mouth falls open.

I almost drop my mug.

"All right, G-ma. We're gonna go in and get ready. Or sit and process this for a year."

"Nope," she says, "no time. Your mom needs your help with the suncatchers for the craft fair today. I'll let her know where to find you. But first—" She looks down and reaches into her sports bra.

Oh, god.

Adam grips my hand.

Grandma fishes a small bottle out of her bosom. "Here," she says, untwisting the cap.

"Please don't be the Heartbreak Tea," Adam whispers.

I snort. He read my mind.

In a flash, she shakes liquid into each of our coffee mugs. "Perfect," she says with a satisfied nod. "Get you all fueled up for a big day at the craft fair."

She takes a swig from the bottle before re-bra-ing it.

"There you all are." Mom calls as she rounds the corner and pushes through the cottage gate, carrying a giant blue bin.

I busy myself by swirling my spiked coffee. Mom saw the roses Adam sent me, but having her witness me with him in our pajamas is on another comfort level.

She smiles between us. "Well, good morning," she says with an inflection.

And there it is, the level of discomfort.

Grandma elbows her. "Told you the cottage was a good idea."

Adam smiles politely. "It's a wonderful place. Thank you so much for letting me stay."

G-ma gives a wicked smile. "Like you had a choice."

Mom and Grandma share a knowing look while I very casually dissolve into the floor.

"Don't be like that, Ben," Mom chides. "You can't fight the universe. What's meant to be will be."

"On that note," I say, grabbing the doorknob, "what's meant to be right now is that Adam and I are going to go shower and—"

"Best way to conserve water!" shouts someone from a yoga mat, followed by a chorus of cheers.

Adam bends over in a fit of laughter. So much for being a team.

"Okay, bye, it's been great," I say, pushing the door shut.

"Meet you by the front fountain at two o'clock so we can head to the craft fair," Mom says.

"Don't forget your lube," Grandma calls. "For the shower, not the craft fair. But actually—"

"Oh my god." I click the door closed, face burning. Adam snorts behind me while I heave a full-body sigh. "Thanks for zero help," I say, smiling.

He wipes his eyes. "Your family is hilarious."

I shake my head and raise my mug. "I mean, what the hell?"

Adam shrugs. "Here goes nothing."

We clink our drinks together then swig.

It goes down like a trail of acid. "Yup," I scratch out.

Adam coughs. "Definitely the tea."

We stare at each other, cheeks full of held-in laughter, then burst into a howling fit and fall against the back of the door.

This is why I'll never let my father near Adam. There's no way I'll let him taint this joy, our safe space.

Chapter 19

That afternoon, Mom meets us by the main merfolk fountain with six giant bins of suncatchers made from sea glass, sea-shells, glass beads, and something she calls spell bottles that look like tiny jars of potpourri.

Adam and I load them into the back of a white passenger van covered with rock-band stickers.

"G-ma's friends are the ones who usually run this booth," Mom says, "but since you two are here, I convinced them to let you take over. The seniors who frequent these craft fairs will want to pay you two attractive masculine folk very handsomely, don't you think?" She pinches my cheek. "Get it? Handsomely?"

"Mom, oh my god."

Adam snickers. "Happy to help, Laura."

"Thank you, Adam," she says, then turns to me, face serious. "Ben, not to put too much pressure on you, but any funds you make are going to go toward Grandma's big finale party."

I swallow hard. "Okay. I will do my best to transform into an extrovert for one afternoon."

"No, I got you help. Forced Proximity has a show at the fair, and they can assist you until then." She nods to the front entrance where Adam's bandmates greet us as they walk down the steps.

Seeing as their matching neon-pink shirts all have a big, bold FP on them, I take it that Forced Proximity is the name of their band.

Adam and I wave back, then he places his arm around my shoulder.

He's with me instead of one of his bandmates. He is showing *me* off. Unless, I'm number seventeen? I shove the thought away and the gut plunge along with it.

Every minute in Maywell Bay with him makes this thing between us feel more and more solid, and I should hold on to that, but what comes after we leave here?

Nothing good happens when people leave.

I heave a sigh and Adam eyes me, brows creasing.

"Okay, Mom. We've got this," I say, voice full of forced confidence. Adam hasn't done anything that should make me worry about the future, so if anxiety could take some time off, that would be great.

She pulls us both into a hug. "Thank you. Love you."

Adam holds the van door open for me. "You okay?" he asks.

"I'm good, promise," I say, placing a kiss on his cheek as I climb in.

Five minutes later, I'm sandwiched between Adam and the blond, California-tanned keyboardist named Ryan in the rear seat of the van, Bouncing Souls blaring on the radio. A guitar spans across all of our laps because that's the only place it'll fit after stacking the suncatcher bins in the back.

"That was not the most outrageous show. Not by far," Howie the bassist says from the front bench seat. Howie has deep bronze skin and wears large metallic sunglasses and a purple backwards ball cap. Their curly brown hair poofs out on all sides. A conglomerate of musical instruments is piled on the space beside them, and each time the van hits a bump in the road, every instrument plays at once.

Shyla the drummer laughs from the front passenger seat. She has deep umber skin with curly black hair and a heartfelt smile. "What about Vancouver?" she asks, twisting around to face Howie.

"Twenty-seventeen or twenty-eighteen?" Taylor adds as he steers the van, his red bowler cap replaced with a yellow one today.

"They're definitely talking about twenty-eighteen," Ryan interjects with a fling of his long blond hair.

Shyla nods vigorously, curls bouncing.

"I have a battle scar from how hard that bra strap hit my face," Howie says, pointing to a dark line on their cheek.

"That was from when you fell off the stage in Denver, you jackass," Taylor says, teeth gleaming.

"Which time?" Ryan asks.

They all burst out laughing.

Adam squeezes my knee, a small smile on his lips.

"So, bro," Taylor says, eyeing Adam in the rearview mirror, "we're a ragtag bunch, but it's not all bra fights and stage diving. We take our music seriously, and we love what you add to the group."

A blush rises high on Adam's cheeks and I can't help but feel a deep sense of pride on his behalf. I squeeze his knee.

"I really enjoy playing with y'all," he says.

The band takes turns exchanging glances.

"There's something we've been wanting to ask you," Shyla says, turning to face Adam.

He tightens his grip on my knee.

"We have a meeting with a manager today," she continues. "They're coming to see our set during the fair. Our latest EP has been really successful. We'd like for you to play with us, and consider joining Forced Proximity full-time, if this works out?"

I hold my breath, chest tight. Did Dad circumvent me by going through the band? "What's the manager's name?" I ask.

"Renata," Shyla says. "She's a big-time Hollywood agent who's venturing into music management. She already represents some major acts."

I sigh. I live to fight Jake Gibbons another day. And this is amazing, because this cuts him out of the picture completely.

But then, a worried expression crosses Adam's face. "I'm happy to play with you at the fair this afternoon for Renata, but I'll have to think about anything more, okay?"

Shyla pulls in her lips and eyes Taylor.

Taylor nods. "Totally get that. We'll have more details for you once we hear from Renata after the set."

Beside me, Ryan leans forward, focusing on Adam. "Take your time to think it over, but you should know that our old guitarist Gavin wants his spot back. We'd rather keep you on. And Renata? She represents acts like the Hedges and Stones, and would have us opening for them on a national tour that starts really soon."

"That is true," Howie adds, peering at us from over an electric guitar.

Adam tenses beside me.

I take him in as he stares ahead. This is everything I was worried about this morning. Now that we're facing it, I need him to know I support whatever decision he wants to make. I would never want to hold him back or have him regret staying in Fern Falls. Like my dad did. "Hey," I say, squeezing his leg again. "I support whatever you want to do. You should go."

"Really?" he asks.

"Yeah," I say, nodding.

He nods back, but I can't read his face. His expression is tight. "Thanks," he says quietly.

"We stan a supportive partner," Shyla cheers from the front.

Adam smiles, but it doesn't reach his eyes.

I have a sinking feeling I've said something wrong. I lean toward him. "Hey, I—"

Taylor makes a sharp turn into a parking lot, and I ram into Ryan's side, Adam jams into me, and the bass guitar on my lap slides across all of us as Howie yells, "Save the Les Paul!"

We park, but Taylor doesn't turn the van off until "True Believers" plays its final note and Howie has inspected every string on the Gibson bass.

Then, the band piles out.

As Adam is about to exit, I tug on his arm. "Are we okay? Did I say something wrong about you joining the band on tour?"

His expression softens and he takes my hand. "I want to talk to you when we can, but we're okay, I promise. Please don't worry."

I nod despite the alarms ringing in my ears. Promise. Like how I promised that I was okay when I was really worried about what happens to us once we leave Maywell Bay?

He hops out and rounds the back of the van, grabbing blue bins with the rest of the crew.

I join, but my stomach churns. I want this to be over so we can talk.

But this craft fair is important for Mom and Grandma, and before I know it, we're carting bins of handmade suncatchers to the harbor, bandmates in tow.

The seaside craft fair turns out to be a few different retail booths and at least thirty boats docked along the pier.

The narrow space is packed with people who are all here to buy fresh fish off old vessels, and that's exactly how it smells.

I grip the handles of the plastic bin tighter. Pier planks, softened from years of weather and wear, give beneath my feet like my shoes might leave tracks in the wood.

Adam lifts his bin higher, adjusting his grip, and his forearms flex. I want to reach over and touch him, to feel connected, but it would mean dropping at least sixty pounds of suncatchers on my toes.

Our space is marked by a plastic table with a sign sitting atop it that says, ELIZABETH'S AND CLAIRE'S SEA GLASS WARES. On one side is a stall selling hand-painted driftwood signs and on the other is a table with succulents planted in everything from teacups to motorcycle boots.

"I know it smells awful, but it's charming in a quirky way, huh?" Adam says, placing his bin on the pier.

Farther down, there are booths of farm fresh produce and artisan foods. There's an old lady running a face-painting station, and I cannot tell if she is napping, or taking an extra-long time on a toddler's yellow cheek daisy.

"Yeah." I stack my bin on top of his, but I really want to ask, *Are we okay? Can we talk now? I can't wait hours wondering what I did wrong.*

"Let's get our craft fair on," Taylor says, dropping his bin next to mine and Adam's. Shyla, Howie, and Ryan open their boxes and start pulling out all the colors of the rainbow in sea-glass form.

Adam and I lay out the turquoise table drape, then lift out driftwood jewelry stands from the bins, and hang the pieces from each white-painted branch.

Ryan steps up beside Adam. "We have to go do a quick sound check for our set, are you okay here, Ben?" He turns toward an open space where a man plays Billy Joel on a portable keyboard.

"Yeah, I'm—"

"I'll stay here with Ben," Adam says, joining me behind the table.

"You sure?" asks Ryan.

"Positive," Adam says.

"Maybe you can talk him into joining the band, Ben," Ryan chides, then heads toward the others as they cart instruments from the van.

Adam tenses beside me.

The murmurs of the crowd morph into a din that the bark of

seals and call of gulls barely pierce. I need to talk to Adam. But what if it breaks us?

The space between us is taut. My heartbeat fills my ears.

If I don't ask, it may break me.

I can be brave. "So what's going on? You've been quiet since the car, and you don't seem at all excited about meeting this manager, about the band asking you to join them."

He braces against the table. "I just . . . don't know if joining them, traveling, or leaving Fern Falls is what I want."

"That's valid," I say. Even hearing him mention the thought of leaving Fern Falls out loud makes my lungs hurt. But like I told him, I will support whatever he wants to do. "Did I say something wrong back in the van?"

He looks up, alarm in his eyes. "No, Ben. I'm so sorry if I made you feel that way. It's my issue."

Relief washes over me. "What's going on in your head? You can tell me."

He grabs the roots of his hair and stares down at the sun-catcher display. "I know I have the means to take off if I want to. Rusty's daughter could fill in at the auto shop for a while, and Rachel is settled with the inn and Morgan now. I don't want to sell the auto shop because I worry about not having that as a fallback in case Rachel or my dad or mom need help. I just . . ." He gasps, like all his worries choke him.

"Adam, you can do things for yourself. Your parents are adults and so is Rachel, and Rachel has Morgan now, too. If you want to travel, pursue your music full-time, you should." The words tear my heart through my throat as I say them. Losing him would be hell. But I'll never hold him back. His future has to be his choice.

"I'm clinging too tightly, huh?" he asks. "Do you want me to leave? Do you need space from me?"

There is so much fear in his eyes. It's the way he looked at me when I said I'd support him joining the band. "Is that what you thought back in the van? That me saying I support you joining the band on tour means I'm trying to get rid of you?"

He exhales. "Before my mom left, she would always try to get my dad to go on outings. Whenever he'd leave on a fishing trip or take a drive to Snow Hill, she got out of bed. She painted again. She lived like she could actually breathe. Then, she left. She's so happy now, without him. And I'm scared because I don't want to leave the people I care about, but I don't want to suffocate them either. And I'm worried I'm coming on too strong and stifling you?"

My heart breaks. I take his hand. "Adam. I want you to know I support you in what you want to do with your life, with your passions, because it's something my parents could never figure out. Traveling doesn't scare me, if we come back together. What scares me is making you stay with me in Fern Falls, and you regretting it later, wishing you would have left."

Adam grips my hand. "Like what happened with your parents."

I hold his gaze. "Yeah."

"So we're both dumping our childhood trauma on our relationship?" he asks.

I chuckle. Even with fear clutching me, he can still make me laugh. "Yes."

"Okay, how is this . . ." he says, looking down at my hand. "We plan the next steps together. You talk to me about the baking show, and I'll talk to you about the band stuff. I'll think about joining them on tour, I promise. And I'll talk to you about it when I decide."

"Agreed," I say, squeezing his hand.

Mic feedback rings in our ears. Taylor's voice booms over the noise of the pier. "Hey, everyone. We're Forced Proximity and we're happy to be here."

I lean into Adam. "You know you want to be up there with them."

He bites his lip. "Okay, yeah. I really do."

I kiss his cheek. "Hurry back because I'll miss you."

The look he gives me could melt ice.

My knees weaken as he hugs me tight. "Thank you," he says, like I brought him back from the dead.

He runs over and joins the band. As he picks up his guitar, Shyla throws me a thumbs-up. I smile. Then Adam takes his place alongside Taylor and fills in the bright summery melody with his playing. There he is, in his element again. Smiling and strumming, more relaxed than he ever is when he rushes through the bakery during his morning coffee runs in Fern Falls. Pain pulses in my chest. If he chooses to leave, I'll support him. No matter how it hurts.

The crowd gathers around the stage and I turn away, realizing I haven't sold one suncatcher.

I check my phone. It's already three thirty and the pressure of making my grandmother's final party a success isn't going to wait on the clock.

The band pauses in between songs, and a few patrons trickle by.

After the music keys up again, I sell two suncatchers. Ranging from twenty to sixty dollars each, it's not a small accomplishment, but I'm sure it's not the boost we need to put on the finale party and make sure Grandma doesn't suspect that something is wrong.

Adam's words from this morning echo through my mind. *Control the narrative.*

I meet his eyes across the crowd. He winks over while he strums, and it gives me the boost of confidence I need.

I pull up Instagram on my phone and go to post a new reel.

Holding my cell in selfie mode, I press down on the record circle. "Hey, Badam fans. I want to thank you for all your support. Adam and I are hanging out at Maywell Pier today, if you want to come by and say hello. Adam is playing with Forced Proximity, and I'm selling suncatchers." I rotate in a circle and Adam throws up a peace sign as the rest of the band waves. The crowd cheers.

I add all the hashtags, tag Delish Dollars Studios, and post.

If I can put my fifteen minutes of internet scandal to good use, why not?

Filming the reel alone draws some people close, and a few patrons step forward.

The band begins playing again and after a few hours of hand-selling suncatchers, the line starts to die down.

The music shifts, drawing my attention to the stage. Adam switches places with Taylor, swapping his guitar for the mic. Then, Taylor thrums and the crowd goes wild over what clearly is the intro to "Don't Stop Believin'."

Adam sways his hips and I snort. He is working this for all it's worth.

He fixes his gaze on me as he sings, "Just a small-town girl. Living in a lonely world."

Oh my god. For all the guitar playing he does, he can sing. Very well. His voice is low and mesmerizing, with the slightest scratch that sends shivers through me.

I swallow hard.

People whoop and holler as he steps forward and makes his way through the crowd. Straight toward me. Never taking his eyes from mine.

Being held in Adam's eyes as he sings is an out-of-body experience.

When he reaches me, I can hardly swallow anymore.

He holds out his hand.

Before I know it, his palm is smooth and solid beneath mine. I abandon the suncatchers and follow him.

I laugh and hide my face in my free hand. People encourage us with cheers as we pass.

We reach the band, but we don't step back among them.

Adam and I are encircled by the hollering crowd. From a distance, a group chants "Badam" over and over.

He holds the mic between us as everyone sings along.

There's so much joy and community in this space and having

Adam here, before me, feeling like he chose me, helps me warm up to being the center of attention, even with cameras flashing.

I don't know the last time I felt this much support.

It's just a show during a craft fair, but it feels like so much more.

I wrap my arm around Adam as the next chorus hits.

Our voices together with everyone else feels like being in sync with something for the first time.

Even after we sing the last line, the people repeat, "Don't stop believin'."

Adam gives Taylor the mic back.

"Thank you all for joining us this evening, we're Forced Proximity," Taylor says.

The crowd cheers again and the band begins tearing down so the last act can have their turn.

Adam leads me back to the craft booth. When we reach the table, he runs his hand up my arm, my shoulder, stopping when he reaches my neck. His fingers are gentle on my skin, as though I might blow away.

I grip onto his forearm.

He leans in, his breath brushing my cheek as he whispers in my ear, "I'll never stop believing in us, no matter what the future brings."

His lips meet mine in the softest, most reverent kiss.

My eyes flutter shut.

With a gasp, Adam pulls back, leaving an unwelcome coolness where his lips just were.

Something behind me has caught his eye, and his expression is icy, like I've never seen it before.

It sends cautionary chills down my spine. "Adam, what's wrong?"

His touch is firm on my arm. "I'm here."

I turn as a voice says, "So this must be the infamous Adam Reed."

Something acrid settles in my gut.

I freeze as my dad smiles in the fading sun. The café lights above us flicker on, glinting off his teeth, the gel in his slicked-back hair.

My throat goes dry.

"Where have you been keeping him, Ben?" Dad fixes his attention on Adam.

I widen my stance protectively, no matter how futile the posturing may be.

Chapter 20

"What are you doing here?" I ask, voice harsh.

Adam's fingers flex on my arm.

Dad tilts his head. "Your Instagram. It was such a great video that I had to come and see the talent for myself. Especially when I saw Renata in the crowd. I didn't want to miss my opportunity to get my offer in." He points toward the redheaded white woman who is approaching Taylor as he ends the set.

Right. The reel I took. So much for controlling the narrative. "That's not a good idea."

"Listen," he says, holding up his hands as if to prove his palms are clean. "I know we've had our differences, but this is our chance to bond here. To move forward."

I swallow hard. Could this be a gesture of goodwill? My nerves spark alarms through me. No. He's using our past to get to Adam, and he wants to use Adam to fix his career. Especially after what he texted me the other night, I have to keep my head clear.

I lean into Adam.

"So, what'll it be, son?" Dad asks.

I'm about to answer when I realize he's looking at Adam. He called Adam son.

"I'd love the opportunity to represent you, be your manager," Dad continues. "I can take you to heights you've only dreamed of. I've worked with up-and-coming bands for years and toured all over the world. I can make your music career dreams happen."

Adam takes my hand and holds my gaze. Then, he faces my dad. "To be honest, Jake, I would never trust you with my career."

Dad shifts his stance. Puts his hands in his pockets. "And why's that?" His voice is strained.

Adam searches my face with a question in his eyes, as if asking permission to speak up. I swallow. Nod decisively.

He squeezes my hand and faces my dad again. "I can't trust a manager who doesn't see what matters when it's right in front of him." His tone is flat, determined. Protective.

Dad's face scrunches up like he's stumped on a riddle. "I'm looking at you, son. I see that you matter."

Something in me dies each time he addresses Adam as *son*. A swipe at my guts with a serrated spoon. A Ben-o'-lantern. I can only stand here, gripping Adam to stay upright.

Adam shakes his head. "You valued a career over Ben. Ben, who is talented beyond belief. Who keeps his family business afloat, who brings joy to a whole town every day." His voice rises. "Who is now on the most renowned baking show in the nation. And now you're trying to weasel your way back into his life for your own gain." His chest heaves as he says the last word.

From the corner of my eye, people stop and stare, but I can only focus on Adam, my lungs reinflating with everything he says.

"That's not fair," Dad insists, glancing side to side as more people eye us, holding up phones like they might be recording.

"I wouldn't trust someone like you with anything." Adam tightens his grip on my hand.

"You're making a terrible mistake," Dad spits out, backing away.

"You'd know how that feels, wouldn't you?" Adam says, voice forcibly hushed like he's trying to keep from full-on yelling.

"Ben." Dad eyes me desperately. "Talk some sense into him. I'll take down the Instagram post."

People in the crowd murmur.

I blink as if emerging from a stupor and take him in. His polished exterior that disguises a conniving, selfish heart.

"Stay out of my life," I say, voice firm. "And stay away from Adam."

Dad glances between us, stunned. Then, he turns on his heel and pushes through the people.

The noise of the crowded pier mutes as I process everything. I can't stop staring at Adam. His nostrils flare as he takes quick breaths. His eyes read me like an open book. No one has ever stood up for me like that, championed me like that. Made me feel proud of myself.

"Are you okay?" he asks, his hand curving across the nape of my neck.

I shouldn't be, right? I should want to cry. But with the way Adam stood up for me, and the way I stood up for myself, I feel alive. I want to be with him in ways I've never been. "Let's get out of here," I say, voice low.

He gives a sharp nod and heads over to Taylor. While he wraps things up with the band, I pack the remaining suncatchers in the bins in a hurry, close up the lockbox.

Adam rushes over. "Taylor and the band will get everything to the van. You want to walk home?"

Home. I answer by taking his hand. I pull him behind me and stride down the pier.

Adam's footfalls double to keep pace with mine. "Ben? What's going on?" he yells. "Are you all right?"

The sun sets around us, painting the sky in violent, fiery shades. People with cameras snap photos as we pass, but not even the paparazzi can bother me now. I am more okay than I have been in a very, very long time. The farther we get from the crowd, the lighter I become.

I grip Adam's hand and pivot, facing him. I pull him to me and drill my gaze into his. I could eat him alive. "I need to get you home. Now. If that's okay with you." My chest heaves with desire.

His expression morphs from pinched with concern to wide and stunned, then dark and hungry as hell. Famished, like me. "Let's go." His voice is velvet, caressing every part of me, sparking life into every cell.

I smirk at him in challenge. "Race you."

He bites his lip and smacks my ass, then we're off.

As we sprint down the pier and onto the boardwalk, cool bursts of wind chill my cheeks, pelt sand at my skin like tiny needles. The slight pain is invigorating.

My lungs burn as we chase the setting sun along the coast, Adam beside me. Our laughs meld and join the chorus of all that belongs here: waves, wind, birdcalls, summertime magic.

We reach the edge of Grandma's property, our purple cottage in sight up the sand from the boardwalk. I stop and bend over, gripping my knees, laughing.

Adam braces a hand on my shoulder and joins in. "I can't keep up with you," he says between laughs. "Are you sure you're okay?"

I stand up and pull him in by the opening of his jean jacket. "I have never felt like this."

His eyes roam over my face like he's memorizing every inch. "How do you feel?"

"Alive. Free." I walk him backwards beneath the cover of a tree. "Wanted. Wanting."

His fingers dig into my sides. "Good," he says with a rasp, like he's forcing the word out.

I push him against the trunk of the palm.

He slips his legs between mine and slides down the tree until our mouths are level.

I crush my lips to his.

He whimpers into my mouth, melts beneath my touch.

My body takes over.

My fingers clutch the thin cotton of his shirt, drawing him into my kiss, deeper.

His back thuds gently against the tree as he pulls me in right back.

A deep groan rumbles from his throat as he removes my glasses, tucks them into my shirt pocket. Grips my waist. Drills me against him.

My hips grind against his. The way we want each other, hard and clear.

I press in as close as I can get, my nose skating his, chin grazing his jaw.

"I want you so badly," I breathe.

My lips meet his, urgent and desperate. Showing him how much I need him with teeth and tongue and soft skin scraping stubble. Nails digging into muscle.

I place frantic kisses on his throat. Grip his neck. Fingers in hair. Clutch. He hisses in a breath through his teeth.

"Ben," he rasps. "Ben." Like a song. The cracking give of his voice makes me hold him tighter. My weight against his body. Not close enough.

I answer him with each press of my lips to his cheek: *I'm yours*. His clavicle: *Yours*. His chest: *Always*.

He angles back. "Wait. I want to make sure you want this? You feel ready? It's not too much? Too fast?"

"I've never been more ready."

A muscle clenches in his jaw. He straightens, puts his hands on my shoulders and adds space between us.

My stomach drops. "Did I do something wrong? Do you not want this?"

He takes a deep breath. "I want this." His voice is hoarse, gravelly.

I sigh in relief, but then squint at him. "Is this about our courtship?" I tease. "Upholding my honor?" I run my hands up his arms, lean in until my mouth grazes his ear. "Because I've already touched myself thinking of you in a most dishonorable way."

His breath hitches and his fingers dig into my shoulders. "Ben." His voice is stern, shooting a jolt of electricity through me. "I need to stop for a second, because the things I want to do to you are not suitable for a public space." He trails his gaze down my body. "We'll get arrested."

I catch fire. "Take me into the cottage right now, and I'll let you handcuff me." My voice is low, almost unrecognizable.

He growls and lunges forward, scooping me into his arms. He hauls me up and bends me over his shoulder.

I laugh and reach down, smacking his ass.

He strides up the dunes, and his foot catches on a divot. Tumbling into the sand, we're feet and limbs and laughter.

"Are you hurt?" I huff out, propping up on an elbow, ruffling his hair. Specks of sand fly out.

He winces, lying flat beneath me on the sand. "I wanted to be the heroic love interest sweeping you off your feet. So, despite my disappointment, I am fine."

I lean down. Hovering just above his lips I say, "You're still heroic." I stroke his cheek. "No one has ever stood up for me like you did with my father."

His expression softens as he reaches up and brushes my hair with his fingers. "He never deserved you, Ben."

There's a stab in my center, the last layer between us. "He wrote me the other night about representing you. I told him to stay the fuck away. I'm sorry."

He tilts his head. "Sorry for protecting me and my career from a narcissist? You should be saying you're welcome."

Tension unspools in my limbs. "I should have told you, though."

"I mean, yeah, because then I could have told him to stay the fuck away and saved you the trouble." He smiles softly. "Let this worry go, okay?"

I choke back a sob, lower my mouth to his, and fall into his lips.

He kisses like it's the last time, savoring every stroke and nip, paying attention to the slightest shift of my weight, gasp, moan. I don't know if I'll ever get used to kissing Adam Reed. Each time is a free fall into something decadent and all-consuming. I sigh into his mouth. He pulls back, smiling, and brushes his thumb along my cheek. He focuses on me so tenderly in the most ordinary moments, transforming them into something magical.

He sits up and offers me his hand. We rise together, dusting sand off our jeans.

Entwining our fingers, I pull him toward the cottage. We walk up onto the back patio, and the stars shine down above his head. I want to freeze this moment in time. The salt in the air. The dreamy look in his eyes. The warmth of his hand in mine.

He bites his lip and pink tinges his cheeks.

Raging need returns to my core.

"That's not fair."

"What?" he smirks.

"I wanted to bite that lip." Then, I lift up on my toes and do just that.

He grips my hips and we back into the patio door, fumble for the handle, and head inside, kicking off our shoes.

We take turns nudging each other farther into the privacy of the house, nipping lips and earlobes and chins. Adam traces his teeth along my jaw. I grab the hem of his shirt.

We stumble through the dark, cool air blowing in from the back door, casting goose bumps across my skin.

Adam's hands roam beneath my top, fingers tracing the waist of my jeans.

I suck in a sharp breath and back into my bedroom door.

Adam presses his hand flat against the wall beside my head.

"Ben." His chest heaves against mine.

I love hearing him say my name like that. Breathy. Low. "Yes, Adam?"

"Do you want me to open this door?" He angles his gaze. "Do you want me to throw you onto the bed? Do you want me to have my way with you?"

I whimper. "God, you make consent extremely sexy."

"Consent is sexy." He bends down and kisses my neck.

I reach behind my back and twist the door handle, push open.

He picks me up, and I straddle him, grinding my pelvis into his.

He moans into my mouth, and the sensation rumbles down my spine.

"Oof," he grunts as we reach the bed, places me on the mattress.

"What's wrong?"

He reaches down. "I stubbed my toe on something."

He kneels between my legs and holds up a metallic item. It shimmers in the moonlight.

He tilts his head to the side. "Do you know you have handcuffs beneath your bed?"

I snort and cover my face. "There was this box in the closet that I accidentally knocked over as I was getting ready for a party, and the lid popped off, scattering sex toys everywhere." I peer through my fingers. "I must have missed those."

His eyes turn hooded and he runs a hand up my thigh. "Do you want me to use them, darling?"

Pleasure cascades through me and I nearly roll my eyes back. "Say that again. Please," I rasp.

His grip tightens on my leg. "Do you want me to—"

"Not that."

Adam pulls me forward so my pelvis grinds into his torso. He stretches up until his lips are at my ear. "Darling," he whispers.

Something in me snaps and I grab his face in mine. Kiss him so hard it'll leave a mark. Mark him as mine. I suck on his neck. My Adam.

I heave a sigh, and press my cheek to his. I . . . didn't realize mine was wet.

"Hey," he says, pulling back slightly. He runs a thumb beneath my lower lashes, my tears shining on his skin. "What's going on?"

"You."

"I'm here." He pulls me in, wrapping his arms around my back so blissfully tight.

I cling to him. "You. Just you."

He kisses my cheek as he joins me on the mattress, cradling me to his side. I sling my legs across his lap.

I've always wanted to be this close to him. Closer still. "It's like I want my fill of you and it's never enough. I can never get enough of you. I want you to be mine. I want to be yours. You see me. You stand up for me." I close my eyes. "You are loud for me, the way you care for me."

"Ben."

I open my eyes and take him in. The moonlight glints off his swollen lips.

"I'm yours if you'll have me," he says softly.

My breath hitches. "There is something I want to ask . . ."

"Yeah?" he says, shifting on the bed.

I loose a breath. "How would you like me to go from your guy to . . . your boyfriend?"

Adam takes my hand in his, rubs his thumb over my knuckles. "Boyfriend is beyond the beach."

I let out a rush of air. "Exactly." I search his face. "Do you want that?"

He smiles. "You are asking me, the one who asked to court you, if I mind being called your boyfriend?" He huffs a laugh, shakes his head. "It's the greatest moment of my life, to be honest. But what about you? Is it what you want? After we leave here?"

I fill my lungs, squeeze his hand. "Of course it is. But I don't want to hold you back if you feel like putting a label on this would do that?"

His brow creases. "Hold me back, how?"

"I want you to be able to pursue your music. I don't want you to feel stuck." I blink hard. "That's how I made my dad feel, that's what drove him away."

He takes my other hand. Fixes his gaze on me. Holds. "Ben. I want you to hear me."

I nod. Swallow.

"You could never hold me back. Having you as my boyfriend, or whatever label makes you comfortable, only enhances my life. You make every good thing even better. I want to share everything with you because you make me happy. You always have."

I inhale. The soft light from outside my window blurs. I blink hard and a tear hits my cheek. "I just . . . I don't want to ruin things for you like I did for my dad."

Adam's stare doesn't flinch. "I knew that's where your head was at." He squeezes my hand. "I could take that guy out for making you feel this way." He shakes his head. "You are not a burden, Ben. Do you hear me?"

My breaths shudder.

Adam pulls me into his arms. Strokes the back of my head. "You are a blessing."

I clutch his jacket as a sob rips through me. "I should be over this."

Adam pulls back, cups my face. Wipes my tears with his thumbs. "There is no *should* here. And it's completely normal that you would have all these fresh feelings after dealing with him. I don't know how I'll feel when I see my mom. You are entitled to however you feel right now. But those negative thoughts are false."

I nod. "Okay."

"I'm glad you talked to me."

I smile. "I'm glad you're my boyfriend."

His face breaks out in the biggest grin. "Me too."

Something in me becomes whole. I can be myself with him, and I don't want to hide. He sees me, and I want that. I want him to see all of me. I rise up and push against him until I'm sitting, then straddle his lap. I cross my arms before me and grab the hem of my shirt, lift it, cast it aside.

His eyes shimmer as he takes me in. "You're so fucking gorgeous," he whispers.

I reach forward and slide my hands over his shoulders, pushing his jacket off. He removes his shirt and it joins our growing pile of laundry on the floor.

I take him in, reach forward, trace my fingers over each ridge and plane of his body like he's made of glass.

He grabs my hand and presses it to his heart. It races beneath my palm.

"This is yours," he says.

Then, he flips me over and climbs on top of me, kissing my mouth, neck, chest.

He slides his hands around to my lower back and lifts me up against him, my pleasure increasing with each pulse of our hips.

I pull him into me and exhale in his ear, "I'm yours tonight. Tomorrow. However long you want me for."

He flinches, moves his hands to my face so fast that I gasp.

"Ben," he says, voice gravelly and commanding. "I mean it when I say I will always want you. I always want to be with you. I never want to leave you. I'm here. I'm not leaving." A tear shimmers at the edge of his lashes.

I shake my head, his hands holding me tight. Then he pulls me into him and we lie back against the pillows.

"Darling," he says, stroking my cheek.

"You didn't say that word."

His expression turns wicked.

He kisses his way to my collarbone, lingers. "Darling," he breathes over my skin. I grip his shoulders.

He kisses down my torso. "Darling," he says between licks.

He unbuttons my pants, pulls them down, and before his mouth meets my most sensitive part, I grip the sheets in one hand, a fistful of his hair with the other.

I'm already gone. Gone for Adam Reed. Forever, for always. Gone.

Chapter 21

The rising sun streams through the blinds, striping Adam in gold. His stubble, the hairs on his leg that sticks out of the sheets, gilded in sunlight. He sleeps like he's racing time in tangles of sheets, and lopsided pillows, and limbs everywhere.

He is so goddamn beautiful.

Last night with him was ours, and all mine.

He is mine. My boyfriend.

I bite my lower lip, savoring the memories of his hands, mouth, body on mine.

As if my brain called to him, he stirs, swipes a hand across his forehead, pushes aside his unruly hair.

One warm brown eye peeks out from beneath his bangs, lid puffy from sleep. "Good morning." His voice is deep and scratchy.

I smile and feel its warmth down to my toes.

We stare at each other for a while, taking in our bare chests, bare limbs, bare appreciation of each other.

"Do you want coffee?" I ask, like it's something I always do. Ask Adam Reed if he wants coffee while we're naked in bed.

"Later." In one smooth, lithe motion, his mouth is at my throat. The surprise of it shoots straight through me.

"Hi," I rasp.

He gently clutches my rib cage, circles his thumbs over my nipples, then drags his fingers lower, lower—

"Oh my god," I rasp.

"So, I have another coffee-related fantasy I have to confess."

I laugh with a puff of air. "Your coffee fantasies are the best part of waking up."

He cocks a brow. "Folgers in your cup? Way to sexualize a commercial."

I squeal with laughter and smack him with a pillow. "Listen, they should hire us for marketing."

"Sometimes," he says, on a laugh, breath warm on my neck, "the steam from the espresso machine makes your cheeks red and I always wondered . . ."

He smiles, shakes his head.

"What? Tell me." Tell me everything.

"I've always wanted to make you all flushed like that before you went to work, before you started brewing coffee. Give you the best morning sex ever."

Shivers fire down my neck. "That's um, very generous of you. You're incredibly thoughtful."

Darkness dances in his eyes. "Just you wait and see."

Then, he dives beneath the sheets and I'm done for.

Soon, Adam is in the shower, and I'm a pile of sated limbs and stupid smiles and yes, very flushed cheeks.

Folgers has nothing on his coffee fantasies.

A knock sounds at the front door.

"Hold on!" I yell. Scrambling out of bed, I grapple for my shorts and nearly face-plant on the hardwood floor.

I'm out of breath once I reach the door.

Mom enters, walking straight by me without pausing. "I need to speak with you."

"There are phones? It's like six a.m."

"No, it's really impor—" She squints at my face. "Are you okay? You're very"—she runs a hand through the air—"flushed."

I cough. "Yeah. I was just cooking."

We both eye the empty, spotless kitchen.

I wince. "Exercising, I mean."

She nods slowly. "M'kay. Sorry, I should have called, but I really needed to talk to you without Grandma hearing, and she's finally sleeping in for once."

I snort. Giving the sunshine some time off from pelvic thrusts. "What's going on?"

Mom sighs. "I hired security to stave off the paparazzi and now, even with the funds that the band brought back from the craft fair, money is really tight, and I don't know if we can pull off the finale. Not in a grand way."

My stomach sinks. "I'm so sorry, Mom."

Her brow creases. "No, this is not your fault."

I can't help but feel responsible, though. I want Mom to be happy. I want Grandma to be happy. I want them both to feel secure. I want to look out for them. "She deserves to have the full party of her dreams."

"Is someone at the door?" Adam emerges from the bedroom with nothing but a white towel around his waist. His hair is wet and his skin glistens and I want to throw him back in bed immediately, except that my mother is standing beside me.

"Oh, hi, hello, Laura. Good morning." He crosses his arms, which makes his pecs pop, and hunches back halfway behind the doorframe. "Everything okay?"

"Hi, Adam," Mom continues, as if we're all fully clothed. "I need help pulling off the final party for Grandma, and I need her to be none the wiser."

Adam gives me a knowing look, and I'm so grateful that he's fully in on this with me.

He smiles. "I think we both know some people who saved an entire town with a single party?"

I laugh, hope tingling through me. All of Fern Falls came together last winter to save the Reed Family Tree Farm when Morgan spearheaded the fundraiser. We all donated our talents to make the event happen. "You think the Fern Falls crew would come? That's such a far way to drive," I say. Today is Monday and the party is scheduled for Saturday. "That's asking a lot in a short amount of time, especially with the commute."

He tilts his head thoughtfully. "Morgan has her old event-planning connections here in LA, yeah?" he asks. "Maybe we can start there? I can call Rachel right now."

"Your boyfriend is smart and sexy!" Mom says, jumping up. "Good job, Ben!"

I pull in my lips.

She hops up and bounds to the door. "Let me know how this progresses. We don't have much time. And good luck with your exercising." She winks, and thank god, finally leaves.

I close the door and lean against it, wincing at Adam. "I'm so sorry."

"For what? Your mom calling me sexy?"

I groan and cover my face with my hands.

He walks over.

"The Parrish family having meddling ways? The shock, the horror."

I laugh and playfully smack his arm. "What do you think of that, though?"

"No, sorry, not into a MILF situation here."

"God, gross," I laugh, smacking him again. "She called you my boyfriend. Do you still like the sound of it?"

He pushes me back against the door, tilts my head up. "I think I need to take my boyfriend back to the bedroom."

I smile, pulling him close. "Don't we have some phone calls to make?"

He runs his hands beneath my robe. "Like you said, it's six a.m."

"Doesn't Rachel wake up at like five?"

"Please do not talk about my sister right now."

I laugh. "Payback for the MILF comment. Our family members are way too involved this morning."

He raises a brow. "You sure you want to make those phone calls right now . . . darling?"

That. Fucking. Word. "What phone calls?" I rasp. "Don't know what you're talking about."

He snickers as I tug him toward the room and pull him back into bed.

Chapter 22

After a few days of utter crisis, Adam and I have run through our respective contact lists, and this isn't a situation I can Instagram Reel my way out of. Because of the influx of tourists in Fern Falls due to the TV show, Morgan and Rachel are fully tied up at the resort, but Morgan did make some calls for us, and now her old boss, Johanna Barnes, is sending over an intern from The Barnes Events Company in Santa Monica to help us however they can.

"So, they'll be here tomorrow?" Adam asks.

We stand in front of the cottage, overlooking the courtyard like the place is about to combust.

My insides are in knots. The finale party is the day after tomorrow, and if we don't pull it off, it really is all my fault. Some paparazzi are still out front, and Mom is inside with Grandma, baking last-minute items for Saturday.

"Yes." I hope. But something else eats at me, too. "Have you heard from the band? About the manager? Have you thought about it?" He hasn't mentioned it all week, since the craft fair on Sunday.

Adam puts his hands in his pockets and fixates on the court-yard. "No. Nothing yet."

I don't take my gaze from him. "Promise me you'll think about it when you do hear?"

"Okay," he says, toeing the ground.

His expression is closed off and there's a heavy set to his brows. "Adam, is everything—"

"Ben?" Mom materializes on Grandma's back porch and waves at us. "May you and Adam come help us out for a bit?" she hollers.

I don't want to leave this moment with Adam. I want to know what is bothering him. "Sure," I reply anyway. I need to give him some space. If he wants to talk to me, he will. I don't have to ask him directly like I did on the pier. Space doesn't always have to come with horrible consequences like it did growing up.

Adam takes my hand, a comfort in itself. We cross the yard and walk through the doors into Grandma's kitchen.

The counters are laden with ingredients and Mom and G-ma are in full baking mode: Cher, candles, margaritas.

For a moment, there is only this.

"Alexa, volume down," Grandma says, cutting Cher off. "Good afternoon, you two," she says, engulfing us in a huge hug. "It's just like when I'd visit Fern Falls and bake with you when you both were young, except now you can have alcohol!" She hands us each a tequila-scented drink.

Adam holds his up to me. "To old times."

I smile. "And new."

We clink glasses. One sip is equivalent to a shot, so we set our drinks down.

"All right, you two get working on this," Mom says, bring-ing us to the dining table where ingredients for chocolate chip cookie dough are spread out.

"Can't beat a classic!" Grandma says. "Only time-honored traditions for my finale, because that's what I am. A classic."

Adam claps. "That's perfect, G-ma Parrish."

I say a silent prayer that the party planner will show up early tomorrow and with reinforcements, or this party will be a classic fail.

Mom and Grandma work at the counter, turning their backs to us.

I take a deep breath, trying to calm my nerves about the funding for the party, about what will happen afterwards. The Zoom call with Delish Dollars is the next morning. So far, they seem happy with how social media has come around, but nothing is guaranteed.

I pick up the stick of butter with shaky hands. It drops into the flour, dusting my face.

"You're adorable," Adam says, wiping my cheek with his thumb.

I laugh. "I'm a mess."

Adam leans in close. "You're perfect."

If only this was the cottage kitchen, I'd press him against the counter and give him something sweeter than chocolate chip cookies.

He kisses my cheek.

I could melt. Swear all this off and go hide in the cottage with him. Through the party, the weekend, hide in there forever and never have to think about the two of us leaving Maywell Bay. "You're trying to distract me from worrying, aren't you?"

He hugs me around my waist. "Is it working?"

I laugh and nuzzle into him, fishing the butter out of the flour. I set it down and pause. "Adam?"

"Hmm?" He straightens and reaches for the recipe card in the center of the table, studying it like he's practicing for a speech.

My lips quirk up. "You know how you told me to take the narrative into my own hands?"

"Yeah." He turns his attention to me. "You did fantastic. The Badam fan base is well fed." He smiles.

I chuckle. "Well, what if I did that literally? Took it into my hands?"

He tilts his head to the side, placing the recipe card down. "How do you mean?"

I take a deep breath. "What if I experiment with my own recipe?"

He turns toward me. "For the show?"

"Right." I nod. "Still a cinnamon roll, but with a twist that's all my own." I check over my shoulder where Mom and Grandma run loud hand mixers to the tune of "Believe." "So my dad doesn't have another chance to claim it as his."

He props his hand on the table. "Will the show let you do that? Will they still let you compete with an altered recipe?"

I shrug. "I have a Zoom call with them on Sunday. If our PR efforts weren't enough and they say I can't compete, I could pitch this recipe change as a backup plan."

"It's an excellent idea," he says, but his voice is soft and he stares at the bag of sugar instead of meeting my eyes.

Concern scrapes through me. "Am I overlooking something?"

He shakes his head. "No, no. I'm just sorry, Ben. I blame myself that you're even in this position."

I turn toward him, leaning my hip into the side of the table-top. "What are you talking about? This isn't your fault."

He faces me, eyes full of regret. "I should have agreed to sign with your dad when he approached us on the pier. All of this would have gone away. He would have dropped the C&D, your spot on the show would be secured along with your business and"—he glances at Mom and G-ma—"everything else."

A pain pulses in my core. This is what's been on his mind, eating at him. How dare my father make him feel this way. Everything that man touches is tainted. "No, Adam. I would never want that. Ever. No matter what."

His shoulders lower. "I acted rashly. I was so pissed off at how he treated you that I didn't think through all the consequences, and how much you'd have to do to circumvent this issue. I could have handled it for you. Signed with him, then dropped him after the baking finale."

I reach forward. "Please. Don't do this to yourself. Giving my father what he wants only deepens his hold on my life. You did the right thing, Adam. You stood up for me, and yourself. I lo—" I stop short, pull in my lips. I almost told this man that I love him. Before my mom and grandma and Cher. "I love that about you. That you stand up for what's right, even if it's hard. You do it for your family and friends, and you do it for me. And you should also do it for yourself. I'd never want you to be subjected to my dad for anything."

He hugs me tight. "Thank you for saying that."

I rub his back. "I mean it."

He sighs, pulling back. "How can I help? With the cinnamon roll twist?"

I smile. "Let's get these cookies done and then we can go to the market?"

"Perfect." He looks down at his bowl and smiles. "I've always wanted to have a baking day with you."

"Me too," I say, grinning.

I'm even excited to go to the grocery store with this man. He makes ordinary things into something special. I mix ingredients and try to push down the guilt that I didn't even notice how bad he was feeling since the interaction with my father. I hope I haven't been so absorbed in everything else, that I'm missing cues from him.

Chapter 23

We return from The Gull's Loot, a little seaside market up the boardwalk, arms laden with bags. I place mine on our cottage counter as Adam steps up beside me.

"You think we cleared out the store?" he laughs, slipping three totes from each arm and setting them on the counter with mine.

I scoff. "I stuck strictly to the essentials."

Adam smirks. "You gonna use gummy worms in your cinnamon roll recipe?"

I hold up a hand. "Those are necessary for the baker. For inspiration."

He pulls a package of red licorice from a bag and places it on the counter. "That's why I got these. To inspire."

I laugh as we unpack and splay the ingredients across the countertop. There are two types of gummy worms (regular and sour because balance is important), Oreos, five different kinds of chocolate, and basic baking ingredients: butter, salt, spices, vanilla and other extracts, eggs, milk, cream cheese, instant coffee, and last but not least, the licorice. The cottage kitchen was already stocked with some pantry staples, which is good for my wallet.

I cross my arms, examining our haul. "I admit I may have gone overboard."

"At least you have a ton of options," Adam says, stepping close. "What do you want to make?"

I scan the ingredients, overwhelmed by choices. Panic grips me. The recipes at the bakery, from Mom's cookbook, are my safe space. They have steps, measurements, and rules to follow, all laid out for me. The products they produce make people happy, which means I make people happy, and that makes me valuable.

I don't want to venture beyond those recipes. I like my day-to-day routine. Bake, deliver cinnamon rolls, bake again, home. It's not exciting, but it's predictable, and predictable means safe and secure. Everything is pushing me out of my comfort zone lately. What if trying new things—and failing again—makes people I care about give up on me? Discard me? My hands shake. I cross my arms. "I can't do this."

Adam's gaze falls on me. "Why would you say that?"

I can't meet his eyes. "I've only ever baked according to a recipe. I won't be able to do this on my own, without my mom and grandma overseeing it. I'm such an idiot for not telling them about this. I'm going to ruin everything."

"Ben." He tilts my chin toward him. "Listen to me. You can do this. You bake every day, and it's not just about the recipes in your family's cookbook. You modify orders. You add ingredients when customers ask for it. You are more capable than you believe. I want you to believe in yourself like I do."

I sigh. "You've been my hero, you know that?"

Adam blushes. "Let's not go that far. You're the one doing all this to help your family. You see that, right?"

I swallow hard, shoving down feelings of guilt, shame. That constant voice that says if it weren't for my mistakes, my family would be fine. "I'll try to." *I'll try to see myself like you do.* I scan the ingredients. Jessica would tell me to take one thing at a time. I'm not ready to tackle a cinnamon roll twist just yet, but I could start with something different. "Right now, I'm feeling . . ." I reach for the container of instant coffee. "How about some chocolate espresso cupcakes, to warm up my independent baking muscles? Will you be my taste tester once this is done?"

"I'll taste anything if it involves you and your muscles," he whispers in my ear.

Shivers race down my neck.

Oh, okay. This will be fun.

With all the goodness that radiates off him, I'm reenergized.

I wash my hands, then select items that complement the coffee. Chocolate, vanilla. Set the oven temperature.

"Put me to work," Adam says from the bar side of the counter.

I smile, heat filling my face. Why does everything sound like an innuendo right now? I do not hate it. "Can you grab the flour?" I point behind me to the top shelf, cheeks flushed.

Adam walks over and reaches up into the pantry, pulling down the bag. It tilts and flour dusts his hair. I rush over and brush it off, unable to keep my hands off him for another minute. He turns, brow raised, then takes my hand in his. He swipes the residue off my finger, leaving a trace of heat across my skin. Smiling wryly, he dabs flour onto the tip of my nose.

I squint at him in challenge, transfer flour from my hand onto his cheek.

"You know if you keep touching me, we're not going to get any baking done." he says, voice strained.

"Would that be so bad?" I tilt my head, bite my lip.

His eyes darken. "It's taking all my restraint not to press you up against that counter, Parrish. Bake. Quickly. This is important to me. I want to taste what you make." He leans in. "And then I want to taste you."

I swallow hard. "Who said baking can't be foreplay?"

He chuckles low. "Wouldn't that break a hundred health code regulations?"

I scan the kitchen. "I don't see any inspectors here. You?"

He cocks a brow and smiles wickedly. "Okay. How do you want this to go? You're in charge."

In charge. When he says it like that, it's not intimidating. A thrill shoots through me. "With each ingredient we add, we remove an article of clothing?"

Adam glances between us, in nothing but our T-shirts and shorts, that evil grin beaming.

"Good point." I laugh. "Wouldn't get through one recipe."

He nods. "Why don't you go with your gut?"

I snort. "I mean, that's not the body part that'll guide me, but yes."

He smirks. "And you're sure you don't want to strip bake?"

I press a hand to my chest. "I was referencing my heart, Adam. My heart. I am a gentleman."

He lowers his lashes. "Maybe I don't want you to be."

I clear my throat, give myself a shake.

He pulls his hair back, slides a band off his wrist, and ties it up. "Okay, focus." He nods, eyes closed. "Baking."

When he opens his eyes, he laughs.

"What?"

He points at my mouth. "You um, might be drooling."

I snap it shut, swipe at my chin. "I reject societal gender norms, but you make a good case for man buns everywhere."

He smiles. "I like you like this."

"Like what?"

"Happy. Talking without filtering first. You being you. In your element."

I shift on my feet. "You make me feel free, comfortable to be me."

He comes close. "Like I said, you're in charge. Tell me what you need."

I flush with heat. *In charge.* "Cinnamon."

He goes to the counter, flexing as he reaches into a bag for the spice.

This is what I call foreplay. I could watch Adam gather ingredients until the day I die.

He skims my arm as he reaches past, placing the cinnamon beside me. "What's next?" he whispers in my ear, raising goose bumps along my neck.

I swallow, leaning toward him. "Eggs? Brown sugar?" He runs a finger along my collarbone. "Uh, granulated sugar?" My words are slow, lazy, buzzed. "Butter. Always butter."

"Uh-huh," he says, voice rough. "What else?" That devilish finger traces my jaw.

"Chocolate," I rasp. "Cocoa powder, salt." My head lulls back.

He cups the base of my neck, runs his fingers through my hair. His other thumb traces my throat, breath hot on my neck.

"Okay." His voice is a deep rumble against my skin and I'm semi-hard at the sensation. "I'll be back."

He's gone in an instant. I blink and grip the counter, trying to inhale.

After a few moments, I regain enough composure to grab the powdered sugar, milk, a bowl, a whisk.

Adam returns with the requested items and places them on a free spot of yellow countertop.

I measure everything out and combine it all in my bowl.

There's a flash of movement, and his shirt falls to the floor.

I grip the whisk and beat the frosting so hard I'm going to break this glass mixing bowl.

"Sorry, I didn't want to get that shirt dirty. I really like that shirt," he says, voice teasing. "Is this distracting?"

I huff a breath and set down the whisk. "I'm going to kill you."

He makes a low chuckle.

I lift my finger to lick off some splashed icing.

He grabs my hand midair, casting currents up my arm.

Never taking his eyes from mine, he brings my hand to his lips.

Then, that fucking bastard sucks the icing off my finger, long and slow.

A sound erupts from my throat that I didn't even know I could make.

"Why aren't you baking, Ben?" he asks, then he runs his teeth across my skin.

My eyes roll back. I half growl, half laugh. "Fuck you, Reed."

"Fucking *please*," he begs, dragging my wet fingertip down the center of his chest.

I come to and pull back, reclaiming my finger. It's my turn to be evil. "Where?"

He smirks in question. "Library? Definitely not with a wrench."

I laugh and the tension thins enough to afford a deep breath and fraction of focus. I sort through the ingredients he placed on the counter, filling spoons and bowls with a fury. "Tell me your fantasy. Like, a place you'd love to fuck in." I pass him a bowl and measured ingredients.

He mixes them. "Are you really gonna make me talk about my sexual fantasies while I have to combine ingredients?"

I slide him a daring look. "Let's see how long we can keep this going without tearing each other's clothes off." I gulp, taking in his bare upper half. "The rest of them, anyway."

He shakes his head. "Good thing the cleaning products are far away from all this. I can't think straight just standing next to you."

I smile, beating the eggs in a small bowl. "When have either of us ever thought *straight*?"

He tilts his head back in a roar of laughter. "Touché," he says, wiping at the corner of his eye. "Remember when we first watched *The Mummy Trilogy* together that summer around junior high?"

I meet his eyes. "And you went through the twenty stages of queer panic in my mother's living room?"

He snorts, nodding. "Yeah."

"That was a great night." Rachel and Morgan had to cancel on movie night last-minute, and I sat next to Adam on the couch until two a.m., having a queer panic of my own.

He tilts his head and eyes me softly. "That was the first time I'd ever told anyone I'm pansexual."

I smile at the memory. The way he couldn't stop staring at the screen, spanning between the romantic leads. I'd told Morgan of my bisexual ID a couple years prior, and I knew exactly what he was going through. When he fixed me with wide eyes and said, "You know what? I'm pan," I shoved a handful of popcorn in my mouth, nodded, and said, "That's awesome," around chewing. Then, my heart proceeded to punch through my chest because Adam. Reed. Was. Not. Straight. And my crush went from tolerable to, well, what we have now. I wouldn't change a thing.

My heart might burst with pride and honor. "I love that you told me first."

His smile broadens. "Me too."

"So now," I say with a sly smile, "you can tell me about your fantasies, right?"

His normally ruddy cheeks deepen to raspberry as he focuses on the ingredients before him.

"C'mon," I prod. "I've heard your morning coffee fantasies, but I want to know them all."

"I'd love anywhere with you," he says softly, mixing with a spoon.

I eye him. "Smooth."

"No, really," he says, facing me.

I smirk. "Where specifically?"

"Honestly?" He shakes his head. "Ah, it's dumb."

I pause my stirring, fix my attention on him. "It's not."

He holds my stare, clears his throat. "I want you to fuck me in the bed of my truck."

My mouth goes dry. Him. Me. His '77 Chevy Silverado. Visions take over my mind and I drop the spoon.

He picks it up. "Did that make you uncomfortable?"

The only discomfort is how tight my pants are growing. "No, Adam. You did not make me uncomfortable." I stare at the batter. If I so much as meet his eyes, I will take him to the driveway, where his truck is parked right now, and that would be quite the topic at Saturday's party.

"Are you sure?" His voice is wary.

I level the batter into cupcake tins, hands shaky. "Hun, my brain is half gone in that truck bed with you. Let's get these damn cupcakes baked."

"Here, let me." He takes the pan and bends over, placing them in the oven, giving me a full view of his gorgeous ass.

I cross my arms and lean back against the counter. "You're wicked."

He casts me a smirk over his shoulder. "So, now we . . ." He raises his brow suggestively.

I grin like a devil. "Have to wait fifteen minutes."

He closes the oven and straightens. "Fifteen minutes. No big deal." A muscle twitches in his jaw.

"Yeah?" I say with the slyest voice I can muster.

He nods, face stern.

"Okay. Stand over there." I point to the opposite counter.

He goes and leans his back against it, folding his arms.

I keep the same stance. This is fine. I'm fine.

We stare each other down for what feels like twenty-four hours.

I blink, and eye the timer. It's down to ten minutes. Not agonizing at all. "Let's mix this up," I say. "Each minute down, we take a step closer to each other with one rule." I grin. "No touching."

He glares and growls, actually growls. "Fine," he bites out, lips hardly moving.

Nine minutes. I step forward. So does he. His arms are still crossed, biceps swollen against his chest.

We hold each other's stare like this is a competition.

Eight minutes, step.

Seven minutes, step.

Six. Adam's eyes bore deeper into mine and I can't take his full attention without combusting, so I let my own gaze trail his bare skin, memorizing each strand of dark hair that leads from his lower torso to the waist of his shorts.

"Four," he says.

I blink. "Huh?"

"You missed a minute." His smile goes crooked.

I check the timer. "You didn't step forward."

"Ben," he says, voice strained. "Look at me." He steps back. The hard length of him is evident through the soft fabric of his shorts.

I breathe hard. "What . . ." I swallow any words when I take in his stare. His eyes burn with a dark intensity I've never seen. I couldn't form words if I tried.

"I want you to see," he rasps. "I want you to see how much, how badly I want you." He strokes himself through his shorts. "I'm not breaking the rule."

My mouth goes dry as I trace each movement of his fingers. Then, I let my own hand fall, stroking myself lazily.

The timer wails.

I rush and turn it off, fling open the oven door. I meet his eyes again, and a white-hot heat consumes the edges of my vision.

"Time's up," he says, smiling like sin.

I rise and face him, full of confidence. "I see you," I start, a slight warble in my voice. "What I do to you." My voice gains strength as I step forward, lessening the distance between us. "Now I want to feel . . ." I reach out, hovering at the waist of his shorts. "What I do to you."

His chest rises. I haven't even met his skin, and he hisses in a breath through his teeth.

I lean in close enough to be warmed by the luscious heat radiating off him. "I want to touch what I do to you."

With a drunken expression, he gently grabs my hand and guides my fingers to skim along the tender skin of his stomach. His head lolls back, and he hums with pleasure.

Empowered, I trace the lines of his muscles, savor the scent of him on my tongue. Musk, sea salt, sugar. "I want to taste what I do to you."

I push him against the counter and clutch his body against mine.

After a lifetime of knowing someone, you think you've learned every part, but this is a brand-new Adam Reed.

This is Adam, unafraid.

He comes up beneath me, then forms his mouth to mine. I flick my tongue against his lips, and he enters my mouth greedily, savoring me like the last lick of batter from a bowl.

His kisses are hard and fast, then tender and seductive. His tongue does things to my mouth I can't even grasp until they're done. I'm reeling. I'm flying. I'm high.

"I want you to know," I gasp, clutch at his arms, his shoulder blades. "You don't need to ask. I want to do everything with you."

He pulls back, searching my face. Strands of hair fall loose from his bun.

My cheeks heat. "Sorry, was that off base?"

"No, don't apologize, babe." He cups my face.

God, I could hear him call me that forever. I nuzzle into his palm.

He tilts his head. "It's just, no asking, huh?" He grins slyly. "What if I was into some freaky shit?"

I snort. "I mean, what if I was?" I tease, raising my brow.

"That's actually, well . . ." He bites his lip.

My stomach clenches. Did I say something wrong? I'm never this daring. Maybe I'm terrible at it.

He moves his hand to my chest. "I want you to lead this."

I swallow hard. "What do you mean?" My heart hammers against his palm.

"Tell me what you want." He moves his hands to my arms and trails his fingers along my biceps. "How you want it."

"Oh." I nod. He wants me to be in charge. Like I have any clue what to do first. "Okay." I wipe my palms on my shorts.

Adam laces his fingers through mine. "Boss me around, Parrish. I'm yours." He growls the words and nips my ear, whispering, "In case that wasn't abundantly clear."

I melt at his words. At the pleasure ghosting across my skin. The heat of his sweet breath on my neck makes me relax into his touch. "I like that."

He nips my ear again. "That?"

"Yes," I whimper.

"What else do you like?" He traces the shell of my ear with his nose. "Tell me. Give the command."

A thrill shoots straight through me and I moan. "Will you do that again? Please?"

He pulls back, shaking his head, smiling. "You and your manners. Forget them right now." His grip tightens on my arm. "Don't ask. Tell me."

I loose a shuddering breath and any last tie on my restraint along with it. This is what I've dreamed of. "I want you on the couch." My voice is hoarse.

He smirks then crosses through the kitchen, the living room, until he reaches the green velvet sofa. The roses he sent me are vibrant on the coffee table before him.

"Stop," I command, swallowing *please*.

He does. Turning, he faces me, eyes dark and raging.

I swallow. "Strip," I whisper.

He raises an eyebrow, angles his head back as he stares through his lashes, fingers working the closure of his shorts until they fall.

"Boxers, too," I choke out, bite my lip.

Adam steps out of his underwear, one leg at a time, then rises, bare before me.

The soft glow from the kitchen light casts him in gold, and I grip the counter.

He is the most beautiful person I have ever seen.

"Sit," I rasp.

He lowers onto the couch and spreads his arms across the back, letting his knees fall apart. He brings up a hand and drags it over his hair. "Like this?"

"Yes," I answer, voice rough with desire. Seeing how much he wants me over and over is a drug. After years of questioning, witnessing it now, feeling it now, is everything. "Lace your hands behind your head."

He smirks, eyeing me questioningly. "Okay."

I approach him slowly, stopping once I stand between his open legs. Then, I clutch the hem of my shirt and pull up.

He reaches for me.

"No," I say, stomach half-exposed. "Hands behind your neck."

He moans. "No touching you?"

"Not until I say." Each command I give makes me more bold, more confident.

"Please. Hurry," he begs.

I strip off my shirt and toss it on the floor.

Adam's eyes glaze over as he takes me in. "You know you're so fucking beautiful, right?"

I pull my lips in between my teeth. Bite down.

"You're so beautiful, Ben." He says each word with care, like a hymn or gospel or song.

I hold his stare as I unbutton my shorts, let them fall, then remove my boxers. I place my glasses on the coffee table. Then, I stand before Adam completely bare in every way. This man can have all of me. My whole wasted broken heart, every part of my body. He makes me come alive in ways I never knew I could.

His pupils blow wide. "Tell me I can touch you," he rasps, swallows. "Hurry."

I shake my head. "I'll take all the time I want."

He gives me the most pitiful look.

"Now," I say, bending down. "I do the touching."

I rub my hands up his legs.

His stomach pulses with each sharp intake of breath.

I near the crest of his thighs and hold his gaze as I wrap a hand around his shaft, coax a bead of wetness from his tip, and rub it down the length of him.

He hisses, chest rising. "Babe."

I work him with my hands, loving how my touch makes his whole body sigh.

The dazed look in his eyes drives me wild. I meet his tip with my lips, then take him into my mouth.

"Oh my god." He clutches my hair by the roots.

I stroke and press my tongue along the most sensitive skin down the length of him. Over and over.

"Ben," he groans.

I take him in as deeply as I can, pumping up and down to the rhythm of his breathing, not neglecting a single part of him with my touch.

Time dissolves as Adam's pleasure becomes my addiction.

"Ben, I—"

He comes for me with the sweetest moan. I want to memorize the sound. Play it on loop.

I wipe my mouth and search out his eyes, but he stares at the ceiling. A tear shimmers down his temple, soaks into his hair.

My gut hollows out. "Hey. Hey. What's wrong?" I lift up on my knees, hold his arms. "Was that not okay?"

He focuses his attention on me, eyes brimming with tears. "Please don't think that." He leans forward and strokes my hair. "I should have told you so long ago. I was such an idiot. I wasted so much time."

"Adam, it's okay." I wipe a tear from his cheek. "You can tell me now. What is it?"

He takes my face in his hands.

"I love you." His breath hitches, like he's in wonder of how it sounds. "Ben, I love you."

I grip his wrists and hold on for dear life.

He presses his forehead to mine. "I have loved you for years, and there's this part of me that has loved you for always, like even before we met, my heart was waiting for you."

His words fill me back in, all the erased parts of me, like bright color to a rough sketch. My entire soul shines gold as the sun.

His muscles tighten and he lifts his head. "Take your time. You can process this. You don't have to feel the same. You don't have to say it back."

"I am so fucking in love with you, Adam," I breathe on an exhale, voice shaky.

He melts in my hands, and his eyes glimmer with fresh tears.

I clutch his shoulders. "I have loved you from the day we met. You were the first person who didn't look at me like something broken. You heal parts of me that have been numb and forgotten for years. You make me stronger and braver and you see me how I want to see myself. You are selfless and loving. You make me laugh when laughter feels far away. You're so talented and so humble—" I take a sharp breath and lean into his touch. "And you're excruciatingly hot. It should be restricted by city ordinance. We're in a drought."

"Ben." He laughs through his tears and pulls me up, arms tightening around me. He kisses my forehead. My temples. My cheeks. When he reaches my lips, he pulls me onto his lap. "This okay now?"

"Hmm?" I ask, dazed.

He smirks. "Touching you? It's allowed?"

"Yes," I blurt out. "Strike that rule from the record."

He smiles. "So stricken." Then, he flips me over, lies me across the couch, and straddles me. He kisses and licks and sucks in so many ways, in so many places, I lose track.

This man devours me, and I am gone, spent, finished. He grips my shaft and the shock of pleasure is so intense, I jolt.

"How do you . . ." He eyes me questioningly, still stroking.

"Hm?" I try to concentrate on his words.

"What would you like?" he asks, eyes glazed.

My head falls back. "What you're doing. Is great. Everything you do is great."

"How about that?" he asks, pointing to the bowl of icing on the counter. "I'd love to taste it some more." He casts me a devilish grin.

I exhale and nod, unable to speak the words, *Wow. Okay. Jesus fucking Christ, yes, ice me like a Christmas cookie.*

He retrieves the bowl and is back so fast I have to catch my breath.

Then, there's no chance of breathing.

He paints the frosting across my skin.

"I love you," he says, in sync with a stroke of his fingers. "I love you, I love you, I love you."

Then, he takes me into his mouth, and I fall into bliss.

Chapter 24

The next morning has Adam at an eight a.m. rehearsal, while I direct vendors in the courtyard like a party contractor.

After maybe two hours of sleep, both of us are love-wasted, and I wouldn't change a goddamn thing.

I sip on the hazelnut coffee he made and smile over at the stage on the far side of the courtyard where he practices with the band.

He winks, like he has the past five times I've caught his eye.

But this time, he sits on the edge of the stage with my cousin's son beside him, and Janet standing nearby. Adam turns back to Matthew, and helps him hold his yellow guitar in his lap. The instrument is almost the size of him. Adam plucks some strings, then Matthew copies him. The squeal of joy that he makes when he hears the music makes my heart swell. When Jason returns from filming in South America, he is going to love seeing his little boy with a brand-new passion for music. Jason will have him playing show tunes in no time.

Adam glances over, face full of joy. That same joy he gets

when he plays music onstage. The same he has when he tells me he loves me.

His voice echoes in my mind: *I love you, I love you, I love you.*

I'm high all over again, flushed, light-headed. I take a sip of the iced coffee in my thermos to come back down to earth.

"Mr. Parrish? Where would you like this placed?"

I take in Steve and two assistants from Steve's Party Stuff.

After taking charge in the bedroom last night (er, kitchen and living room), I could command Starfleet. Or, at least suggest to three men where to place a five-foot-high bust of Athena.

"Beneath the willows would be perfect," I say, pointing to the gardens beyond the hedges.

They haul the statue in that direction, struggling beneath the weight of the Greek goddess.

The decorations will be sparse, but with the intern coming from The Barnes Events Company and a few folks from Fern Falls that Whitney said she sent down today, I trust we'll be okay. I have to. I don't want Grandma catching on that anything is wrong, and I want her to have the best, most elaborate party yet. The grand finale of her dreams.

Mom exits G-ma's back doors and crosses the yard. She's in yoga pants and a lavender sweatshirt that says WITCH, PLEASE GIVE ME COFFEE. "Thank you for all your help, honey," she says when she reaches me. "I just got G-ma settled in the kitchen. Said we needed more pastries for tomorrow to keep her busy." She leans in. "Word to the wise, I'd be wary of the brownies unless you feel like having an extra-trippy party experience."

I laugh. "Good call. And, of course. Helping is the least I can do when all this paparazzi is because of me." I chuckle. "Kind of like when I was a kid, huh?" I sip my coffee. So, that just slipped out.

Mom's expression turns serious. "Ben. First of all, this is not your fault. And it wasn't when you were a child, either."

I stare at the lid of my thermos. "You have to say that, you're my mom."

She shakes her head. "No, I—"

"Laura?" A person in green coveralls with tattooed forearms, black cat-eye glasses, and a messy blonde bun stops next to Mom, arms overflowing with faux wisteria blooms. "Where would you like these?"

Mom looks around, then points to the stage and the columns around the pool. "How about those areas, and then wherever you think? Thank you so much, Alex."

Alex gives off major bi vibes and we exchange a knowing smile before they head off in the direction Mom pointed.

"Ben." Mom turns back toward me. "Listen to me. None of this is your fault. You can't control what the media feeds on just like I can't control whether that bartender over there is going to drop a third glass on the concrete. Or, like I can't control Grandma's finances."

I swallow hard. "I know."

She touches my arm. "I also hope you know how much of a help you've been to me. I couldn't have done this without you. You've helped fix so much."

Fix. That's all I ever want to do. My throat grows thick with emotion. "I'm really glad to hear that."

She pulls me into a hug. "I mean it."

Beyond Mom's shoulder, Uncle Tim walks toward us. He is in light pink tennis apparel, complete with very short shorts. "Ben," he hollers, "don't you worry." He points a tennis racquet toward the front gates. "This person was looking for you, but I sent them off. Damn paparazzi."

"Looking for me?" My chest tightens. Please don't be Dad. "How'd they get past security?"

Uncle Tim shrugs. "Said they're here from a barn? Those vultures will say anything."

"Oh, shit." I give my coffee to Mom and take off toward

the front to try and catch the person from The Barnes Events Company.

I run through the gate, pushing past paparazzi as the security guards make a path for me, but it's still a mess of flailing arms, flashing lights, yelling.

"Ben, over here, Ben—"

"How are you feeling about the altercation with your father at the pier last weekend?"

"Have you heard from your dad, Ben?"

"Are you worried about the *Take the Cake National* finale in a couple weeks?"

"What's next for Badam?"

I try my best to block out the questions, but each one pecks through my newfound confidence, embedding my walls with worries.

The past week has felt like a calm before the storm when it comes to my dad, but I can't worry about something that hasn't even happened yet.

Right now, I'm only concerned about finding the intern from The Barnes.

I gain distance from the media, and spot a person in a hot-pink jumper with long, straight black hair and tawny beige skin opening the door to their silver Mercedes.

"Excuse me," I call, passing by the merfolk fountain, "are you from The Barnes?"

"Hi." They pause, the car door half-open. "I'm Ivy, they/them." They hold out their hand. "Are you Ben?"

I shake their hand, smiling. "Hi, Ivy. I'm Ben, he/him. Thank you so much for coming, and I'm sorry about the confusion." I gesture to the crowd behind me. "It's been a bit chaotic."

"No problem at all," they say with a wave of their hand. "May you show me around the property? I want to get an idea of layout before I bring in the vendors."

"Vendors?"

They nod. "Johanna said to go all out for this. Our decorators and costumers are on standby, waiting for the green light to come on in." They reach in their car and pick up a tablet from the front seat. "We will have our social media manager here to gain coverage so we can allocate this as a marketing expense, keeping the accountants happy. Will that be okay?"

"Absolutely, wow, thank you so much." I try my best not to get choked up, but it's a challenge.

I walk Ivy around the property, and they take notes on their tablet, drawing diagrams like a party architect.

Ivy makes some calls, and in a couple hours, the courtyard bustles with activity like the first day I arrived, as it's transformed into what looks like a Regency Era movie set.

A chorus of screams sounds from Grandma's patio, and I whir around, fully expecting to find paparazzi scaling the gates.

Instead, my heart might burst from joy.

Mom sprints to the back deck as three of her best friends exit the house.

The owners of Fern Falls' naturals shop, Tea and Tarot, engulf Mom in a group hug, their red, blond, and black hairstyles smashed together like the fur of a calico cat as they all jump and squeal.

I run forward, internally bracing to be poked and prodded out of all my dignity. "Aunties!"

"Ben!" they yell in unison, and pull me into their black hole of a hug.

"What's this?" asks Mari, my pseudo-aunt with a black pixie cut and deep brown skin. She points a long purple nail at my light blue T-shirt. "No more button-ups?"

"I'm dressing a bit more casual lately," I say, smiling.

"Ah. I have a feeling it's the influence of a certain musician?" Adelaide, my auntie with pale white skin and long blonde hair, raises her head above the others, peering where Adam rehearses across the courtyard.

"That is the only musician I will make an exception for," Florence, my aunt with red hair and rosy white skin says, her face stern.

"That's also what she said about her second husband," Mom chides.

Florence scowls.

"And her third," Mari adds.

"Don't you dare start this," Adelaide shouts, which for her is the volume of most people's speaking voice.

I laugh and hug them tight. When we pull away, all the women talk at once but somehow carry on a conversation only they comprehend.

I desperately miss home.

I love Maywell Bay, but I can't wait to return to Fern Falls. With Adam.

My chest warms at the thought of the future that awaits us.

Once our friends and his sister get past the initial Big Deal of Ben and Adam Together After All This Time, life will settle into a wonderful kind of normal. Almost like we have here, but better because it won't have an expiration date.

Maybe we'll live together in his little apartment above the auto shop. Or at my house. For the first time in a long time, it could be a home again.

"Ben?"

I blink to find my mom and aunts staring at me. "Oh, sorry."

"Where would you like them to help out first?" Mom asks.

I take in their expectant faces, waiting for me to decide, to take charge. I take a deep breath. "I think you should all settle into your rooms, and then may you please check in with Ivy over there? They're with The Barnes Events Company, and they're here to help us out."

They all nod and smile.

"I'll show you to your rooms," Mom says.

The women disappear into the house and I take in the busy

courtyard, pushing down a worry that hasn't loosened since I passed by the paparazzi.

Something in me braces for loss.

Loss of this time together, just Adam and me.

While I love all the dreams we could realize together in Fern Falls, I can't help but worry it would mean him sacrificing other dreams.

I find him on the stage. He sets down his guitar and joins Taylor and the band in what looks like a serious conversation, probably about tomorrow's set.

I don't doubt that he loves me, but what if it's not enough? What if his life will be more fulfilled away from Fern Falls?

If that's the case, I need to prepare to let him go.

After a long day of directing high-tea settings and deciphering the ambiguous rules of pall-mall, I retreat to the cottage and dive into the remaining ingredients from yesterday's Gull's Loot market haul.

Grabbing the basics plus three different kinds of chocolate, I whip up a small batch of cocoa cinnamon rolls to have ready for Adam when he finishes rehearsing. This Regency Era theme has them learning all kinds of new songs.

Once the baking is done, I can't sit still, so I thoroughly clean the cottage, which includes fishing out any missed sex toys from beneath my bed (a blindfold). Thanks to Ivy's costumers, my wardrobe for tomorrow's party is ready to go, and I don't hate it. A big part of me will miss dressing up every Saturday night. I can't wait to see what Adam will be wearing.

When it reaches ten p.m., he still isn't back, but I have packed up my duffel bag to leave on Sunday, after my Zoom call with Delish Dollars Studios—which is not something I'm going to spiral about late at night.

The front door opens and Adam walks in smiling, as if he knows he saved me from doom-scrolling social media on my phone. I put my cell on the coffee table and get up from my spot on the couch.

"You're a sight for tired eyes," he says.

His greeting is a verbal hug. "It's good to see you, too."

He points to the tray on the counter. "I was talking to the cinnamon rolls."

I hit his arm playfully and we laugh.

He grabs two plates from the cabinet and places a bun on each. Then, he hands one to me and takes his own. We tap them together in a toast.

"I really love this," he says around a bite.

I blush. "Thank you. I added a chocolate schmear in the center, and drizzled a chocolate sauce, topped the cream cheese frosting with chocolate shavings."

"It's absolutely delicious." He swallows. "But I mean, I like this." He gestures between us. "Being together. I love coming home to you."

My blush deepens. "Me too." I lean my head on his shoulder. Will we be able to do this back home?

We eat in a silence that's only partially strained by my own burning questions about what happens come Monday.

When we're done, Adam takes our plates to the sink.

He washes the dishes, humming "Don't Stop Believin'." I smile, recalling how he serenaded me last weekend.

What happens next weekend?

"Adam?"

"Hmm?" He faces me, drying his hands on a dish towel.

How do I ask such a big question? I take a deep breath. There's only one way to find out. I slide onto a barstool and grip the counter ledge. "What happens when we get back home?"

He sets the towel down and returns, hoisting up onto the stool beside me. "I've been thinking a lot about this. I'm glad you brought it up."

My muscles relax. "Yeah?"

"Yeah." He props an elbow on the counter and rests his chin

on his palm. "I know we live, like, a mile apart?" He takes my hand. "It's too far. Anywhere I'm not sleeping in the same bed as you is too far."

I nod, running my thumb over his fingers. "Do you want to go between our places?" I meet his eyes, warmth flooding my veins. "Until we want to stay in one? Together?"

He squeezes my hand and smiles. "I love that plan."

"Me too."

I search his face, and even though this is the happiest moment, his eyes are so tired.

"Is everything okay?" I ask.

He nods, focusing on our interlocked fingers. "It was just a long day with the band."

A sense of unease creeps through me. They were talking pretty intensely this afternoon. "Did you all hear back from the manager? Are there plans for a tour?"

His brow furrows. "They're still working out a lot of details." He clears his throat and brings his free hand to my face, cupping my cheek, expression softening. "I'm more concerned about this detail right here." He brushes a thumb across my bottom lip, lighting sparklers across my skin.

I stand and press up between his legs.

His gaze darkens and before I catch a full breath, his lips are on mine, the perfect pressure that reassures every part of me that we are in this together. The future is ours, and we are each other's.

I want to get closer to him than I've ever been, I want to crawl inside his skin. I delve beneath the hem of his shirt and crush him to me, his own arousal evident and hard against mine.

He pulls back slightly, lips a bright berry red. "Before this trip, I always, always wanted to untuck those collared shirts of yours. See you come undone." He takes me in. "Now, all I have to do is . . ." In one smooth motion, he lifts my T-shirt over my head and sets it onto the counter.

I smirk. "I can go get a collared shirt, if you prefer."

He bends forward and takes one of my nipples in between his teeth and nips, casting shivers down my spine. "Don't you dare."

Something in me breaks open. Something he sets loose each time he touches me, kisses me, talks to me, looks at me. I'm free.

I devour his mouth with mine, plunder with my tongue. I bite his lower lip and pull, scrape my teeth across his jaw, savor the tenderness of his throat with my lips.

Adam stands.

I clutch his shirt. "No, I'm not letting you go."

His brow kicks up. "Even to follow me into here?" He whips off his shirt and winks as he backs up into his bedroom.

I stare with a burning heat as he disappears into the darkness beyond the door.

Don't let him disappear.

Don't let him go.

I follow him like our future depends on it.

Chapter 25

From my spot on the side of the stage, I watch the exquisitely dressed crowd dance beneath a canopy of string lights and dripping wisteria. Against a lavender dusk, candles glow in glass teardrops that hang from willow branches, glittering off crystal garlands.

Grandma's version of "classic" is *Bridgerton* brought to life. Every guest is a unique Regency Era fantasy with parasols and tightly curled updos, plunging bustlines and half corsets, all awash in a vibrant candy-colored palette.

Per G-ma's request, the band plays an instrumental version of "Electric Love."

Adam owns the stage. He plays like every feeling he's ever held in his chest flows straight from his veins to his guitar strings. I'll never tire of watching him. Especially not in this outfit.

He wears a post–French Revolution masculine look, but each fabric from his shirt and cravat to his embellished waistcoat, tailcoat, and trousers are all in varying shades of teal. His tighter-than-is-historically-accurate pants are paired with high black boots, and his gold watch fob sways as he plays. His longer waves are styled back and parted to the side.

If we weren't in public right now, my matching lavender ensemble would be with his on the bedroom floor of the cottage.

I may have to push him into the pool to watch him climb out Anthony Bridgerton style.

The Hot Boyfriend Show and breathtaking atmosphere are almost enough to distract me from the Zoom call with Delish Dollars studios tomorrow morning. And the Zoom call is enough to distract me from this creeping sense that my father isn't finished with me yet.

The paparazzi is still camped out at the front gates, and I don't dare go near for fear of them unearthing my most terrifying thoughts and yelling them for all to hear. Again.

Grandma waves over from beside the pool, her giant white wig swaying with the motion. I take a deep breath and straighten my waistcoat. I can't hide at the edge of the stage forever.

Adam inches toward me, still strumming his guitar. "Are you going to be okay out there?" he asks, knowing that I needed a second nap today to prepare for all the socializing.

"I'll survive," I say, then kiss his cheek.

"Just stay away from the tea," he quips, eyes sparkling.

I laugh and descend the golden steps of the stage—which is actually shaped like a traditional stage tonight, complete with elaborate pastel-pink curtains.

I skirt the crowd but stop short when someone calls my name.

Before I know it, three pairs of arms are pulling me into a pastel hug. My mom's best friends all wear suits like mine in shades of peach, periwinkle, and sage green.

"Thank you so much for helping to bring all this together," I say.

Adelaide flips her blond hair over her shoulder. "We hardly did anything except keep your grandmother occupied and Laura less frazzled."

I chuckle. "Well, that's everything, and I cannot thank you enough."

"You go on and have a great time now," says Florence, her red hair braided up and studded with purple rhinestones.

"We're off to find her husband number ten," teases Mari, looping her arms through her friends', slicked back pixie cut gleaming beneath the twinkle lights.

I smile after them as they cut through the crowd in a full-on Sanderson Sisters stride.

Now that I've seen part of my Fern Falls family, my steps are light as I reach my grandmother.

"There's my strapping chaperone!" she says, embracing me with layers of bright pink fabric. "You look great, hun," she says, pulling back.

I shake my head. "Not as good as you. You're rocking that ball gown, G-ma." At least fifty silk rainbow butterflies are incorporated into her white wig and trail the cap sleeves of her dress.

"Thank you, but I called you over for more than compliments." She puts her arm around my shoulder, and her full magenta skirts tilt to the other side. "It is most dishonorable for a lady of my stature to be unchaperoned at an evening ball."

I smile. "What is your stature? Single?"

She looks aghast. "No, sober. Come, let's promenade."

We hook arms and follow the trail around the pool—which can no longer be called a pool.

The entire body of water is filled with lily pads, underlit by bright purple lights. The perimeter is bordered by willow trees in pastel planters. Wisteria blooms and twinkle lights mark the cobblestone walkway that leads to a massive bridge suspended across the pool.

Ivy and The Barnes Events Company pulled this off in a way I could have only ever dreamed of.

"Now," she starts once we're farther down the path, "I want to talk to you about your future."

I huff a laugh. "G-ma, have you been spending too much time with the aunties' tarot deck?"

She pats my arm with a gloved hand. "Is your guitarist going to put a ring on it?"

I sputter. "Grandma."

She raises a brow.

"G-ma."

She nods in approval. "More importantly, is that what you want?"

"A future with Adam?"

"That, and everything else." She leads me onto the bridge. "Tell me what you want, Ben. You are always so busy taking care of everyone around you. Even while here, you've been running around handling so many things. What do you want?"

Whitney's words from two weeks ago replay in my mind: *You deserve to go for what you want in a way that feels wonderful to you. You deserve wonderful things.*

I pause and take everything in. All the guests, enjoying themselves. Yes, it's overwhelming to be among so many people, the noise and stimulation, but it fills my heart with joy to see so much happiness in one place. "I want to be happy," I say.

She squeezes my arm. "And what does happiness mean to you?"

"Not being tethered to my fears." The words fly out of my mouth. That's what these past two weeks have shown me, during my time with Adam, at these parties, in these costumes. Even with the outside pressures, and everything that is still pending with the baking competition, I've been happiest when I've been brave and fully seen. With Adam, but also with Mom and Grandma. The talks we've had. Facing Dad for the first time in years. Overcoming a serious bout of depression. Controlling the narrative. Making my own decisions, my own recipes. Taking charge.

"There you go," she says, patting my hand. "Go slay your fears, my dear."

We step off the bridge and arrive at the other side of the pool as the band transitions into an instrumental "Don't Stop Believin'." I search out Adam, and he meets me with a bright, shining smile. Our song. I grin back as wide as my face allows.

"But first," Grandma says, "let's go get a drink."

We approach the bar, a giant gilded countertop covered in a rainbow of pastel-filled martini glasses.

She grabs a pink one and hands me a lavender.

I smirk. "G-ma, why are you always trying to get me drunk?"

She clicks her tongue. "I am trying to keep my grandson well hydrated." She clinks my glass with hers. "But I hope you know, you never needed liquid courage." Then, she winks, and heads to the stage.

I huff a laugh, recalling the first night Adam arrived, and eye my drink with caution. Thankfully, it actually tastes like lavender.

I catch a glimpse of Grandma's pink gown as she ascends the stage, where Taylor hands her the mic.

"Thank you all so much for being here!" she proclaims, free arm spanned wide. "I couldn't imagine celebrating my eightieth year with anyone but a few of my closest friends."

The giant crowd cheers. She is a legacy of a person.

"And I'd like to introduce you to a very special musical act we have tonight, in addition to the incredible Forced Proximity. May I get a round of applause for our talented musicians?"

I clap and yell along with everyone else. Adam's cheeks are thoroughly pink from the attention, but he is beaming. My chest fills with pride.

"And now, please welcome to the stage, the Pretty Pixies because there is no way in hell I'm having a finale party without the best drag show in Maywell Bay!"

Grandma steps aside, and three drag queens enter stage left to uproarious applause.

Each member has rich brown skin, and wears a pastel-pink ball gown with a matching wig. Their makeup is a marvel, and when the prerecorded music starts, everyone rushes to the dance floor.

The queen in the center wears massive, iridescent wings and begins a pop rendition of "The Boys of Summer."

I shake my head and smile. I'd recognize that person anywhere.

My fairy godmother from Greaser Night.

Despite all the outside stressors, this really has been the best two weeks of my life.

I catch Adam's stare as he heads toward the back of the stage.

Come Monday, when we return to Fern Falls together, the best days of my life are still waiting for me.

My whole body fills with the warmth of gratitude.

"Ben?" a soft voice sounds beside me.

I turn to find Mom, dressed in a simpler pink dress than Grandma's, but looking like she stepped out of a Jane Austen film adaptation. Her expression though, isn't festive at all.

"Is everything all right?" I ask, setting my drink on the bar top.

"Not really. Not at all." Her tone is tight, words rushed.

My stomach plunges as she lifts up her phone and displays the screen. I know what it is before I even look, but having the image confirm my fear is another level of horror.

It's an Instagram post from Jake Gibbons Music Management. The image is of the C&D letter he served me—the one I showed him, and left with him at his office nearly two weeks ago.

I scan the caption, hands balling into fists:

I didn't want to go public with this, but as I've said previously, the Parrish Family Cinnamon Roll recipe belongs to me. I've already given them the courtesy of a C&D, pictured here with a date that precedes the show recording with @DelishDollarsStudios, and yet my recipe is being developed into a brand without my consent. I'll see them in court.

I gasp for air. "Mom, I can explain."

"What do you mean?" she asks, face twisting. "Your cousin Betty just showed this to me. She came across it on her Instagram feed and texted me this screenshot. Did you already know about this?"

My stomach lurches into my throat. I might be sick.

The scenery spins.

"Ben." Mom grabs my arm, steadying me. "Talk to me. We can fix this. Together."

Her eyes are full of desperation. The same look she wore when search and rescue brought me home from the woods. When Dad left. When I told her the bakery was failing. When I convinced her to let me go on *Take the Cake National*. So much for being fearless when each fear I tackle regenerates like a hydra.

"I ruined everything," I say, voice cracking. "I can't explain right now. I need Adam. I have to talk to Adam." I turn, and push my way through the crowd, leaving Mom gaping after me.

If I can get to him, he can steady me. He can talk me through this.

He'll see the best in me, even though I fucked everything up. Again. Like I always do.

I make it to the stage just as the band exits.

Shyla, Ryan, and Howie pass me in a flurry of pastels, but Taylor stops on the bottom step. "Whoa, you okay, bro?" he asks.

I nod, body numb. "I need to talk to Adam."

"Oh, thank god," he sighs. "Talk some sense into him for me."

My brain scrambles. "What do you mean?"

Taylor runs a hand down his yellow suit. "He's passing up the opportunity of a lifetime by not leaving on tour with us next week. I know how supportive you are of his dreams. Don't let him give them up. He'll regret it for sure."

I swallow hard and step back as Taylor follows the others

while the Pretty Pixies belt, "After the boys of summer have gone."

From the side of the stage, Adam steadies his guitar on its stand.

How could he have hidden this from me when I asked him about it last night? Why didn't he tell me he'd already said no to the band, that the national tour was really happening? Weren't we going to make these decisions together? After everything he's helped me through, why did he keep me out of this? Does he not trust me like I trust him?

He catches my gaze and his smile stops halfway. He strides over, face full of concern.

My phone rings in my pocket and my stomach falls through my feet. I already know who it is. Bringing the phone to my ear, I don't bother to check the screen. "Hello," I say, tone flat.

Adam pauses at the top of the steps.

"Mr. Parrish. This is Dylan with Delish Dollars Studios."

Dylan. The producer who "misread the heat in the kitchen," right. "Yeah," I huff, like the wind was knocked out of me. My palm grows slick against my phone case.

They clear their throat. "I'm sorry to inform you that your Zoom meeting with John Sawyer, our director of public relations, is canceled. The network can no longer move forward with having you as a contestant in the finale episode."

My stomach cannot drop any farther, so I plop down on the bottom golden step.

"We can't have a competitor on the show who is in legal conflict, especially over a submitted recipe, and especially with proven documentation of an initiated lawsuit."

"Okay," I say, because nothing else will come out. Not: *But I've been experimenting with other recipes, my dad is a fucking asshole, this is bullshit. My grandma is going to lose everything. My business is ruined.* Just okay. Okay like the failure I am.

"Our legal team will reach out in the coming days to settle the contract and one hundred thousand dollar financial obliga—"

I hang up before they can say another word. I could have fought, but for what? Why? It's done. Dad got what he wanted, and just like that, the hope I had of helping my grandmother, of securing the business, of finally making things right for my family, is gone.

"Ben?" Adam sits beside me. His agonized expression is fitting for a plunge into the darkest gnashing depths to rescue Eurydice.

An expression like the first search and rescue member wore when they found me in the cold, dark woods, swallowing my sobs so I wouldn't summon predators.

I'm beyond rescuing now.

I won't let anyone sacrifice for me again, not when I'll only fail them in return.

Chapter 26

Beyond the crowd and lights of the party, the sand sparkles beneath the moonlight, peaceful and calm. Our little lavender cottage is empty, a shell for the ghosts of the time we spent there. Nothing staying, nothing growing, only leaving.

Everyone continues partying, living in a momentary fantasy, like my whole world didn't just implode.

I want to scream for everything to stop, everyone to leave. Leave me alone.

Adam shifts closer on the step. I startle.

"What's wrong?" He places his hand on my knee. "I'm here."

I'm here. It stabs my chest. He should be leaving with the band next week. "Why didn't you tell me about the tour?" My voice is raw.

He sucks in a breath and curls in his fingers, fist balling on my thigh. "Because it wasn't important."

I shake my head. "I think you kept this from me because I'd encourage you to go."

He takes my hand in his, bends his head lower, trying to

catch my stare. "I was worried you wouldn't believe me when I say that I want to stay."

The image of our hands in my lap blurs. "You only think that right now because we're in this honeymoon phase, this mini vacation. You will regret this years from now, when your feelings for me have settled, when you're stuck in Fern Falls, working a job you don't like."

"That's not true," he says, voice cracking. "I love the stability of the auto shop, and I love playing at The Stacks. I'm thinking of giving guitar lessons for the local kids when we get back. I wasn't lying when I said that I'm here for the long haul, Ben. This isn't an infatuation for me." He covers my hands with his. "I have loved you for years. I will love you for every year to come."

I choke out a whimper. I have to stay strong. I can't give in to this no matter how much I want to, or how much I long to drag him back into our cottage and make love to him until I forget everything and everyone. Until this feels solid enough to keep. "I know you weren't lying. I just don't think you're seeing this clearly right now."

He rests his arm on my thigh, tightening his hold on my hands. "I am, Ben. Tour or no tour, I'm here. This is where I want to be. With you."

I snap my gaze to his and regret it instantly. His eyes brim with unshed tears. I will never forgive myself for making him cry in his gorgeous costume with his gorgeous hair on this gorgeous night. "Adam. Please." My voice breaks. "You need this time, this opportunity. You've never had something like this. You've never had time to explore your heart and mind without it being anchored to someone else's needs. If we jump into a commitment, I want it to be because we are truly ready." I search his face. "Can you say that you are ready right now? Or are we clinging so hard because we're desperate to not lose each other like we've lost other people?"

"I don't know how to answer that." His voice is small.

My stomach clenches like it was punched. "Exactly," I exhale. "You have to go."

He shakes his head, staring at our hands. "I don't know how to answer in a way that will convince you this is what I want, that I don't want to go on tour or leave Fern Falls. That I'm fulfilled." He meets my eyes. "I am happy with you, Ben. I am happy in our hometown."

A sob breaks loose. "You're not going to want to stay forever," I raise my voice, forcing my words past tears.

"Ben." He brings our hands to his chest. "Can't you see that you're pushing me away?"

My knee jerks. "Can't you see that you're staying because you feel you have to? Because it hurt you so badly when your mom left that you don't want to do the same to me?" My voice is thin and high.

He shakes his head. "This is different."

"Are you giving up a piece of yourself to stay?"

He pulls in his lips. "I'm giving up an opportunity, that's it."

I clutch his hands for strength to keep going. "Adam, you're fighting this so hard because you're scared, but you can do this. You deserve to do this for yourself."

He leans in. Our bent arms meld together. "You're scared, too," he whispers.

I touch my brow to his. "I know. I don't . . ." My voice gives out. I gasp for air. "I don't know what it's like to not be afraid." Not until earlier this week. Not until Adam. But I can't hold on to him, suffocate him, make him sacrifice everything else in his life because I need him. That's not how relationships work. That's how they end.

He comes in even closer. Our legs part and intertwine. Teal, lavender. "So, the only way for us to conquer our fears is to keep reliving them? I leave like my mom left me, and you push me away because you're terrified of me taking off like your dad did?"

I stare at him, unable to speak.

His brows arrow together thoughtfully. "What if you come with me? What if we travel together?"

I want to say yes. I want to let that be the end, let that be everything. But leaving would mean letting my family down. I shake my head. "I can't leave my mom and grandma right now. I have to run the bakery. It's the last thing I have to try and help my family with."

He shakes his head. "You still have me." His chin dimples and he takes a shaky breath. "Making me leave isn't fair."

I shift forward. "You'll regret not doing this. I know you will. And I won't be the source of your regret. I won't have you resent me. I couldn't take it, Adam."

Resent turns to coldness and coldness turns to hate and hate turns to ignoring cries for help from the dark backyard while on a business call, shutting the window. Leaving.

Adam takes in a sharp breath. "That won't happen. Ever. Ben, I'm staying."

I pull my hand from his and pick up my phone from the step, open my dad's Instagram post, hold it up for him to see. He takes my phone with his free hand and reads it, eyes wide. "Shit. What's going on with the show? Is that who called you just now?"

I nod. "It's over."

"Ben, I am so, so sorry." He hands the phone back to me. "What can I do?"

"You can go on that tour, because this," I wave my phone, "is what happens when people sacrifice their dreams to stay in a place they outgrew."

"I would never do something like that to you." He stares at the step.

"I know," I say, placing my phone in my pocket. I take his hand again. "You're too good, Adam. You'll spend your whole life being good, then look back only to realize you didn't do anything for yourself."

He exhales slowly and fixes me with a soft look. "You won't accept that I want to stay, will you? It's going to take me leaving, going on this tour, for you to believe me when I say I want to be with you, isn't it?"

I pull in my lips and sniff back tears. "It's going to take you going on this tour to see it's what you've always wanted, to realize that you deserve to do things that fulfill you. You, Adam. Apart from your family. Apart from Fern Falls. Apart from me."

He nods slowly. "I love you, Ben." He bends forward and rests his head on my shoulder. Pine and musk. "I hope one day you can accept it, that you can trust me when I say I want to be here. I want to be with you."

I swallow hard and lean into the scent of him, the warmth of him. Soft hair against my wet cheek. "I want us both to know we did everything we wanted to do in this world. No regrets. I want you to know you went after your dream."

His shoulders shake. "You're my dream," he whispers, voice thin and breaking.

My throat tightens. "But I'm not your only dream, nor should I be. You owe this to yourself to do this."

He breaks his grasp on my hands and wraps his arms around me, pulling me in tight, tighter. I bury my face in his shoulder as we clutch and grip and dig our fingertips into pastel coats and cry.

"I love you," he whispers.

"I love you, too," I choke out.

Adam kisses me, and it's different than all the other times. It's not a beginning, it's goodbye.

Then, with one last agonized look, he leaves me on the steps and follows after the band.

This time, when someone I love leaves me behind, it's not an untethering or free fall or chaotic outward spiral.

This is a sinking and settling of deep, anchored pain. A

breaking and spreading of roots. A spike in the earth, foundation laid, firm stance of stubborn boots.

I'm the one who made him go. I am in control.

Even if I hate the way we end, at least I saw it coming.

Safe. Secure. Predictable.

Chapter 27

I can't stay in this cottage another minute. Thankfully, my bag is still packed from last night, like I had some premonition that everything would come to this.

I change, throw on my jean jacket, and hang my costume in the closet. *My feelings for you are not fragile.* This stupid party theme, making me think of some Regency Era courting bullshit.

I need loud music, my power tools, need to drown out his voice ringing between my ears: *Can't you see that you're pushing me away?*

I grab my duffel and sling it over my shoulder. The weight of it grounds me as I charge toward the door. I need to get back to the bakery. Make sure it stays afloat, and that I have enough funds to help Grandma out however I can. Now that I've lost all support from the show, and probably the internet, I need to get into my kitchen and figure out how to keep everything going. I have to help my family. I won't abandon them. I am not my father.

I freeze as I pass the coffee table.

The roses Adam sent me shrivel at the edge of their petals. I tear my attention away and reach for the door, but it flies open before I touch the knob.

Mom rushes in, pink gown flowing. "Don't tell me you were going to leave without saying anything. Ben?" She searches my face, takes in my duffel bag. "What's going on? Please. Talk to me."

Her expression is frantic and regret grips me as I walk to the couch and sink down into it, setting my bag at my feet. "It wasn't supposed to happen like this." I clutch my head in my hands.

The cushion shifts as she settles beside me, places her hand on my back.

"I told you all would be fine when I went on the show. I promised." My voice cracks. "Then, all this shit came that I never saw coming. That's what Dad does, you know? That's how he works."

She rubs my shoulder.

I spill everything about the cease and desist, social media, the contract violation and fees I have to pay, how the bakery will most likely go under because of me, again.

"I'm sorry," I say when I'm through, which would have been the best place to start.

"Oh, Ben." Mom pulls me into a tight hug. "I'm so sorry you went through this alone, that you felt like you couldn't come to me."

I shake my head, grip her arm. "I wanted to handle this, not cause more stress in your life because of another one of my mistakes. This was my chance to fix everything, on my own."

She pulls back and turns my chin to face her. "What are you talking about?"

I lean forward, elbows on knees. "Dad wouldn't have left if I hadn't run into the woods that night and cost him that deal. I'm the one who ruined everything then, just like I have now."

She is silent for several breaths. "Ben, this is not your burden to carry." She leans forward. "Do you hear me? I want you to lay it down here and leave it."

My vision blurs, turning my brown boots into mud puddles.

She sighs. "My only regret is staying with your father for as long as I did." She shifts on the sofa. "I am the one who made him leave. All those years ago, I made him leave."

I face her and her expression is tortured. "What do you mean? You were devastated after he left."

Her throat bobs. "I was heartbroken for the mental and emotional abuse he subjected you to, that I put up with him for so long because I was afraid to leave him. That was why I grieved." She exhales sharply. "It was little things over a long period of time. Jessica, your therapist, helped me see that when I went to her. The way he withheld affection or didn't talk to me for days if I didn't please him. He belittled me if he disagreed with the smallest things, poked at my deepest insecurities with cruel comments. He tried to take control of shared things, like our finances, and he made frivolous purchases but told me I couldn't spend money. I put up the biggest fight just to keep my car so I wouldn't be stranded when he left town for work." She fixes her gaze on me, tears studding her lashes. "That night you got lost? He said I was a selfish mother for taking a business trip and it was my fault you were gone. That was when I realized he was never going to change, and that staying with him would only harm us both even more than it already had."

Party lights sift through the front blinds, like the first night I was here, casting the room in filtered pastels. Her words swarm in my brain, like the little specks of illuminated dust in the air before me.

She puts her arm on my shoulder. "I'm so sorry that it took almost losing you for me to make him leave. I'm sorry you have carried this pain for so long. I'm sorry I wasn't frank about this before. I thought sharing this would make it worse. I . . ." She worries at a loose thread in her dress, pulls. "I was scared you would never forgive me for making him leave. I tried to spare my feelings, and I now realize that came at the cost of yours. I'm so deeply sorry, Ben."

I turn to her, pink light stripes across her blue eyes, winking off her tears. "Mom," I start, barely able to speak.

The destruction my father caused hurts, it scarred me. But this woman right here? She loves me with the love I always wanted from him. She fights for me, believes in me, does the hard things. For me. I hug her tight and sob into her shoulder. "I love you."

She presses her hand against my hair. "Ben, I love you."

We hug each other until the muted music from outside shifts through two songs.

She sniffs and straightens, wiping her eyes. "You don't have to leave."

I eye my duffel bag and dry my tears with the back of my hand. "I do."

"Is this about Adam? Are you two okay? I hope this didn't come between you."

I shake my head. "No, it's not like that. He has a chance to tour with the band, and I want him to take it."

"Is that what he wants?" she asks.

I flinch. "I don't think he realizes it yet. I don't want him to regret passing this up."

She nods slowly. "Ben, your grandma is doing great health-wise now, and I can come back to Fern Falls, take over the bakery for a bit. We can sort out this situation with Delish Dollars Studios together. I'll meet with financial advisors regarding Grandma's finances. This whole situation has shown me that I should have brought up the bank issue with her first thing. I'll talk to her next week. Let me take over for a while. You can go with Adam on tour. You deserve to be happy, too."

Something unwinds in my chest. This is what it feels like to not be alone. The whole time, I've had this, right here. Be with Adam. I could go be with Adam.

I search through the blind slats and take in the blur of the party outside. Bright lights against dark sky. A part of me leaps at the idea of running across that courtyard and into his arms, kissing him hard, and telling him that I'm coming, too. We're traveling together. We're doing everything together.

I take a shuddering breath. But there is this other part of me, this slashed-up side of my heart that screams and cries to let him go. If I join him, he can never really know if a life with me is what he wants. And I will always worry I held him back.

"I think I'm the one who needs him to go on without me," I admit, voice quiet.

"Okay," she says. "But you know people have long-distance relationships all the time? Phone sex exists, and FaceTime makes it even easier to—"

"Oh my god, Mom." I barely resist the urge to cover my ears. "You sound like Grandma."

Her eyes go wide. "Oh, shit. You're right."

We both loose a much-needed laugh.

Once we relax, she studies my face. "What is stopping you from holding on to your relationship with him, Ben? You two are so good together. You deserve good things."

I grimace at those words. You deserve good things. You deserve wonderful things. You deserve to be happy. Why am I so uncomfortable when people tell me that?

Something like understanding washes through me. "There is something in me that needs to heal." I nod as the words come out, the truth of them sinking to my marrow. "Something I can't pinpoint, but it hurts still. And if I commit to him, I want it to be with every part of my heart, even the broken pieces. And I think . . ." Fresh tears carve warm trails down my cheeks. "I think that I still have healing to do on my own. I need to learn how to love myself first, and I'm not there yet, but I'm trying. The distance will help."

She rubs my back. "That is incredibly self-aware of you, and a giant step, sweetheart."

"Thanks to years of therapy," I chuckle, rubbing my cheeks.

"I'm proud of you," she says, "and I'm here for you, however I can help."

"Thank you, Mom."

We stand and hug.

"Please tell Grandma goodbye for me?" I ask, bending down and retrieving my bag.

She nods. "We'll see you soon. I'll keep you posted on everything."

I smile, then open the door before I can change my mind and do a complete one-eighty on everything.

What I need is space to heal.

What I want is to crash into Adam right now and never let go.

This is so fucking hard.

I breathe as deeply as my tight lungs allow and make my way past Clare West, my stone mermaid friend with her conch shell raised high.

Skimming through the crowd, head down, I open the front gates and pass the flashing cameras and loud catcalls of paparazzi.

Their questions morph into a mangled tapestry, and I refuse to decipher any threads.

I don't owe them a thing, and I will not let them make me care anymore.

With the media held back by the hired security guards, I near my car, and reach into my jacket pocket for my keys.

When I retrieve them, something falls onto the sandy sidewalk.

Bending down, I pick up a small white and amber figurine.

The glass cinnamon roll that Adam gifted me on our first date.

I give it five minutes until photos of me crying on the curb make it to social media.

Chapter 28

My eyes will barely stay open as I round the final bend into Fern Falls, high beams lighting up the dirt road of Maple Drive. The back of my little house with purple eaves nearly disappears in the three a.m. darkness.

I park and don't budge.

I'm back, but what has changed?

I don't feel like a new Ben, a better Ben.

I feel like I was on the losing end of a fistfight.

Grabbing my duffel bag, I exit the car and don't bother to lock it, a perk of being home in the mountains.

My feet move like I'm trudging through deep snow as I make my way up the back porch steps and head inside.

Dropping my bag on the floor, I close the door and take in the space.

Maybe it's because of the dark, or the silver-gray moonlight that casts a murky hue through the windowpanes, or the stale smell of a home put on pause for vacation, but everything here has an overwhelming sense of being hollow, like a mausoleum to my past.

I don't know if I'm a better Ben, but something has changed, and this space cannot stay the same.

Sleep suddenly feels far away as I flick on the lights and open the curtains and windows, allowing the cool pine-tinged air to sweep through the room. I was never going to sleep anyway, with my heart breaking over Adam, my mind picturing him alone in the cottage bed tonight. All I want to do is get in my car and speed back into his arms.

Which is why I set my phone on the counter and pick an upbeat playlist, letting the music's energy flow through me as pop songs blare.

I can't control anything in my life right now, but I can create my own space.

I grab a cardboard box I had set aside from Mom's old internet orders for Mountaintop Mystic, and start with the mugs in the kitchen cabinets. The red one with the Rolling Stones tongue? Gone. The white cup with MUSIC IS MY LOVE LANGUAGE? Bye. The pink one that says CAT PERSON? Keep. Obviously.

I pick up the box that now holds past demons and cart it into the living room. There's a gray blanket Dad used to drape over his office chair. In it goes.

Books on a shelf about music marketing? They land with a thud in the discard pile.

I keep up this way, clearing built-up cobwebs that Mom and I never got to because life got in the way, until the box overflows and my chest isn't as tight.

If I do this every day, get rid of more and more things that cling to the past, maybe my future will be clearer.

Ping.

"Dover Beach" by Baby Queen is interrupted by a text notification. With not a little trepidation, I abandon the box and go to my phone.

Please. Don't be a studio or a post or a tweet or a Jake.

My breath hitches and I sit on a barstool, reading the text over and over again.

Adam: Did you get home safely?

My fingers shake as I type back.

I did.

He checked on me. The least I can do is check on him.

Are you okay?

My breaths turn shallow.
Those damn typing dots appear then vanish.
I put my phone down, head in my hands.
Exhaustion descends upon me in an aching weight.
Ping.
I swipe up my cell.

Adam: I miss you already.

I exhale on a whimper. I miss him. I. Miss. Him.

Adam: I can tell you need this space, though, and I respect that. Rachel is bringing me my stuff. I'll be staying in Taylor's and Shyla's guest room, but I'll let you know when we leave on tour.

I text back a red emoji heart then lay my head on the countertop. Tears collect between my cheek and the tile.
Did I do the right thing in letting him go?
I love him.

Sometimes, doesn't that mean letting go? That's a whole saying. People write songs about it.

I take the glass cinnamon roll out of my pocket, set it on the counter before me.

I started my bakery, did the show, faced my dad, fell in love. Now it's Adam's turn to do something big, step out, and I won't be the one to hold him back.

It's my responsibility to take care of myself, to heal. But that doesn't mean it's easy, and there is nothing I can do about it but cry.

Tears fall until I should guzzle a Gatorade to rehydrate.

I stride to the fridge and stop short when a knock sounds at the back door.

I wipe my face with my jacket sleeve.

Before I can grab the knob, a hollered "Ben, you there?" echoes through the wood.

I open up to find Morgan, Whitney, and Tanner on the front porch holding all kinds of recreation equipment, like they're about to drag me to a summer camp. I don't even care. I couldn't be happier to see them.

I slump against the doorframe, barely able to keep from sobbing all over again. "Y'all? It's five in the morning. You didn't have to come."

Tanner shrugs, the green thermos and cups in his hands lifting. "You know what they say. Seventy is the new thirty, leopard print is the new pink, day's the new night."

"I, no, I don't think that's a thing." I laugh, shaking my head. A small, relieved smile tilts my lips as they all enter.

I shut the door and Whitney drops sleeping bags onto the living room floor. "What Tanner is trying to say," she says, arranging the bags into a square, "is that none of us slept last night thinking about you and Adam, so now we're here to sleep with you." Her eyes widen. "I mean—ha—you know what I mean." Her face reddens and she focuses extra hard on the sleeping arrangement.

"What Whitney is trying to say," Morgan says, holding up a tabletop s'mores kit, "is that we brought breakfast and do you have a lighter?"

I huff a laugh and head to the kitchen to retrieve matches.

Tanner follows, clearing a stack of paperwork on the counter to empty a thermos into four tin cups. The beverage smells like cinnamon and apples.

"How do you know about Adam and me?" I ask, rifling through a junk drawer. "Or, um, what do you know?" My voice is thin.

Morgan comes up beside me, leaning on the counter. "Pretty much all of it. Adam called us at the inn. Rachel is on her way to be with him now, get him settled in with the band."

I grab a box of matches. Swallow hard. "How was he doing?"

"Like shit," Morgan says, at the same time Whitney calls from the living room, "Like you."

Morgan places her hand on my back. "He's worried about you, Ben. I am, too."

I take in a deep breath and fight back another onslaught of tears. "Did he tell you about the Bake-Off?"

"Yes." She rubs my back.

"And we're here to support you," says Tanner, coming up on my other side.

I take out the matches and place them on the counter, shut the drawer. "Thank you for being such good friends. I—" Tears choke me off.

Morgan closes in, then it's all arms around me, tight, tight. Morgan's voice in my ear, "Honey. It's going to work out. You'll see."

"It's okay to cry," Tanner says, rubbing my back.

"We've got you," Whitney adds, running up, completing the group hug.

Eventually, my breaths steady and we pull apart.

Before I know it, I'm bundled in a down-feathered cocoon stuffing marshmallows into my mouth. "Breakfast of champions," I say, wiping melted chocolate off my chin.

Whitney and Tanner both build their second s'mores in the center of our sleeping bag huddle, and I pretend like I don't see them glance my way every other second.

"Started clearing out some of my parents' old things," I say, nodding toward the box of junk in the corner.

"Oh my god, home makeover!" Whitney squeals, face alight.

I snort. "You know what? Yeah." The idea fills me with satisfaction, something to look forward to. Something to fix. "Would you all want to do that with me? When you have time?"

I eye the space. The chipped blue paint along the molding. Faded floral window valances. Dried herbs strung from the kitchen ceiling collecting dust.

Golden sun peeks in, proclaiming the new day.

There's no reason this house can't feel like my office does back in the bakery, cheery and cozy. No reason I can't make this mine, reclaim it as something new.

For a new me.

"We'd love to," Tanner and Whitney say in unison.

"Oh, I am about to HGTV this place up," Morgan says with a wide smile. "But first"—she reaches beside her, grabbing a toiletry pouch—"I'm gonna go brush my teeth." She heads to the bathroom.

"And I'm going to sleep," Whitney says, wiggling down into her purple bag. "Pretty sure this level of tiredness is what inspired the seventh circle of Dante's *Inferno*."

"None of us need to see Whitney Collins driven to violence," Tanner says, settling in.

She smacks him with a paisley throw pillow.

I laugh for the first time in what feels like fifteen summers.

"Sorry, Tanner," Whitney whispers.

"It's all good, Whit. It's all goo . . ." he replies, drifting off to sleep.

"Yeah. It's all goo," I echo, smiling.

I roll onto my back melting into the sleeping bag like my limbs are literally made of goo, and stare up at the ceiling, counting the knots in the wooden beams.

Ping.

My heart leaps despite the tired ache in my bones.

Adam.

I reach for my phone and pull it to me. It scrapes across the wooden floor.

One look at the screen makes me want to shatter the device.

@JakeGibbonsMusicManagement sent you a message request.

I pull up Instagram, hands shaking.

Sorry for how this went down. It's really between your mother and me. Although, you could have prevented it by connecting me with Adam Reed. We're all to blame here.

I no longer shake.

My heartbeat steadies in my ears. Strong, solid, sure.

Angry.

It takes me one second to respond.

Then, I block his account.

A FUCK YOU has never felt so good.

Chapter 29

It's been a month since our living room campout, and the bestie renovation crew kept their promise. A rented storage pod half-filled with old family skeletons now sits in my back drive, and part of me is resurrected. Especially since I gutted the garage and Tanner helped me paint the interior walls pink. Bubble-gum Sky pairs great with power tools. After we tossed the old boom box in the storage pod, Whitney gifted me a new Blue-tooth speaker. It's bright purple and blares my playlists like a charm. I make those a lot now, playlists. Forced Proximity is a top choice, and every rendition of "Don't Stop Believin'."

There really is something to be said for the space you keep. I even started burning Mom's old herb bundles every night after the decluttering I fit in with Morgan and Rachel between their hours at the inn and mine at the bakery.

Thankfully, the bakery still exists largely due to my home-town. Just like Mary Sue's customers were not ready to let go of the old bakery, Fern Falls isn't abandoning Peak Perk Café. Or me.

Mom and I talk every day since she took over the contract issues with Delish Dollars Studios. She's also working with G-ma on her financial situation, and they are both due to arrive within the hour so we can discuss everything here, at the café.

Then, of course, there's Adam.

I eye my phone on the bakery's pink countertop like it's about to sprout arms and hands and strangle me. I've been avoiding this thing like oversalted dough. I'm so happy for Adam, but the missing gets to be too much when I descend into the black hole of Forced Proximity's Instagram profile.

I have commented on his personal posts over the past weeks, cheered him on from a distance. I still want to be in his life, just not too close. I don't want to hold him back. There's also the issue of self-preservation. What if he wants to date somebody new? What if he meets the love of his life on the road, at a charming dive bar where they share a beer and talk late into the night and dance to a jukebox song? Hypothetically. It's not like I've imagined that exact scenario lying in my bed at two a.m. staring at the ceiling. I couldn't handle watching all that play out across my social feed. Best to avoid the phone almost entirely. It does nothing good for my anxiety.

The bell above the front door chimes.

"Where are those hot buns at?" Whitney hollers, strolling in like a ray of sunshine in light yellow coveralls and pink Doc Martens, hair in two blue-tipped, braided pigtails.

"And good morning to you, too. Here's a brand *spankin'* new batch, fresh from the oven." I chuckle and push a fresh tray of cinnamon rolls across the front counter. If you can't beat them, join them in the buns jokes.

Her laughter brightens the room.

A few regular patrons look up from their newspapers and coffee mugs to wave at her as she passes by.

Reaching the counter, she leans over and grabs a roll, bites, moans in pleasure as she chews.

"You know I'm gonna have to charge you for those eventually."

She smirks. "We both know you're lying."

I smile. Obviously, I'm full of shit. After my therapist advised me to limit my social media engagement for a while for my mental health, Whit took over the café's social accounts in exchange for nothing but iced lavender oat milk lattes for life. And cinnamon rolls. And lemon bars.

"Where's Tanner today?" I ask, wiping a drip of glaze on my teal apron.

She lowers her pastry and raises a brow. "What? Like I know his location at all times?"

I smirk. "I mean, you two have gotten a lot closer lately."

"If you consider not being hostile as being close, then yes. We have." She becomes very interested in the icing on her roll, examining it thoroughly.

I shrug. "Listen, if my own love life is on pause, I'm gonna meddle. It's the rules. I'm a Parrish."

She squints. "And a queer Parrish, so is that like, an official license to meddle, stamped, sealed, delivered?"

I loose a hearty laugh. "What can I say? I'm Certified Bisexual."

She snorts. "From one bi to another, meddle all you want, just keep these coming." She shoves her cinnamon roll back in her mouth.

Izzy, the owner of the local flower shop Mountaintop Florals, waves over from a front table, her red hair brightened by the sunny window, which matches her cherry-print dress and latest rose tattoo on her pale skin.

Whitney waves back and goes to join her.

I pick up the tray of cinnamon rolls—instant *Take the Cake National* déjà vu. No, I won't be dropping these on anyone's head today. In fact, I've never felt more sturdy and solid in my skin.

In my white Vans sneakers and dark wash jeans, I brought some Maywell Bay home with me. Beneath my apron, I am in a blue button-up shirt because I'm not a monster, but it is short-sleeved.

I lean over to the pastry case and slide in the tray of cinnamon rolls just as the door chimes and a very flustered Tanner Monaghan strides in, face flushed, and he's wearing—

"Tanner? Where is your white shirt?" I ask, straightening. I have never seen this man in anything but white tees and jeans, and here he stands in mustard-yellow shorts and a hunter-green tank top—and okay, guess those five-inch-long T-shirt sleeves hid a substantial amount of muscle.

His cheeks redden. "I enjoyed helping you paint your garage pink, ya know? Thought I'd try some new colorful things. I'm exploring myself a little." He runs a hand through his still-tousled dark blond hair—freshly polished fingernails gleaming in a midnight purple.

I glance over at Whitney and my heart bursts into a thousand meddling pieces. Her hand is frozen midair, clutching half a cinnamon roll, and her mouth hangs open as she stares at Tanner like he's Kristen Stewart incarnate.

Izzy and I exchange a knowing smile.

I clear my throat, turning my attention back to Tanner. "You want your usual iced vanilla latte?"

He shakes his head. "Maybe later, but I need you to come with me to The Stacks. Um, right now." He juts a thumb over his shoulder in the direction of his bar.

Okay . . . talk about déjà vu.

"I don't think I can leave the bakery during our morning rush."

He scans the tables.

Mayor Park stands up. "I was actually about to leave," she says with a knowing smile.

Beside her, Becca Rae, our local author, rises, placing her napkin on the table. "Me too."

The others in the café stand, grabbing their mugs and heading toward the door.

Izzy slips out with the crowd, and Whitney holds the door open, gesturing for me to join the exodus.

I shrug. "Okay, well, that solves that?" I untie my apron.

"No," Tanner says. "You'll need the apron."

My face screws up. "Do you need help in the bar kitchen?"

"You'll also need your family cookbook," Whitney hollers from her spot as door monitor.

I squint.

She makes a shooing gesture toward the back.

I sigh and follow instructions, returning a few moments later, clutching my leather-bound heirloom. "Let's go, I guess?"

I throw my cell phone into my apron pocket and Tanner leads me out the door, Whit close behind.

The sun warms my face and the air is fresh and alive with summer pine.

All this familiar scent needs is musk, motor oil.

I swallow past a pang of longing.

"There he is," a shrill voice calls.

No sooner do I look up than a middle-aged blond white woman bounds over. I last saw her in a purple velvet cape and corset, but today she's in a red summer dress.

I stop in my tracks. Does she seriously still think I have an agent I can connect her with? "Cousin Betty? What are you doing here?"

Paying no attention to my question, she cuts between Tanner and me. "You ran off, little scoundrel," Betty coos, giving his bicep a firm pinch.

Tanner clears his throat and casts me a look that clearly spells out *help*.

That explains his flustered state when he entered the bakery. He was on Mission: Escape Cousin Betty.

"What are you doing here? Did my mom and grandma already arrive?" I ask, but I may as well have screamed into the void because she only gazes at Tanner like tiny hearts and blue-birds encircle their heads.

In a flourish, Whit comes up and loops arms with Tanner. "Betty? Hi. I'm Whitney, Tanner's very good friend. So nice to meet you." She smiles extra sweetly.

I've never seen a person actually deflate, but my cousin transforms from twitterpated into a popped tire.

Then, in the span of a second, she faces me like a shiny new object. "All right, let's go." She hooks her arm through mine and drags me toward The Stacks in a full-blown sprint she is somehow capable of in stilettos.

"Whoa, what's happening?" I inquire to no avail, gripping the cookbook, grateful I chose sneakers today.

I look back at my friends to yell a demand for answers, but they take their precious time strolling down Main Street arm in arm. Tanner stares at where their elbows loop like their point of contact is the eighth wonder of the world.

Soon, they are far behind, and Cousin Betty has me in front of The Stacks, which appears to be empty, patio deserted, green doors closed.

Betty halts, but I propel forward.

She grabs me by my apron straps and pulls me upright.

Now that I'm firmly on my feet, she stands before me and squints, adjusting the collar of my shirt.

"Seriously," I pant, trying to catch my breath, "what is going on?"

She brushes off my shoulders. "If there is one thing I've learned as Cousin the Elder, you don't ask questions when G-ma calls."

I nod. I mean, true. "But what—"

"Plus," she continues, picking a spot of lint off my apron, "theater has taught me that you don't need to see the audience past the spotlights to know they love you, so just keep going."

"Okay?" I hold the cookbook to my torso so she'll stop prodding at me.

Betty steps back, assesses me, shrugs. "So get in there and smile through the glaring lights."

I tilt my head. "That's a metaphor, right? What are you talking abou—"

She smacks my behind and shoves me through the doors of The Stacks.

I stumble in and throw my free hand in front of my eyes as a glaring light takes over my vision.

Not a metaphor, then.

I stumble forward, squinting. "Hello?"

"Over here, sweetie," Mom's voice calls from the far side of the bar.

Wait— "Mom?" My vision clears with dancing orange spots, and I take in the bar—if it can still be called that.

Mom stands with Grandma along the back wall, where the stage normally is, where Adam usually plays. Today, it's transformed into a spotlit set straight out of the Home Shopping Network. It's a bright white half-shell of a kitchen with a giant yellow counter in the center, covered with neatly arranged baking supplies and ingredients. Along the back wall, above a sink and stove and fridge, is the banner that hung out front during the day of my filming montage. A cheery pink backdrop emblazoned with HOMETOWN PRIDE FOR PEAK PERK CAFÉ!.

Mom and Grandma wear aprons that match mine—teal with a pink cupcake—and they both smile, like they're waiting for me to speak.

I hug our family cookbook tight as Whitney and Tanner enter behind me. Whit's voice is at my shoulder. "Go put on your very own baking show, you star," she says, then pulls Tanner to the side.

My own baking show? What is—? How did they—?

"You are not going to stand there and gawk while my life is ticking away, are you?" Grandma calls from the stage, hands on her hips.

The crowd breaks out in laughter and I take them in.

Rows and rows of chairs face the stage and are filled with my friends and neighbors and not-really-cousins, whom I should call cousins after today.

I walk down the center aisle as they call my name and wave.

Morgan and Rachel sit near the aisle with Morgan's father, Warren, and her old boss, Johanna. Morgan beams and Rachel throws finger guns.

Not far from them are my three aunties, smiling and waving and dabbing Kleenex beneath their eyes. Adelaide clutches a very large purple crystal to her chest.

Uncle Tim sticks his arm into the aisle with a boisterous, "Go get 'em, tiger," as I return his high five.

Little feet run up and two tiny brown arms encircle my legs. "Ben, I missed you!"

I bend down and give Matthew a one-armed hug. "Hi, buddy, it's so good to see you."

He fixes me with wide eyes. "Where's your love?"

"My love?"

He nods. "Adam. He said I could play his guitar again."

My throat aches and my eyes sting. "He's traveling right now, but I bet his sister, Rachel, would let you play her guitar."

"Okay," he says, then runs over to his parents.

Janet smiles and waves from the front row, and beside them is Jason, suntanned with shaggy bleached hair and a tangerine orange T-shirt.

Growing up, Jason always made me feel seen in the warmest of ways, and time hasn't changed a thing as he pushes over to me, beaming.

I sit on the edge of the stage to be eye level with him as he brings his wheelchair to a stop.

"Don't you look like a tropical vacation," I say, leaning in and giving him a hug.

"So good to see you, Ben," he says, patting me on the back.

I settle onto the ledge, and place my cookbook down, glance up at Grandma and Mom, who smile at us.

"I take it you're about to fill me in on all of this?" I ask him.

He laughs. "I just returned from filming in South America for Nat Geo, and G-ma"—he leans forward—"it's G-ma now, right?" he whispers.

I laugh and nod.

"Okay, G-ma informed me of all the bullshit that went down between your dad and Delish Dollars Studios, and I'm so sorry."

"No, it's okay," I say.

"It's not," he replies, "but I want to try and make it better."

Janet lifts up a handheld camera and grins, while Uncle Tim raises a cell phone haloed by a ring light.

Before I can ask what all this means, he says, "We're gonna film you three making your cinnamon rolls and live stream it to my social accounts. Afterwards, we'll upload the higher-quality recording. I'll then edit it and put it on my website and YouTube channel, and put my multimillion follower base to good use, yeah?"

I blink. Swallow. Breathe. This is another chance I have to control the narrative, to take things into my hands, to take charge. Another time when people I love are proving how much they believe in me.

There's still an impulse, a gut reaction that warns me to run out the door, but beyond that, there is Jason's smiling face, the preparations that all my friends and family have made, and the hundred-plus people crammed into this bar to show their support.

If everyone I love believes in me so much, I should, too.

I lean in and give my cousin a tight hug. "Thank you, Jase."

"You've got this." Then, he pushes back to his spot in the front row where Janet hands him the camera.

He throws me a wink, props the camera on his shoulder, and points it at the stage.

I grab the cookbook, ascend the side stairs, and take my spot between my mom and grandmother behind the counter, placing the book before us.

"I have so many questions," I say through a wide smile.

"And we have answers," Mom replies. "But first, we bake."

"Wrong," Grandma says, handing each of us a shot glass. "First, we cheers."

I laugh as we clink glasses of what is thankfully plain old bourbon.

"To us," I say.

"To you, Ben," Grandma replies.

Joy sparkles through me.

Mom nods in agreement, and we drink.

Pushing our emptied glasses to the side, I crack open our cookbook to the page Mom created years ago.

Her cinnamon roll recipe is still covered in her handwritten additions, measurements, and notes in purple ink.

I glance between the women who raised me. Their smiles encourage me to take the lead.

Jason nods, and a red light blinks to life on the front of his camera.

I smooth my apron, breathe deep, and grin. "Hi, I'm Ben Parrish, and today, I'm making my family's famous cinnamon rolls for everyone to enjoy."

Chapter 30

"Why does this smell like foot?" Grandma inquires, frowning down at her teacup.

From across the tile counter, Mom finishes pouring hot water from an electric kettle and rolls her eyes. "My best teas for leaf readings are not the tastiest, but you'll survive."

G-ma clicks her tongue. "It's expired."

"Says the woman who serves formaldehyde as a signature cocktail," Mom quips.

Grandma glares at her as she settles onto the barstool beside me, all three of us in a row at the kitchen counter of my little house.

Mom clutches her mug and slides mine before me. Steam hits my face with the scent of vinegar? Gym bag? No, that's definitely . . . "I'm not one to meddle," I say, "but this really does smell like foot."

Mom looks aghast.

Then, we all howl with laughter.

"Not one to meddle, that's rich," Mom says. She goes to grab a hand towel, dabbing the corners of her eyes.

Behind her back, G-ma pulls a tiny amber bottle from her purple blouse and adds a squirt of liquid to her cup. Then, she recaps and replaces it.

I meet her eyes and she winks.

I try not to laugh and give her away.

"Okay," Mom says, returning to her stool. "Sip away and our futures shall be revealed." She brings her cup to her lips.

"Revealed to be glued to the toilet after drinking this," Grandma says.

Mom sputters, swiping her chin. "Yeah, no, that's definitely expired." She gets up and confiscates our cups. "Don't drink that."

I laugh as Grandma mumbles, "Waste of perfectly good formaldehyde." Then, she sneaks a swig from her bra-bottle.

Mom slowly waters a houseplant with the bad tea, careful to not disturb the leaves at the bottom of the mugs. Then, she grabs three watermelon hard seltzers from the fridge, handing us each our own.

"That's more like it," G-ma says, popping the can.

Mom salutes us with her drink and sips.

A simple pendant light hangs above the kitchen island, and the indoor ambience turns glowy as the windows grow black from night. It's about eight thirty p.m., and my whole body is exhausted but sated from the joy of the afternoon.

The recording went great, and we stayed afterwards to help clean up and make sure our extended family got to their cars and on their way safely. My friends lingered at the bar for a while, but I wanted to bring Mom and Grandma back to the house to get them settled for the night, and get caught up on everything.

I sip my drink.

Anytime now . . .

The clock on the wall ticks.

They'll fill me in . . .

Mom hums a tune that I'm sure is Lenny Kravitz.

Grandma taps a lime-green acrylic nail on her seltzer can.

"Is anyone going to tell me what the hell is going on?" I blurt.

"Whoa, there, angry little sea star," Grandma says.

Mom faces me, turning on her stool. "No, that's fair." She eyes Grandma over my shoulder. "Where do you want to start, Mom?"

G-ma snorts. "How about where you thought I was broke."

I look between them, which requires pivoting my entire body, so I stand up and cross my arms. "But Mom said your bank account—"

She raises a hand and a perfectly penciled brow. "I'm a six-time divorcee. You think I only have one bank account?"

I snap my focus to Mom. She winces, nods.

"But didn't the bank say—"

"You think I only have one bank?" Grandma huffs.

Mom shakes her head. "I should have gone to her first thing, Ben."

"Damn right," says Grandma.

They both raise their cans, sip.

I take a tight breath. "So G-ma, you don't have to liquidate your estate?"

Her face screws up. "No. Your mother was working with one account in one bank I deal with. That was my party funds account at my party funds bank. If she would have come to me, I could have transferred the money."

I close my eyes and loose a held breath. Party funds bank. Right. Who doesn't have a party funds bank? "Thank god," I say.

"Thank my fourth husband, Rodrigo," Grandma replies.

"Thank you, Rodrigo," we all chant in unison.

I reach for my seltzer and take an extra-long pull.

"Mom, what about the Delish Dollars contract?" I wait expectantly like I'm getting project updates from a marketing team.

"I'll take that one, too," G-ma chimes in. "I don't know if you ever saw it, but after your father left, he published an article—"

"The one where he said he'd sue the DCFS for defamation?" I say, chest aflame.

Mom's expression fills with sorrow. "Yes," she says, voice quiet. "That one. I'm sorry you saw it."

I shake my head. "It wasn't your fault."

Grandma rises, clutching her seltzer can. "Once your mother filled me in on everything that rat bastard did, I marched down to his shitty office and told him that if he didn't vanquish that pitiful excuse for a C&D and cough up five hundred thousand dollars for the loss he caused the studio, I'd bring him to court, citing that DCFS article as evidence that this isn't the first time he's tried to ruin our family with malicious intent. And, after my expert team of lawyers was done with his sorry con-man ass, he'd be using his tears for toilet paper." She gulps down the rest of her drink and crushes the can in her fist, breathing watermelon flames.

I gape at her. I am equally in awe and terrified of my own grandmother. "You really did all that?"

She snaps her gaze up as if just noticing me. "I didn't actually march to his craphole of an office, I drove, but yes, yes I did. And that dumpster fire coward had the wire transfer processed in no less than twenty-four hours, because he knew my lawyers would come for millions if he so much as whimpered. And I don't give a flying baboon where he got the money, and don't waste one more thought on him, Ben, or on Delish Dollars Studios. It's done." She pulls me into her Wonder Woman hug and says into my ear, "Listen here, sweet child. Whatever gives you joy in this world, that is what you do. That is what you deserve. Every good and wonderful thing. We love you, we love you, we love you."

Mom comes and embraces us both. I cry in their arms, holding a half-empty can of summer-flavored alcohol, barefoot in my kitchen, like a goddamn adult.

We pull apart and wipe our eyes.

"Okay," Grandma says. "I'm gonna walk this off in the fresh mountain air." She heads to the door.

"G-ma?" I ask, something she said flagging in my brain.

She looks back, hand on the knob.

"Did you say Dad is paying you five hundred thousand dollars? Wasn't the studio contract for one hundred thousand?"

She waves a hand dismissively. "Laura, you fill him in on all the details, and wait for me before you watch *Dateline*." Then, she's out, door clicking shut behind her.

"Mom?" I ask, taking her in. "There's more?" I slump onto a stool, setting my drink on the counter. "I don't know if I can mentally, emotionally, or spiritually handle any further details."

She retrieves our empty mugs from the counter, then sits on the stool beside me. "This is the fun news, promise," she says, sliding my cup over to reveal dried herbs marinating in the dredges of expired tea.

"This is the news?" I squint at the mush like I'm trying to decipher shapes in cloud formations. "Is that a finger? I think my tea leaves are flipping me off."

She laughs and wraps her hands around her own cup. "Mine's an acorn." She smiles. "For happiness and contentment."

"I love that, Mom."

"I do, too. It's perfect for everything I want to tell you." She turns her attention toward me and holds my stare. "Over the past few weeks, your grandmother and I have put our heads together to think of an appropriate way to thank you for all you've done for us."

"All I've done for you?" I snort-laugh. "Were you not just standing in this kitchen two minutes ago? You are the ones who deserve the thanks."

She shakes her head. "Ben, you have handled my naturals business and maintained this household for the entire time I've been gone. You have run the family-owned bakery completely on your own, even when it fully took you out of your comfort zone on live TV. In many industries, efforts like that would come with a substantial promotion or bonus."

I clear my throat. I guess I did do all of that.

She flattens her palm on the countertop. "So, here is what your grandmother and I want to do. I bought this house years ago. It is now paid off, and I want to sign the deed over to you."

I gasp. "Mom—"

She holds up a hand. "Maywell Bay is where I belong now, near your grandmother as she ages. We want you to take the remaining four hundred thousand dollars to use as you please. Renovate the house as you wish, travel, invest, build a nest egg for your own business ventures, whatever you please."

I grip the edge of my seat and brace against building emotion. "But—"

"Not done."

I nod.

"While I'm here," she continues, "I'll pack up my old inventory from Mountaintop Mystic and bring it with me to Maywell Bay. There, I can shift the business fully online or open an apothecary, but most importantly, you will no longer be tethered to it. And finally—"

"Mom. This is already too much."

"Almost done." She adjusts on her seat. "Your grandmother and I will be making many more trips up to Fern Falls. To help in the bakery so you can take vacations—that is, if you still want the bakery, we can sell it if you prefer, but the bottom line is, we want to be more present in your life. We love you."

I let out a long and deep sigh, staring at my tea leaves.

"I know. Take a minute to process," she says.

My brain scrambles to catch up. "I definitely want to keep the bakery," I reply. "It makes me happy. And I'm glad you can still run your business because I know that makes you happy."

She smiles. "Me too."

"Of course I want you to come up, but I also want to visit you and Grandma a lot more often."

Her face softens. "We'd love that, Ben."

I take a pull of my seltzer. I could finish renovating the house. I could tackle all the paused DIY projects in the garage. Maybe I'll open an antique shop in the front when it's emptied out. I could call it Fixed Up Things. All the possibilities sing through me. I take a deep breath. "I'll have to process the rest? Take some time to think it over."

She nods. "Totally understandable. We can talk about it as many times as you need."

My attention shifts toward my teacup. I love this house. I'd love to make it my own. Accepting the money though . . . "How do people accept gifts, Mom? How do people accept that they deserve things without doing something to earn them?"

She hums as she leans toward me. "I think, sweetie, you need to ask yourself, why you feel like you don't deserve love, because this is where that's coming from. Our gifts to you are an act of love. You do not need to earn that. It gives us joy to love you, Ben."

I take deep breaths as my chest tightens and wrap my hands around my mug to ground myself.

My whole life, I've thought that if I could only do things perfectly, not make mistakes, then people would stay, people would love me.

Mom rubs my back.

I can no longer use my father as a goalpost for my self-worth. I can no longer believe that the actions of a toxic, harmful narcissist were spurred by something I did or didn't do when I was eight years old or twenty-six.

My father is not capable of giving the love I need, and that is not any fault of my own.

Because the people I love do love me.

Everyone who showed up at The Stacks cares about me. My family loves me, my friends love me.

They love me no matter what mistakes I've made.

And maybe, sometimes, our mistakes are nothing but unavoidable side effects of reaching for something bigger, something better. I may have failed the bakery in the beginning, but I tried to start a business. I ruined the TV show, but I stepped out of my comfort zone. I lost Adam, but I love him.

And Adam loves me.

Adam. Loves. Me.

I blink through tears as the dark green and brown leaves in my cup blend together. "It's a butterfly," I say. "The leaves. They form a butterfly."

Mom's hand stills on my shoulder as she peers over. "You're exactly right. I see it. Do you want to know what it means?"

I nod, swiping at my eyes.

"Butterflies symbolize success and happiness, but they also represent transformation or rebirth."

I laugh into my hands. "A little on the nose."

She chuckles. "The universe is pretty clear when we're listening."

I let out a deep sigh, exhaling the weight of so many misconceptions I've had for so long.

She pulls me into a hug. "I'm so proud of you, Ben."

"I love you, Mom."

We hold on tight for a bit longer.

Pulling back, she sighs and clears our cups.

As she makes her way to the sink, my phone buzzes.

I pull my cell from my pocket and shake my head, a giant stupid grin on my face. "Mom?"

She turns the water off and faces me.

"Would I possibly be able to use some of those funds to purchase a plane ticket?"

She smiles knowingly. "Got a musician to get to, huh?"

"Yeah." I beam. "Yeah, I do."

I get up to go pack my duffel bag, but before I re-pocket my phone, I read Adam's text again:

Missing you.

The attached image is of a neon sign against a sunset sky. At the top is a deer. The middle says PORTLAND OREGON, below that: OLD TOWN.

In the foreground is Adam's hand. Between his fingers is a tiny, yellow, glass guitar figurine.

He'll only have to miss me through the next flight out.

Chapter 31

Part of small-town living is having an equally small airport an hour's drive away in good weather. But, when the weather is good, the meager flights are booked solid.

My grand gesture options are limited to: wait until next Saturday to board a plane from Snow Hill to PDX, or drive six hours to LAX and fly out tomorrow night.

Obviously, I'm not waiting a week for the Snow Hill option, but arriving a whole twenty-four hours post-receipt of a romantic text? Not the adrenaline-fueled concert entrance Adam deserves.

The tour schedule on Forced Proximity's website has them listed as playing at a Portland venue right now. So, even if I do make it there tomorrow night, there's a chance I could miss him before they all leave town. Austin is their next stop, but there's a weeklong gap, so I'm not sure when they're leaving the West Coast.

I could call him.

No. Out of the question.

I get one shot to tell Adam how I feel, to make things right, and I have to do that in person.

Plus, I desperately want to hold him.

My arms ache for him just imagining his warmth pressed against me.

His musky pine scent.

The firm, grounding pressure of his palms against my back.

Yeah, I'll take a red-eye from Portland to catch him in Austin if I have to.

"Honey?" Mom calls over from the front door to where I sit on the porch swing.

The patio sconce halos her blond hair as tiny winged insects swoop too close to the lightbulb. "You coming in soon? It's already ten."

I pull my pink knit throw blanket tighter around my shoulders and rock forward as the swing gives a peppy squeak. "I think I'll stay out here a bit longer."

"Okay," she says. "I'm almost done making a game plan for the shop stuff." She jabs a thumb toward the room at her back. "Then, Grandma and I are gonna finish *Dateline* and head to bed. Maybe we can drive to Los Angeles a little early tomorrow so you can show me that romance bookstore you found. The Torn Corset?"

I smile. "The Ripped Bodice. And yeah, that would be amazing."

"Love you." She smiles.

"Love you, too."

Then, it's me and the sparkling expanse of constellations, the sparse buttery squares of distant cabin windows, and the wanting, wanting, wanting of Adam Reed.

Always wanting that man.

I pull out my cell phone and it's crickets. Literally. They chirp louder than city traffic on these summer nights.

Adam is playing a concert. There will be after-parties. Fans lined up to meet the fresh new opening act for the Hedges and

Stones. Forced Proximity doesn't seem like the vandalizing type of band, but who knows, maybe there are hotel rooms to thrash.

I laugh out loud at the idea of Adam throwing a pillow on the floor as an act of destruction.

On that note, it's time for me to head in. Thinking about Adam and bed linens will only lead to me sobbing or needing to scratch an itch that should not be um, scratched on my front porch.

I let out a cheek-flapping sigh and heave myself forward to disengage from the backward pull of the swing, leaving the blanket behind.

The wooden deck creaks beneath my steps, and there's a scuttle beneath the slats. Racoons. I should leave some orange slices out for them.

I grab the door handle.

Gravel crunches at my back as the screen door illuminates with the glow of approaching headlights. That, at least, is not raccoons.

I turn as a red truck slows to a stop in front of my house.

The headlights die as the engine cuts off, and I squint through the windshield.

It's Rachel, driving the official Reed Family Tree Farm truck.

The truck door opens, but it's not hers.

Someone exits from the passenger side.

I'm hallucinating.

That's what this is.

I need to masturbate so badly that I am in some lusty haze where Adam Reed walks toward my porch.

A raccoon scurries out from beneath the deck and runs into the silhouette of nearby forest.

Not a sex mirage, then.

"Ben?" Phantom Adam asks.

I blink hard.

Maybe-real Adam steps onto the porch, black boots creaking the slats, black T-shirt now caught from the night by the porch light.

His mussed hair is spotlit to a toasty chestnut, and that crooked smile is as red as a summer strawberry.

"Holy shit," I exhale. Because I'm suave as hell. I wince.

He makes a hum of a laugh and steps near, the porch appreciating his presence with each happy squeak.

"Adam? How are you here?" My voice is too thin.

He halts. "Rachel drove me."

I smile. "Yes, but your text."

He takes in a deep breath, understanding dawning on his face. "I messaged you before I boarded the plane, and it must have sent once I landed in Snow Hill."

I inhale sharply, breathe out. "But don't you have a show in Portland? Right now?"

"Yes," he nods. "That's why I'm here."

I squint. "So you can play in Portland?"

He lets out a small laugh and shakes his head. "Sorry, I'm screwing this up. I had a whole speech planned on the flight over." He holds my gaze. "I went, Ben. You wanted me to give touring a try, so I went." He stops before me and the moon sparks a cool copper in his eyes. "I know it was short, but it was long enough for me to ask Taylor to give my spot back to their old guitarist."

Shivers rush through me. "Don't you love playing with them? Why would you give that up?"

He shifts his stance and a breeze ruffles his bangs, parting them to reveal the sharp set of his brows, the intense longing in his eyes. "I came home to tell you that with every beat of my small-town heart, that life is not for me. The crowds were suffocating, the bus smelled and gave me motion sickness, the shows felt hollow, the Continental breakfast danishes were so terrible your cinnamon rolls would sue."

I laugh through my nose.

He runs a hand through his hair, steps closer on a sigh. "What I'm trying to say is that I'm a one town, one auto shop, one local gig once a week and teaching guitar one day . . . One man for one life kind of guy." He takes my hands in his. "It was empty without you. You are the one I wanted to celebrate with, hug after a show, come back to at the end of the day. I wanted to look over and see you in the wings. I want you." His thumbs run across my knuckles. "Please. May I have one more chance to prove my love to you? To help you trust that I don't want to leave?"

I am on fire in the cool night air.

If he were not clutching my hands, I would fall to my knees.

"I . . ." How do I tell him that every minute apart has been an agony he just flung to hell with his presence, his words, himself? That I've changed my pillowcase each morning because I cried myself to sleep every night he was gone? That I never want him to leave like this again? "I bought a plane ticket."

He flinches. "You're leaving?"

The panic in his voice makes my heart lurch. "I have a flight to Portland tomorrow night."

"I could go with you."

I shake my head. "No, sorry, this isn't coming out right." I take a deep breath and squeeze his hands. "I was coming to tell you that I love you."

The man shrinks two inches in a full-body sigh.

"And I am learning how to love myself, too." My voice cracks.

He smiles and little lines crinkle beside his eyes.

I take a sharp breath to stop tears. "You don't have to prove your love to me, Adam. You show me in the way you treat me, speak to me, believe in me, look at me. You always have. But I had to allow myself to see it, and I had to heal to believe it, and I have to continue healing, every day, to keep trusting it." I tilt my chin toward his. "But I love you back with every piece of my heart. The broken pieces and the mending pieces, the healed parts and the parts you've helped me heal—" My voice gives as my vision blurs.

He bends and touches his nose to mine. "And I love every single piece of you, Ben Parrish."

With a breath that passes from my mouth to his, Adam kisses me.

Tender pressure on my lips, tender touch against my back.

Strained muscles beneath my fingertips.

Loud applause from the window to my right and the truck to my left.

We break apart and our laughs dance off the trees.

He reaches up, eyes shining, then runs the backs of his fingers down my cheek. "My darling. My Ben." He sighs. "I love you."

I lunge into his arms and cling tight. With my mouth against his ear, I whisper, "I love you, Adam Reed. I love you. I love you. I love you."

He hoists me up, spinning around until the landscape swirls.

Then, he stops, and his mouth meets mine.

I grip his arms as he lowers me to my feet. His clenched muscles yield beneath my touch in an unwinding, melting, final release of every last worry.

We mold together.

I hold his face in my hands and kiss him back in a way we'll remember when our hair turns gray.

It's Adam, me, here, now, tomorrow, next month, next meteor shower, life crisis, failed recipe, written song, holiday, birthday, every day. It is everything.

Every good and wonderful thing.

Acknowledgments

There were a thousand moments when I truly believed I wouldn't be able to finish this book.

Fortunately, anxiety lies, and I had the best support system pulling me through.

Thank you is not enough:

Michael, for being my rock in all things. For holding me tight even and especially when everything threatens to spiral out. Life is best with you. I love you, I love you, I love you.

Aisley, for making me feel like a rock star in sweatpants. You deserve every good and wonderful thing, dear one. I love you times infinity.

My therapist, Julie, for reminding me that first and foremost, I have to create for the truth in myself, that I'm not here to perform.

Kels, Mom, Dad, I love you.

Grandma. You are my idol. G-ma is for you.

Carol, Brock, Jordan, Julia, E&M, thank you for always believing in me.

Erin Connor, Carlyn Greenwald, and Sonia Hartl. Thank you for your early feedback when this story was nothing but alphabet soup. I cherish your friendship.

The friends who saved me in the chats and beyond: Jessica, Megan, Elsie, Liana, Heather, Jenny L. Howe, Renée Reynolds, Samantha Eaton, Rachel Lynn Solomon, Melanie Schubert, Angela Montoya, Jessica Parra, Nikki Payne, Regina Black, Maggie North, Ella Sinclair, Sarah Burnard, Susan Lee, Falon Ballard, Alison Cochrun, Helena Greer, Timothy Janovsky, Ruby Barrett, Meryl Wilsner, Ashley Herring Blake, Anita Kelly, Ava Wilder, and many more. If I missed your name here, please know it's on my heart. I'd be lost without you. Thank you for keeping me together. Oof, I'm tearing up. Thank you for seeing my heart even when my brain is a mess. I love you.

Claire Friedman. I am forever grateful to have you by my side. Thank you for championing my work and prioritizing my well-being. I appreciate you more than you could ever know.

Elizabeth Trout. Your insight and support kept me strong when the outline fell apart, and during every rewrite. Thank you for always seeing the heart in my stories and helping them shine.

Jane Nutter, Michelle Addo, Carly Sommerstein, Lauren Jernigan, Kait Johnson, Alexandra Nicolajsen, Matt Johnson, and every amazing person at Kensington: You are the best team an author could hope for.

Hannah Schofield, Kate Byrne, and Sophie Keefe: Thank you for believing in this series.

To all the booksellers I've been so fortunate to meet: You are my heroes.

Book influencers and the HoliGays22Crew: Your talent knows no bounds. Thank you for being loud about stories you believe in.

You, dear reader. Thank you for supporting queer stories and queer creators. Thank you for being here.

I love you all.

In the Case of Heartbreak

Courtney Kae

The suggested questions are included to enhance your group's
reading of Courtney Kae's *In the Case of Heartbreak*

Discussion Questions

1. Maywell Bay holds the happiest memories for Ben. Is there a place that conjures instant sunshine for you?

2. *In the Case of Heartbreak* is filled with tropes: forced proximity, friends to lovers, unrequited crush to lovers, meddling family members, "May you reach that button for me?", and found family. What are some of your all-time favorite tropes?

3. What songs would be on Adam's Summer Playlist for Ben?

4. In the beginning, Ben is terrified of failure. Has there been a time in your life when you pushed through fear to accomplish something?

5. Despite the pain his father causes, Ben has a beautiful community of loving people. Are there people in your life whom you've leaned on, whom you consider your close family or found family?

6. If you could take a summer vacation anywhere, where would you go, and whom would you bring?

7. Ben ultimately finds deeper healing through himself, therapy, medication, Adam, family, and friends. When was a time you felt seen and accepted for who you are? When was the last time you did that for another?

8. What summery treat or drink would you ask Ben to make for you at Peak Perk Café?

9. Describe your perfect summer outing or date.

10. What are things about yourself that you love? What are things that make you proud and give you joy?